THE GIRL IN THE WOODS

A JOE COURT NOVEL

BY

CHRIS CULVER

ST. LOUIS, MO

First paperback edition February 2019.

www.indiecrime.com

Facebook.com/ChrisCulverBooks

A Joe Court Novel

To Roy, my friend.

Other books by Chris Culver

Ash Rashid novels:

The Abbey

The Outsider

By Any Means

Measureless Night

Pocketful of God

No Room for Good Men

Sleeper Cell

Gabe Ward Novels

Counting Room

Stand-alone novels:

Just Run

Nine Years Gone

Joe Court novels:

The Girl in the Motel

Contents

Chapter 1

Nick Sumner's boss paid him to kill people, but he was more of a salesman than anything else. When he was a kid, everybody thought he'd follow his daddy's footsteps and become a Southern Baptist preacher. The ministry had held little appeal for him, but he liked standing in front of crowds and talking. He had a knack for it, too. Even at twelve years old, he'd been able to crack up entire rooms full of people. It gave him an edge in his current occupation.

He shifted in his black leather seat, pointed his ass toward the kid in the driver's seat, and farted. Logan darted his eyes in Nick's direction. The kid's skin was pale, and he gripped the steering wheel with a white-knuckled grip. A clammy sweat had formed on his brow. He looked sick, but he was fine. He just didn't want to kill his girlfriend, their present job.

"Did you fart?" asked Logan.

"Nah," said Nick, hooking a thumb toward the window. "We passed a pack of wild elephants. They were trumpeting."

He expected a reaction, but Logan simply nodded and looked forward again, continuing to drive. They were heading toward St. Louis in the kid's black BMW 3 Series. Nick didn't know Logan well, but they had been in the car together for almost half an hour. They'd never be friends, but a little conversation didn't seem out of order.

"Wild pack of elephants? You're not going to say anything?" asked Nick, smiling and dragging out the words for comedic effect. "Elephants don't form packs. They're not Cub Scouts. That's crazy talk. Elephants form parades."

"Sure," said Logan. His lips didn't crack a smile. To do this job right, the kid needed to relax, and Nick had something that could help. He slipped his hand inside the right breast pocket of his jacket and pulled out a Ziploc bag that held a joint made from a marijuana strain called Granddaddy Purple. He didn't smoke often, but he had purchased it and a lot of other stuff from a shop in Colorado three days ago.

He lit up, inhaled, and held his joint to the man beside him.

"You need this more than me, kid," he said. "Toke up. It'll make you happy."

"Are you serious?" he asked, looking at Nick again. "You want to smoke now? In my car?"

"Yeah," said Nick. "You look like a cancer patient. If we meet Laura with you looking like that, she'll recognize something's up. This will help you relax and make you feel better."

Logan hesitated but then took the joint and put it to his lips. He inhaled for a second before trying to pass it back to Nick.

"Have a real hit, kid. I'm tired of asking."

Logan looked to his right again before inhaling for a count of five. The tip of the joint burned a pleasant orange, and when he exhaled, the car filled with the grape-smelling smoke. He handed the joint back to Nick, who took another hit. Relaxing waves of euphoria washed over him.

When they finished the joint, Nick felt himself almost melting into the BMW's supple leather seats. He glanced at Logan. Nick didn't like working with partners—especially amateurs—but his client had insisted for this job. That was life. He couldn't fight it.

"So tell me about your girl. What's she like?" he asked. Nick didn't care what Logan said, but he needed to get the kid talking to calm him down. Logan's eyes fluttered, and his Adam's apple bobbed as he swallowed.

"Her name is Laura Rojas. She's a lawyer. She's really smart."

"How old is she?"

"Twenty-six," said Logan.

Nick nodded to himself, gaining a fuller picture of the situation.

"So she's a smart, young lawyer," he said. "She pretty, too?"

"Yeah," said Logan. "She's beautiful."

"You screwing her?"

"None of your business," said Logan. "Why would you ask me that?"

"It's my job to ask questions like that," said Nick. "We're not driving to pay her a social call. Your girlfriend is a threat. My employers don't respond well to threats. You're lucky they sent me. Some guys I work with would have killed her and taken out her whole family the moment they got to town. Me, I don't think we need to do that. Do I need to do that?"

"My stepfather tells you what to do," said Logan. "You're an employee. We're in charge."

Nick shook his head and reached into his jacket for his firearm. It was a nine-millimeter SIG Sauer P226 loaded with jacketed hollow point rounds. Upon impact with a target, the tip of the round would expand to inflict a maximum amount of trauma. They weren't great against men in body armor, but they were lethal against soft targets. He pointed the weapon at Logan's head, any sign of conviviality gone.

"I pull this trigger, I'll blow a hole out the side of your head the size of a golf ball. I don't want to hurt you, but neither you nor your daddy calls the shots on this job. Understand?"

"You shoot me in the car, you'll die, too," said Logan, darting his eyes to the right. "I'll drive into the ditch or the other lane."

"True," said Nick, "but at least I'll die with a smile on my face."

Logan said nothing for a few seconds. Then he nodded.

"I was trying to sleep with her. I never got the chance."

Nick nodded. It was a good answer. Already, he was thinking of her in the past tense. Nick holstered his weapon. They drove for another fifteen minutes.

"So what kind of food do people in St. Louis eat?"

Logan looked at him and shrugged. "Whatever they want?"

"What's the city known for? Chicago's got deep-dish pizza, Philly's got the cheesesteak sandwich, Memphis has barbecue. What's St. Louis got?"

Logan shrugged again. "Gooey butter cake, maybe? Why are you asking me?"

"I'm asking because you're the only person in the car and you grew up here," said Nick, looking out the window. The landscape around the interstate had rolling, wooded hills with occasional jagged outcroppings of limestone. It was pretty, but Nick preferred the ocean and white sand beaches of Miami, his hometown. "Where do you get gooey butter cake?"

He shrugged. Nick gritted his teeth and shook his head.

"Don't shrug," he said. "Answer the question. Where do you buy gooey butter cake? A bakery, the grocery, what?"

He straightened and gripped the steering wheel. "My favorite place is Park Avenue Coffee."

"All right," said Nick, nodding. "We'll take care of Ms. Rojas, put her in the trunk, and then get cake at Park Avenue Coffee."

Logan looked at him, his mouth open. "I don't want to have cake while she's in the trunk. What the hell is wrong with you?"

"You refuse cake, and you think there's something wrong with me?" asked Nick, shaking his head. "No, my friend, there's nothing wrong with me. Two things I've learned in this life: One, you never turn down a beautiful woman when she offers you sex, and two, you can never eat enough cake."

"You're crazy," said Logan.

"Some days, I think I'm the only sane man in the world."

Laura Rojas lived in a little house in Mehlville, a suburb south of downtown St. Louis. Nick had scoped it out on the internet, but he hadn't driven by yet. After another few minutes of driving, Logan put on his turn signal and exited the interstate.

"Have you been to Laura's house before?" asked Nick.

"Why does that matter?"

Nick sighed, allowing his frustration to come out into his voice. "This will go a lot easier if you trust me and answer my questions. If you've been to the house before, it won't seem odd if we show up now. If you've never been to the house, you'll look like a stalker."

"Then, yeah," said Logan. "I've been there."

"Good. Have you got a picture of her?"

Logan reached into his pocket for his phone and thumbed through his photographs before coming to one he wanted. He handed it to Nick. Laura was more than attractive; she was gorgeous. In the picture, she wore shorts and a St. Louis Cardinals T-shirt. Logan had his arm around her shoulders, but she looked stiff, like she was hugging her brother.

Nick handed the phone back, and they drove for another few minutes before Logan turned into a residential neighborhood. The homes were brick ranches with covered front porches and single-car garage stalls. The neighborhood looked old but well maintained. It was probably a good place to raise a family.

"Laura is beautiful," said Nick. "Did you ever wonder why a gorgeous twenty-six-year-old lawyer from the suburbs of St. Louis was visiting a college kid from St. Augustine?"

Logan said nothing, not that Nick cared. Logan screwed up; the trick was not screwing up again.

About two blocks into the neighborhood, Logan slowed and gestured toward a single-story brick home with a bright yellow door. Unlike the surrounding homes, Laura Rojas's house had no landscaping, and her yard looked more like a field that a farmer had left fallow for the season than a manicured suburban lawn. No cars parked in the driveway, and none of the lights inside were on.

"Pull to the end of the street. We'll wait for her. When she arrives, I'll do the talking. You back me up."

"Why don't we wait in her driveway? She knows me."

Nick sighed and rubbed his eyes. "This girl was milking you for information about your father's company. She doesn't care about you. She used you, and now she's done with you. How do you think she'll react if she sees you in the driveway?"

"I don't know."

"Since I'm old and wise, I'll tell you. If she sees you, she'll drive by her house and call the police because she doesn't want to deal with you anymore. We don't want that, so we'll stay here and surprise her. When she pulls into her driveway, you will park behind her car so she can't leave. Then, we'll get out, and I'll do the talking."

Logan glowered, nodded, and drove to the street Nick had pointed to without saying another word. There, he parked behind a big evergreen tree to conceal their vehicle. As they waited, Logan drummed his fingers on the steering wheel.

"We won't hurt her, will we? I mean, she may have been using me, but she was still a nice person."

"I will talk to her and learn everything I can from her. Afterwards, I will shoot her in the heart. Is that a problem?"

"Please don't hurt her," said Logan. He swallowed and looked to his right at Nick. "I mean, don't hurt her more than you have to. Make it quick."

"I won't make her suffer."

They waited in silence after that. After half an hour, Laura Rojas's red Honda pulled into her driveway. As she waited for her garage door to open, Nick tapped his young companion on the shoulder.

"Magic time. Drive."

Logan turned on the car and pressed on the accelerator. Laura's house wasn't far, but, by the time they arrived, her garage door was up. She had yet to drive inside.

"Park right behind her on the driveway," said Nick. "Stay calm."

Logan did as Nick asked, and Laura popped out of her car. She looked concerned at first, but then she saw Logan step out. She forced a smile to her lips, but she did a good enough job to fool most people—especially a college kid in love with a woman way out of his league.

"Hi, Logan," she said. "I didn't know you were coming by. I've got work tonight. How about you call me later, and we'll get together?"

"Sorry for dropping in like this, but I'm Nick Sumner. I'm Logan's uncle," said Nick, stepping forward and holding out his hand for her to shake. "The kid's been telling me all about this young woman he's met, and I told him I had to meet her. I didn't believe him, but you are everything he said you were."

She stepped forward and shook Nick's hand. Her skin felt soft, but her grip was firm.

"It's nice to meet you," she said. "I'm sorry, but I've got to work tonight. Rain check?"

"Don't worry about it. We were in the neighborhood and thought we'd stop by," said Nick, nodding. "I'll tell you what. Logan and I plan to get dinner in St. Louis. You want us to bring you back some gooey butter cake?"

She hesitated but then shook her head. "I've never been a fan of gooey butter cake. It's too sweet."

Nick looked to Logan and smiled.

"I thought everybody liked it around here. You're telling me that this young woman, a St. Louis native, doesn't like gooey butter cake? That's absurd. That's unbelievable. That's un-American. I need you to get in Logan's BMW right now—backseat, please—and we will get some gooey butter cake."

"Sorry, but I've got work to do," she said. She turned to Logan. "I'll call you later, okay, hon?"

"Please get in the car, Laura," said Nick.

"I'm sorry, but like I said, I'm busy."

Nick pulled his jacket back, exposing his sidearm. "How's that niece of yours, Ms. Rojas? Emma is such a pretty little girl. I'd hate for something to happen to her."

Laura's smile disappeared. Her skin lightened a shade.

"Logan, what's going on?"

"Get in the car, Laura," said Nick, his voice soft. "If you listen and do as I say, your sweet little niece and your beautiful sister will live long, happy lives. If you don't, their lives will be nasty, short, and brutish. It's time for us to talk. If you answer my questions, I'll tell my employers you cooperated.

I'll recommend that they let you go. If you refuse to talk, you'll have a long, hard day."

Her eyes locked on Nick's, but she didn't move. She had more backbone than he had expected. Good for her.

"Who's your employer?" she asked.

"Not Logan and not his stepfather," said Nick, nodding toward his younger partner. "And nobody you want to meet. Now get in the car, or an associate of mine will pluck out Emma's eyeballs with an ice pick."

Laura straightened and stared into Nick's eyes. Then the first tear fell down her cheek, followed by another. She wiped them away and took a step back.

"You would hurt her, wouldn't you?"

"With the greatest reluctance," he said, nodding, "but yes, if that's what the job required."

She swallowed hard enough that her throat bobbed. "Can I get my purse?"

Nick shook his head. "No. But you can get in Logan's car."

"Don't hurt Emma or Alma."

"You have my solemn vow. If you do as I ask, no one will touch your niece or sister," said Nick, walking toward the BMW and opening one of the rear doors. Laura walked beside him and sat down. He shut her door and looked at Logan, who was wiping tears off his cheeks. "Get in the car, kid. We've got a long night ahead of us."

Chapter 2

I stopped and felt my feet sink into the muck as my radio spat static. My mouth was so dry I couldn't spit, and my head felt light. Given the heat and humidity, sweat should have poured down my back and chest, but I had stopped sweating an hour ago. I was dehydrated and tired, but I had a job to do.

I leaned against a tree to steady myself. The air smelled like mud, stagnant water, and animal shit. I was so deep in the woods I didn't even know where the highway was. Dark clouds covered the sun and sky, so little light penetrated the canopy of leaves and branches above me. We were under a tornado watch, but so far no storms had come our way. Even without severe weather, though, the area's gloomy feel depressed my mood.

"Dispatch, repeat," I said into my radio. "I'm only getting static."

I waited for Trisha to repeat her message. Around me, an early summer breeze rustled the fallen leaves and weeds at my feet. I should have brought a machete to hack through the brush. It would have made the morning a lot easier.

I drank the final gulp of water from my canteen and wiped grit from my forehead with my shirt sleeve before asking my dispatcher again to repeat her instructions. When that didn't work, I took out my cell phone. My connection was weak but stable. Trisha answered on the second ring.

"Hey," I said. "It's Joe. I'm somewhere in grid seven in a hollow in the woods. I didn't hear your message."

"Hey, Joe. Sorry about that. The terrain makes it hard to communicate."

"Yeah," I said, looking around to make sure no one could see me before adjusting the sports bra beneath my shirt. The salt-encrusted fabric chafed my back and sides, but it was the best outfit I owned for a long walk in the woods. "What's going on?"

"A volunteer found a body in grid thirteen."

Even though I had expected this call all morning, I still grimaced.

"Paige or Jude? And please don't tell me one killed the other."

"Neither," said Trisha. "It's a Jane Doe. She's at a little campsite."

I blinked, hoping I had misunderstood.

"You're telling me our search for Paige and Jude turned up a different murder?"

"We still don't know whether someone murdered Paige and Jude, but this girl's dead. Dave Skelton is on the scene now."

Complaining about a body on the ground wouldn't get me anywhere, but I swore under my breath anyway. Our search had started that morning when a hunter found a car belonging to Paige Maxwell deep in the woods. She and her boyfriend, Jude Lewis, had gone missing four weeks ago. They were both in high school, and they were in love. When my station received reports that they were missing, I presumed the two of them had run off together to hook up without their parents stopping them, but after this much time without contact, I feared the worst.

"Tell Dave I'm on my way," I said. "And remind me where grid thirteen is again."

Trisha gave me directions and warned me that the National Weather Service said we had nasty weather coming in. I groaned and cleared my throat.

"If you haven't already, call the boss and let him know about the weather. We've got almost fifty volunteer searchers out here. If we get a severe storm with this many civilians out here, we'll be in real trouble."

"Will do," said Trisha. "Good luck, Joe."

I thanked her before hanging up. Already, mud and sweat caked my shirt and jeans, making them stiff and uncomfortable, while rainwater from crevices and nooks along the forest floor had long since soaked through my cheap hiking boots. Every muscle in my body ached, and every inch of my skin itched from mosquito bites. This wasn't how I had envisioned spending my Sunday afternoon.

I hurried to the staging area where I had parked and then drove to grid thirteen. As I neared the crime scene, I found a marked police SUV on the side of the tiny gravel road. Officer Dave Skelton and a civilian in jeans and a T-shirt leaned against the vehicle. I parked behind them and stepped out. Dark clouds loomed on the horizon to the west.

A mosquito buzzed past my ear, and I slapped it as it landed on my neck. The bug spray I had put on that morning should have lasted eight hours, but it had stopped working an hour ago. Mud caked my arms, protecting some of my skin.

Skelton and the civilian nodded as I walked close. Skelton was in his late thirties and had black hair that had turned gray. He was a local product, and he knew St. Augustine County well because he had smoked weed in every hollow, hill, and valley when he was in high school.

The guy with him was about fifty, and he wore an orange high-visibility vest. I shook his hand and looked to Skelton.

"Got a moment?"

Skelton nodded, and we walked to the back of my truck to talk in private. Officer Skelton wore a St. Augustine County Sheriff's Department T-shirt and an orange high-visibility vest.

"What do we have?" I asked.

He took a notepad from the pocket of his jeans and flipped through a few pages before speaking.

"Mr. Williams is the volunteer searcher assigned to this quadrant. He claims he followed the road and came to a campsite where he found the body. He shouted until another volunteer came with a radio. Nobody touched anything, and nobody walked around the scene until I got here."

"Good," I said, nodding. "What have you done?"

"I checked the victim to make sure she was dead. Then I backed off. I thought you'd want to have the first crack at her. Victim is twenty-five to thirty years old. She's Hispanic, five-two to five-three, and maybe a hundred and twenty pounds. No ID or clothes on her. She has a single gunshot wound to the chest, but there's little blood on the ground."

A hundred-and-twenty-pound human being carried a little over a gallon of blood in her body. If someone had shot her at the campsite, her blood would have pooled around her. This wasn't the murder scene; it was a dumping site.

"Any sign of sexual assault?" I asked.

"I didn't look that closely, but considering she's in the middle of nowhere and nude, I'd say it's a strong possibility," he said. He paused and lowered his voice. "If you're not comfortable working the case, I can bring in Harry. He wouldn't mind, considering everything you've gone through."

I didn't roll my eyes, but I wanted to. Officer Skelton meant well, but the comment still pissed me off. I had grown up in the foster care system. Some houses were safe and stable, but some weren't. When I was sixteen, my foster father—a man named Christopher Hughes—drugged and raped me. It was the most awful experience of my life, one I had wanted to keep private for the rest of my life.

Unfortunately, a reporter from St. Louis told the world my story while I worked a high-profile murder case four weeks ago. Since then, people held doors for me and looked at me as if I were an invalid everywhere I went.

I lowered my voice.

"Thank you for your concern, but I don't need the boss's help to work a murder," I said. "Okay?"

Skelton straightened. "Yes, ma'am."

"Good," I said, looking around. "You know St. Augustine. Where are we?"

Skelton blinked and looked around. "You go north about half a mile, you'll run into the chicken processing plant. East of here, you've got the interstate and the Mississippi River. West of here, you've got farms to the county line."

"You know who owns this property?"

"I'd guess Ross Kelly Farms, but I wouldn't bet my paycheck on that."

St. Augustine had few major employers, but the few it had enjoyed considerable influence with the local powers that be. If we arrested somebody at Ross Kelly Farms, we'd have a county councilor or two knocking on our doors with complaints soon. I could deal with that, but it would waste time I'd rather not waste.

I walked toward the campsite. Rustic benches surrounded a rock-enclosed fire pit, while cigarette butts littered the ground. There were beer bottles everywhere I turned and tire tracks in the mud near the road. As Dave had said, the victim was nude, and she had a gunshot wound to her chest.

"You see any clothes around here?"

Skelton shook his head. "Nope."

I nodded as I walked closer to the victim. The gunshot wound was clean without powder marks or fouling, which meant the shooter had stood at least a few feet from her when he squeezed the trigger. Her brown eyes were open, and they stared at the canopy of leaves above us. In life, she would have been beautiful. In death, she was a statue.

I hated this part of the job. This was someone's daughter. She might have been someone's mom. No matter what she did or who she was, she didn't deserve to die like this. She deserved even less what would happen to her now.

The moment a bullet pierced her chest and killed her, she had ceased to be a human being. She had become evidence, grist for the great machinery of the criminal justice system. The coroner would photograph her, cut her open, and remove her internal organs. He'd tease out every secret her corpse possessed and present his findings to a jury. Twelve strangers would study every inch of her body more intimately than any lover ever could, and only then, when the system had taken every shred of dignity she had, would the courts release her to her family for burial.

To the system, she was an object to study. To me, she was more than that. She was something sacred, something worthy of protection. She was a person. From now until the day we put her killer in prison, I would become her voice. That was my calling; it was why I had become a police officer: I protected those who couldn't protect themselves. For those whom I couldn't protect, those like the young woman in front of me, I sought vengeance. I couldn't bring her back from death, but I could even the scales.

I walked closer to see her. A red hair tie held the victim's brown hair behind her head. The ground surrounding her looked dry, but there were no signs of drag marks, which meant the shooter must have carried her. Neither the victim's wrists nor legs had ligature marks, nor did her hands or forearms have defensive wounds.

I took out my cell phone and took almost four dozen pictures of the body and surrounding area before walking back to Skelton's SUV. Walter Williams—the man who had found the body—was inside, taking a nap. I doubted he had shot her, but we'd hold him until we eliminated him as a suspect. Skelton stood straighter as I approached.

"What do you think?" he said.

"She's dead," I said. "Other than that, we've got work ahead of us. We need additional manpower here right away to search the woods, so call Trisha and ask her for everybody we've got available. I also need someone to verify that Ross Kelly Farms owns the property. If they do, I need somebody to contact them. We'll need their representative out here.

"Second, Dr. Sheridan needs to pick up the body. I want him to ID the victim by the end of the day if possible.

"Third, find out who camps out here. Are they hunters, are they college kids who come here to get drunk and have sex, or are they something else?

"Fourth, we need at least two officers with forensic training to work the crime scene. We've got a lot of evidence to collect, and we need it done right.

"Fifth, call Harry. The sheriff should be here."

Skelton scribbled on his notepad, so I let him catch up.

"Anything else?"

"Do you have any plaster of paris in your car?"

He looked up and squinted. "No. Why?"

"Trisha says we've got storms inbound, and I want to get these tire tracks and footprints cast before it rains."

Skelton looked toward the campsite and nodded.

"Okay," he said. "I'll get on the radio and call this in."

"Thank you," I said, walking toward my old Dodge Ram pickup. The door opened with a creak, and I softened my expression. "And thank you for your work before I got here. You preserved the evidence and kept things clean. I appreciate it."

His expression softened, and he nodded.

"Thanks, Joe."

I smiled before sighing. "Okay. I'm off to the hardware store for supplies. I'll get bottles of water, but do we need anything else?"

He squinted. “Bug spray?”

It was a fair idea, so I nodded. As I did that, thunder rumbled in the distance.

“I’ll be back soon.”

Skelton looked at the sky and nodded. “I’ll tell Harry to bring in the party tent.”

I closed my door. A drop of rain hit the front windshield as I rolled my window down.

“Please do,” I said. I paused and waited as thunder once more rumbled to the west. “And tell him to hurry or we won’t have a crime scene left.”

Chapter 3

Even as they traveled over the keyboard, Aldon McKenzie's fingers trembled. It was Sunday, and the building was empty save for the security guards and cleaning teams. Aldon's colleagues were at home, playing with their kids or gardening or doing whatever the hell else they did on their days off. If he had been at home, he would've been reading a book with his autistic daughter.

Daria loved fish. At times, she couldn't focus on anything else. Many kids with autism developed nearly obsessive interests like that. Sometimes that led to trouble, but for Daria, it became her release. She couldn't talk about herself or her day, but once she started talking about clownfish, she wouldn't stop.

Aldon loved hearing her little voice. She had spoken her first word at two years old. *Table.* It was an odd first word, but Aldon fell in love with her voice the instant he heard it. His entire world shifted when she spoke for the first time. At the time, he and his wife had pretended Daria was a late bloomer. They had hoped that once she started talking, she'd interact with people more. Maybe she'd smile like other kids her age.

Unfortunately, that didn't happen.

They took her to doctors and therapists. The professionals were kind and understanding, but Daria would probably need help the rest of her life. She'd likely never go to a typical school, and when she got old enough, she'd likely have to move to a special facility with appropriate staff to care for her. Even the word *facility* broke Aldon's heart. To him, Daria was perfect. She would always be his baby, and he'd never give up on her and dump her into a facility where they'd warehouse her until her death.

And then, he and Jennifer took her to the zoo in St. Louis. Daria had been four, but she still liked riding in the stroller. They had spent hours at the zoo, but she had hardly looked at the animals. Then they walked into an artificial cave near the end of the elephant exhibit.

Both Alden and Jennifer had been ready to go home. Giggling, happy children had surrounded them all day, but Daria hadn't even cracked a smile. It broke his heart all over again. Aldon wished his daughter could experience that same uncomplicated childish joy. She deserved it. He would have given anything to make her smile.

And then she did.

The cave at the end of the River's Edge exhibit wasn't large, but it had faux stalactites and stalagmites on the ceiling and floor, and there were signs pointing out the different features common to the limestone caves that dotted the Missouri countryside. The cave also held a thirty-three-thousand-gallon fish tank with gar, bluegill, and whiskered catfish. When Daria saw that water, she squealed and clawed at the restraints that held her upright in the stroller.

Aldon and Jennifer thought something had scared her, so they ran her through the exhibit and out the other side. Even when they got back into the late afternoon sunlight, though, she didn't stop fighting. Thinking she'd hurt herself, Aldon unhooked the stroller's straps, and Daria vaulted out and ran back into the exhibit.

When Aldon and Jennifer got to her, Daria had pressed her face to the glass and grinned.

"Fish," she said, looking to her mother and father and then back to the tank. She pointed at an ugly gar near the glass. "Fish."

It was the second word she had ever spoken. It was also the happiest she had ever been. Jennifer cried. Aldon knelt beside his little girl and hugged her tight.

They spent two hours staring at that fish tank. Other families passed through the exhibit, but nobody remarked on the cute, smiling little girl at the fish tank. It became the happiest day of Aldon's life.

Now, Daria spoke every day. Her vocabulary and memory astounded everyone around her. She knew the scientific names for hundreds of fish, and she remembered the exact outfit she wore when seeing an alligator gar for the first time at the zoo.

Unfortunately, despite her progress, God hadn't made Daria for this world. As long as Aldon and Jennifer lived, Daria would have everything she needed, but the two of them wouldn't live forever. Aldon was thirty-eight; his wife was thirty-nine. With luck, they'd live another forty years, but they couldn't provide Daria the help she needed forever.

Between Aldon's job as an accountant and Jennifer's job as a second-grade teacher, the family enjoyed a comfortable middle-class lifestyle. They saved every spare penny they earned for their daughter and put it into a tax-deferred trust. In thirty years, Daria would have several million dollars to live on. That money would buy all the help she needed. She'd be happy and safe.

Now, Mason Stewart had put that dream in jeopardy.

Aldon's throat felt tight as he typed in commands. Six weeks ago, he had found some disturbing discrepancies in his employer's accounting books. Everybody made mistakes, and Aldon thought little of them. Then he looked closer and learned the discrepancies weren't mistakes at all.

Something bad was happening at Reid Chemical.

His fingers trembled as he progressed through the guide his attorney had given him. The first step was to create a virtual private network. That would allow him to upload company files to an off-site cloud server without fear of the IT department being able to track him. He had done this weeks ago, and nobody had found out, but the process still made him nervous.

Reid Chemical advertised itself as a boutique manufacturer of chemical compounds for the pharmaceutical industry. In actuality, the company made cough drops and children's ibuprofen. In the past year, though, the company had branched out.

Aldon was on step five of his attorney's eight-step guide when he heard the elevator ding. Like many modern office buildings, Aldon's floor held cubicles but few private offices. He rose out of his chair to peer over the cubicle walls. Three men walked toward him. Two of them carried firearms and wore the black outfits of security officers, but the third came from IT.

"Shit."

Aldon didn't know how the Reid family organized their business, and on a day-to-day basis, he didn't care. He was just a CPA. He kept his head down, did his job, and drove home when the work was done. It used to be a great job, but then Mason Stewart, the CEO, brought in new partners.

Supposedly, Stewart's new business partners operated an off-shore holdings company, but none of Aldon's colleagues knew who they were. These new partners, though, brought a lot of cash with them. More than that, they brought guns and their own security personnel. Now, men with assault rifles guarded the entrances as if it were a military base.

Aldon's heart raced. He had a story prepared if they caught him, but now it sounded flimsy in his head. The progress meter on his computer said he was halfway through the upload. He needed to stall, but first, he needed to calm down. He closed his eyes and pictured Daria. This was for her.

Once his breath came easily, he stood and forced a smile to his face.

"Anthony, right?" he asked, stepping out of his cubicle and looking at the guy from IT. The security guards stopped near the elevator, but Anthony kept walking. Aldon swallowed hard and pointed to his cubicle with his thumb. "I'm trying to get a head start on a big project, and I'm short on time. You guys need something?"

"Oh, don't let us bother you," said Anthony. "We'll come back later."

"You're not here for me?" asked Aldon. "I mean, you're not here to fix my computer or anything?"

Anthony furrowed his brow. "Something wrong with your system?"

"No, it's fine, but what's with the security guards?"

Anthony looked over his shoulder before darting his eyes to Aldon.

"Mr. Stewart ordered it. My team is installing biometric fingerprint readers on each computer. It makes things more secure. I'm sure you'll get an email about it."

Aldon's shoulders and chest loosened. "That will be a big change. It's past time."

"Way past time," said Anthony, nodding and raising his eyebrows. "The world's changing. Information security has to change with it. Since you're up here, though, I'll tell my team to work elsewhere so we won't bother you. Good luck with your project."

"Thank you," said Aldon, nodding and breathing easier. "You, too."

He watched Anthony go back to the elevator. Once the IT manager left, Aldon's legs gave out, and he fell onto his chair, panting. The upload finished a few minutes later without a hitch, allowing him to finish the remaining steps in Laura's checklist. Then, he jogged to the stairwell and pulled out his cell phone to call his wife.

"Hey, honey," she said. "I'm making lunch for Daria. Will you be home soon?"

"I'm leaving the office now," he said.

She paused before speaking. "Are you all right? You sound out of breath."

He thought about lying to her and pretending that everything would be okay. It wouldn't be, though. Aldon had opened Pandora's box. Unlike his colleagues, Aldon knew Mason Stewart's new partners. He also understood what they planned for Reid Chemical. If they found out what Aldon had discovered, they'd kill him and his entire family without hesitation.

Thank God he had found a lawyer with guts. Once he and Laura, his attorney, had the information they needed, she would contact the US Attorney's Office in St. Louis. She'd keep them safe. Considering the people they were up against, the government would probably put his family in witness protection. Witness protection would hurt Daria, but it beat the alternative of being dumped in a shallow grave in the middle of nowhere.

He cleared his throat.

"Nothing's right," he said. "I'll pick up moving boxes on the way home."

"Why do you need boxes?"

"I'll tell you later," said Aldon. "Think about what you'd want to take with you if we had to disappear for a while. I'll be home as soon as I can. We have a lot to talk about."

Chapter 4

I bought two cases of water, fifty pounds of plaster of paris, and half a dozen tarps at our local hardware store before hurrying toward the highway, ever watchful of the darkening sky. As I drove, the clouds released a slow, soaking rain. Heavy rain would wash away the cigarette butts at the crime scene, but the bottles would still stay in place, and the footprints and tire tracks should survive for a while. As long as things didn't get worse, I'd be okay.

I made good time on the highway, but the moment I turned onto the dirt and gravel road that led to the crime scene, my tires slipped, and the rear end of my truck fishtailed as if I had hit an ice patch. The bags of plaster of paris slid off the seat and to the floor beside my feet.

I spun the steering wheel toward the skid while pumping my brakes. My old truck groaned and came to a stop, three wheels on the road and another in a ditch beside it. Then, the skies opened up. Rain pounded against my roof and windows.

I sighed and got my truck back on the road and crept forward. The campsite was about half a mile from the highway, and with every foot I traveled, my hands grew tighter on the steering wheel. It wouldn't take long in this weather for even the deepest tire tracks to lose their shape. We didn't even know our victim's name yet, and already we were losing the evidence that could put her murderer in prison.

This sucked.

After five minutes of driving—and getting almost nowhere—a shape came into view on the road. I tapped my brake pedal to slow down. It was the coroner's minivan. I parked behind him and grabbed a poncho I kept in my glove box.

St. Augustine wasn't big enough to have its own dedicated coroner, so we shared one with four neighboring counties. As I walked toward Dr. Sheridan's van, his back wheels spun, shooting up a rooster tail of mud and gravel right toward me. I turned and covered my face as the spray hit me. A rock slammed into my forearm. It hurt, and I kicked his bumper, rubbing my arm.

"Lay off!" I shouted. The wheels stopped spinning, and the driver's door opened. Sheridan stuck his head out. I spat mud out of my mouth, raked dirt off my poncho, and then checked out my forearm. I wasn't bleeding, but pain radiated up my arm and into my elbow. If that rock had hit me in the face, it would have broken my teeth.

"You all right?"

"No," I said. "Did you not see me?"

"No. Sorry," he said. "The storm snuck up on me, and the van got stuck in the mud. I was trying to free it."

"Well, it's stuck even tighter now," I said, rubbing my now throbbing arm. I didn't bother hiding the annoyance in my voice. "When you spun your wheels, you dug yourself into a hole. We'll carry the victim out on a back brace. When the rain lets up, we'll get a winch in here to pull your van out. If you've got a rain jacket, grab it because we're walking to the crime scene."

He shook his head. "I've already got a body from Jefferson County in the back. If I leave, I'll break the chain of custody."

I crossed my arms and raised my eyebrows.

"Did you come out here alone, Doc?"

He looked to his right. "Well, no, I've got my assistant—"

"He can stay in the van, and you can come to the scene with me," I said, interrupting him. "The chain of custody on your body will be intact. That satisfy you?"

Sheridan thought for a moment.

"Is the body protected in any way?"

"No."

He nodded and unhooked his seatbelt before looking at his assistant.

"Sam, we've got ponchos in the back. Detective Court and I will carry the victim out by hand, so I need you to get the back brace while I get my gear. You might be stuck here for a while, but I'll try to send somebody to relieve you."

Sam, Sheridan's assistant, unlatched his belt and climbed into the rear of the van while I waited. Within moments, I had the back brace tucked under my arm while Dr. Sheridan carried a fishing tackle box full of medical supplies. We were only a couple hundred yards from the campsite, so the walk didn't take long. Sheridan kept looking up at the sky. The clouds had a green, ominous tint, but I had other things to worry about.

At the campsite, five uniformed officers were busy pitching a party tent over the victim's body, while two others collected cigarette butts and bits of paper before they washed away. The rain had already erased the footprints and tire tracks. I couldn't worry about the evidence we had lost, though; I had to focus on preserving what we still had.

"Sampson, Greg," I called. "You can't use plastic bags for those cigarette butts. You've got to use paper. If you put wet paper in plastic bags, the evidence will mold and rot. We won't be able to use it. Paper breathes."

Officer Sampson looked up and furrowed his brow. "We've already bagged a lot of stuff."

"Redo it," I said. I looked to Dr. Sheridan. "The body's yours. Good luck."

Sheridan nodded and knelt over the body while the team and I put up the tent. It took fifteen minutes, but we eventually got a roof over our heads and vinyl walls around us. That kept the rain away, but it didn't stop water from flowing down the hill.

Dave Skelton stood near the tent's entrance, looking at the sky.

"Hey, Skelton," I said, looking up, "find a shovel and build a swale outside the tent. We need to divert this water."

Skelton didn't look at me. Instead, he shook his head.

"Sky's green, and there's a wall cloud to the west," he said. "We should head back to town. The crime scene can wait."

The team looked up at me. St. Augustine was smack dab in the middle of tornado alley, so we took the weather this time of year seriously. Skelton was right, but we couldn't abandon the scene yet.

"We're under a tornado watch at the moment. If that becomes a warning, we'll seek shelter. In the meantime, keep working."

Skelton hesitated before nodding. For about twenty minutes, I settled into the routine of collecting evidence. Then, one by one, every person in the tent froze. My heart thudded against my chest, and my hands trembled as a deep rolling noise reverberated through the woods. It sounded like a waterfall.

"Skelton, find out what that is. Might be a low-flying plane."

Skelton walked out of the tent and swore.

"Not a plane. We've got a funnel."

"Everybody up!" I shouted, stepping across the tent toward the body. Dr. Sheridan was kneeling near her head, but he shot to his feet. "Dr. Sheridan, help me with the girl.

Skelton, open the back of your SUV. Everybody else, get to safety now."

At once, the men and women inside the tent sprang into frenetic motion. We didn't have time to do this right, so I grabbed the victim's feet, and Dr. Sheridan grabbed her arms. Our uniformed officers gathered every evidence bag they could carry. The rain thundered down on the tent, and the wind howled around us.

As dangerous as tornadoes were in open fields, they were far more deadly in the woods. Every tree, rock, stick, and piece of debris around us could turn into a projectile at any moment. Not only that, we wouldn't be able to see the actual tornado coming through the woods, so we wouldn't know where to run.

Rigor had set in, so the victim's body stayed stiff as we picked her up, making her corpse more like a heavy stack of lumber than a giant water balloon. The fatigue I had experienced earlier disappeared as hail pounded against the tent and crashed against the cars outside. Powerful winds buffeted the tent, threatening to rip it out of the ground.

As Sheridan and I shuffled with the victim, the roar of the storm magnified, and small bits of debris lifted from the ground, forming an opaque cloud around us. Grit hit me in the face, arms, and legs, abrading my skin. The wind pushed my clothes tight against my body. I squeezed my eyes to a slit and hurried to Dave Skelton's marked SUV. Around me, taillights disappeared as the rest of the team hurried away.

I should have listened to Dave Skelton earlier. I should have focused on the living instead of the dead. Sheridan and I slid the victim into the back of Skelton's vehicle, but since her body was stiff, her legs wouldn't bend.

"Head on the ground and feet on the backseat," said Sheridan, lowering the victim's head to the floorboards. I lifted her legs so they rested between the headrests on the backseat. We wedged her in there pretty well. The position wasn't dignified, but it was our best option given the circumstances. Once we had her secured, Sheridan ran to the passenger seat and slammed the door shut.

I sat in the backseat when I remembered something: Sam, Sheridan's assistant, was still in the coroner's van up the road, and he wasn't going anywhere.

I slammed my door shut, hit the SUV's side, and sprinted up the road. Sheridan must have guessed what was going on because Dave Skelton's vehicle shot past me a second later.

The coroner's van—and my pickup—were a couple hundred yards from the campsite, so it only took a few seconds to get there. As I pulled open the minivan's door, a deafening crack echoed around me, even above the sound of the storm. I looked to find an old poplar falling to the ground, its trunk having snapped in the wind. Sam, Dr. Sheridan's assistant, had the wide eyes of an animal caught in a snare.

"My truck. Move. Now."

Sam and I ran to my truck. I couldn't find my keys in my pocket, so I reached into the glove box for my spare as the coroner's technician climbed inside. As I turned my key, a heavy tree branch slammed into the hood, rocking the entire vehicle. Hail the size of lemons and baseballs slammed into my roof and front window, creating a deafening cacophony. My old truck coughed and sputtered to life.

"Hold on, buddy," I said, putting my right arm behind the seat beside me and peering over my shoulder as I accelerated backwards, being careful to keep two wheels on the grass beside the gravel road for traction. Even as I drove, the sky grew darker, and the debris hitting the truck grew heavier and heavier. The tornado was moving faster than we were on these mud roads.

My heart thudded against my chest, and my skin felt clammy. Time slowed as dirt and gravel pelted my car.

"Almost there," I said, more to myself than anyone else. The moment the words left my lips, something slammed into my windshield.

"Shit," said Sam, his hands over his ears. "Go, go, go, go."

I didn't know what Sam saw, and I didn't dare turn my head to look. Instead, I pressed on the accelerator hard.

Please don't get stuck. Please don't get stuck.

My tires spun in the soft ground, but then they found purchase, and we rocketed toward the highway. Something heavy slammed into my door, knocking the car to the right. Sam swore and put his hands on the dashboard, bracing himself for an impact. I tightened the muscles of my legs and back, expecting something to slam into us.

Come on, baby. Keep going.

As if hearing my private thoughts, my truck's engine roared even louder than the storm as we shot backwards. Within seconds, we hit the tree line. Once my tires reached asphalt, I threw the car into drive and punched the gas to the floorboard. The sound from the storm was deafening. Impenetrable, dark clouds surrounded us. The hail had cracked my front windshield. My windshield wipers didn't work, but the other windows were still intact.

A towering black form hovered over the woods we had exited. Branches, bits of aluminum siding, and other debris pelted the countryside. I squeezed the steering wheel and held my breath as I sped up.

"There's a bathtub in the road," said Sam.

His voice was so nonplussed that I didn't process what he'd said until I saw it myself. An enameled cast-iron bathtub sat in the middle of the road as if God himself had dropped it. My tires squealed as I spun the wheel to avoid it. Then they squealed again as I whipped the truck around a tree branch as thick as my waist. Grit hit the sides and windows, making it sound as if I had driven through a cloud of insects at high speed. My broken front window creaked with the force of the gale.

Don't break. Don't break. Don't break.

I kept saying it repeatedly so it became my mantra, a prayer to a God who, at the moment, seemed really pissed off.

Time had no meaning in that black cloud, but then I saw a light ahead. The tornado was moving perpendicular to the highway, leaving us behind. The sky grew brighter. A few moments later, I looked in my rearview mirror. The storm didn't have a tight funnel; instead, it had a V-shape that reached from the sky to the ground.

I drove for another mile before turning into the parking lot of a McDonald's. A crowd of people had formed in the parking lot to watch the tornado tear through the countryside, but my team must have kept driving. The moment I parked, Sam opened his door and vomited outside.

"Easy, buddy," I said. "That was scary."

"We drove through a tornado," he said. He spit and wiped his mouth with his sleeve. "That was terrifying."

I tilted my head to the side and took a deep breath. "We got lucky. I don't think we got caught in the vortex. That was probably the forward downdraft."

He looked at me as if I had opened a can of rotten tuna in front of him.

"I don't care if we were in the forward downdraft, the rear downdraft, the vortex, or anything else. We almost died."

I nodded and lowered my voice.

"You didn't die. You're okay. Why don't you get a cup of coffee?" I asked, reaching into my purse for a ten-dollar bill. "It's on me."

He took my money and stepped out of the vehicle. Once he disappeared, I leaned my head back and closed my eyes.

Once I caught my breath, I called my station. The phone rang half a dozen times before somebody—Darlene, a forensic scientist in the crime lab—picked up.

"Hey, it's Joe Court. My team and I got caught out in the storm. We missing anybody?"

"Mark off Joe. She's alive," said Darlene. Her voice sounded distant because she was shouting to someone else. "Are you injured?"

"No," I said. "I have Sam from Dr. Sheridan's office with me. We were the last ones out of the crime scene. You heard from Dave Skelton yet?"

"He's on his way here with your victim. Where are you?"

Relief flooded through me. Aside from me, Skelton was the last officer out. If he survived, the others did, too. Our crime scene may have been toast, but at least no one had died.

"I'm at the McDonald's on Highway 62. I'll head back to the crime scene and see whether there's anything I can salvage."

"Negative," said Darlene. "The boss needs you to come in. We've got emergency calls all over the county."

"Any word on casualties yet?"

"So far, we know the tornado hit a custom cabinet shop out by Ross Kelly Farms. Their building was a pole barn on a concrete slab. We don't anticipate finding survivors."

I nodded to myself as I processed that. My case and the dead woman in Dave Skelton's SUV mattered, but this storm had shifted my priorities.

"Tell the boss I'm on my way to the station. And tell Dr. Sheridan that his assistant made it out."

"Will do, Joe," said Darlene. She told me to drive safely. I stayed in my car and watched the storm. There were occasional flashes of lightning, but the sky didn't look as threatening as it had a few minutes earlier. I got out of my truck and walked toward the restaurant to get Sam.

As much as I wanted to work on my case, my victim would be as dead tomorrow as she was today. Life was for the living, and my friends and neighbors needed my help.

Chapter 5

I spent the rest of the day knocking on doors, talking to my neighbors, and trying to track down missing persons. No further tornadoes hit the county, but several severe thunderstorms rolled through, causing everyone to flee for cover. St. Augustine lost four people. We got lucky. If that tornado had hit the plant at Ross Kelly Farms, Reid Chemical, or Waterford College, we would have been looking at hundreds of casualties instead of four. As wrong as it felt to be thankful for four dead people, I was.

My adrenaline faded as the sun went down, leaving exhaustion in its wake. I ended my shift twelve hours after it started and drove home to my ancient two-story farmhouse. The man who had built my house had ordered it from a Sears catalog in 1913 and had lived in it with his family until he died. When my realtor showed it to me, its most recent inhabitants had been a family of raccoons.

The real estate listing had called it a teardown on a great piece of property, but it wasn't a teardown at all. Where others saw a cracked foundation and shattered windows, I saw a home waiting for someone to restore it. I saw something broken that I could make beautiful again. I liked that.

As I stepped onto my porch, I whistled and waited for my dog. The tornado had come nowhere near my house, but thunderstorms had left branches and leaves strewn across the front yard. Roger, my aging hundred-and-forty-pound bullmastiff, trotted from his house in the backyard to greet me.

"Hey, sweetheart," I said, kneeling and reaching to scratch his cheek and ear. He barked a contented bark and wagged his tail. I wouldn't be alive if not for Roger. Many people say that about their loved ones, but in this case, it was a literal truth. "Your breath stinks, dude. What's Susanne been feeding you?"

As if in response, he licked my face. I laughed and ran my hand down his back. I'd worry about getting him cleaned up later. For now, I was too tired to care.

"Come on in," I said, fishing in my purse for my house keys. My house wasn't much, but it was all mine. When I bought it, I ripped down the old plaster, replaced both the plumbing and drain systems and installed thick insulation. Now, I lived in a comfortable home. Or at least the first floor of a comfortable home. I had yet to touch the second floor beyond tearing out the plaster and ripping out the knob-and-tube wiring. One step at a time.

The moment I got inside, I flopped onto the couch and pulled out my cell phone to call Susanne, my neighbor, and make sure she was okay and to thank her for looking after Roger while I was at work. That done, I called somebody I should have called hours ago.

Julia Green hadn't given birth to me, but she was my mom. She and her husband had adopted me and given me my first real home when I was sixteen years old. I loved them both.

"Hey, Mom, it's Joe," I said. "I finally got in."

"I'm glad. You have any damage to your house?"

"The yard's a mess, but the house is okay," I said, yawning. "How are you and Dad getting along?"

"Haven't killed each other yet, but it's been close," she said. "Retirement's harder than I thought."

Mom and I didn't talk long, but the conversation grounded me and reminded me of all the good things in my life. My adopted family was my anchor in the world. Without them, I became unmoored. With them, I had stability and love. Meeting them had been the best thing to happen to me in my entire life.

After I hung up, I ate Chinese leftovers from my fridge, showered until the hot water ran out, and then crashed into my bed, where I slept the dreamless sleep of the exhausted.

As was his custom, Roger woke me up the next morning by stretching and shaking my bed so violently it felt as if I had just been through a minor earthquake. As my eyes opened, he left his spot at my feet and licked my face. I pushed him away.

"Enough, butthead," I said, sitting up and stretching. Roger's face was so close to mine, his hot breath hit my cheek. I pushed him away again. "I'm awake. Go get your bone. It's in the kitchen."

I watched and waited as he lumbered toward the stairs I had built for him. Even just a year ago, he would have jumped down from the bed and sprinted through the house like a crazy man at the mere mention of his bone. Now, age had forced him to use the stairs. Time slowed us all down, but it didn't make it any easier to watch.

I closed my eyes and sank into the pillow as the dog slurped his water in the kitchen. Roger still drank pretty well, but in the past four weeks, he had stopped eating well. When he was young, he'd scarf his food down within seconds of me putting it in the bowl. Now, it might take him all day to finish his breakfast. In the past week, he had even started to skip meals. My vet said he didn't have long left. It hurt to admit that, but it was true. Nothing good lasted forever.

Muscles all over my body ached, and my forearm had a purple and black bruise the size of a golf ball. It hurt, but it didn't throb. I swung my legs off the bed and glanced at my alarm. It was a little before seven, which meant I had gotten about ten hours of sleep. I could have used another ten, but I doubted my boss would have appreciated me showing up that late to work.

I got ready for the day, and then I walked Roger to Susanne's house before going to work.

My department operated out of a historic Masonic temple the county had purchased a few years ago. The building held the county's small forensics lab, six cells for prisoners, and desks and private offices for the county's forty-five officers. At the moment, we used most of the second and all of the third floor for storage, but the county promised us that we'd eventually get funding to renovate the entire structure so we could use the spaces for interrogations or community policing functions. I wasn't holding my breath.

When I got in, Trisha, our day-shift dispatcher, locked eyes on me from her desk in the entryway.

"Boss wants a status update on your Jane Doe investigation. There's somebody with him from Ross Kelly Farms. They're in the conference room."

I stopped in my tracks and sighed. "It's too late to call in sick, isn't it?"

"Just a little," said Trisha, winking. "Happy Monday!"

I grunted.

"Yep. Happy Monday."

Trisha laughed as I walked past her desk to the department's bullpen in the back. The Masons who owned the building before us had used the room as an auditorium for gatherings and meetings, but when the department moved in, we removed all the seating and put in a cubicle farm. With ornate stonework and moldings throughout, it was a beautiful room. Unfortunately, the cubicle partitions, wooden desks, and buzzing phone lines robbed it of some of its grandeur.

I crossed the floor and walked to the first-floor conference room, where I found my boss and a tall, Hispanic man who looked as if he were in his mid-forties. They were talking to one another as I entered.

"Hey, Harry," I said. Harry Grainger, St. Augustine County's recently appointed sheriff, glanced up from a document he was reading. Crow's-feet ran from the corners of Harry's deeply inset eyes nearly to his scalp line, making him look older than his sixty-one years. His hair was curly, gray, and thick, and his hands were big enough to palm a basketball. The County Council had appointed him sheriff two weeks ago after the previous sheriff, Travis Kosen, retired. I liked Harry. He stayed out of my way and gave me the resources I needed when I needed them. He had only been my boss for two weeks, but I couldn't ask for more.

"Morning, Joe," he said, glancing to the man beside him. "This is Lorenzo Molina. He's the chief of security at Ross Kelly Farms. He's here because your Jane Doe's body was found on company property."

I crossed the room to shake his hand. "Detective Joe Court. Nice to meet you."

"You, too, miss," he said, smiling. Few wrinkles marred the olive-colored skin of his square face, and very little gray flecked his black hair. He would have been handsome had it not been for his cold, black eyes. After shaking my hand, he looked at Harry. "Unless there's anything else, I'll head back to work. You have my contact information if you need to get in touch with me."

"Thank you for stopping by, Mr. Molina," said Harry. "We'll call you later today."

Molina left, and I looked to Harry. "Is he running interference, or is he here to help?"

"He gave me a list of troublemakers at Nuevo Pueblo for you to check out. He also offered to act as an interpreter. I'm leaning toward saying he's helpful, but I wouldn't put my paycheck on it."

Nuevo Pueblo was the company town Ross Kelly Farms had constructed for its largely immigrant workforce. We rarely made it out there, so I didn't know it well.

"Give me the names, and I'll check them out. Do I get a partner on this case?"

"If you need another detective, I'll fill in," he said. "We're short-handed right now."

And by that, he meant we had half the officers we needed to run our department. Though many wealthy people lived in St. Augustine, the majority of our population lived paycheck to paycheck. We did our best with the resources we had. Most days, it was enough.

"Sounds good," I said. "Unless you need anything, I'll get to work."

He walked around the table and slid a piece of paper toward me.

"You've got seven suspects so far. Have at it. Good luck."

I picked up the list and nodded my thanks. Since I didn't know the victim's name, and the tornado had destroyed most of our physical evidence, a little good luck would have been nice.

History had taught me not to get my hopes up.

Chapter 6

I had met most of the troublemakers around town, but I knew none of the men on the list Harry had given me. According to the Missouri license bureau, four of them lived in the state and had active Missouri driver's licenses, one had a suspended driver's license, and two weren't in the license system for any state. None of them had convictions for violent crimes in the United States, but several of them came from countries with which we didn't exchange criminal records. I had work ahead of me.

Since I didn't speak Spanish, I called Sasquatch and asked him to meet me on the outskirts of town. After that, I called a repair shop that offered to pick up my truck and replace the front window. They promised to return it by the time I finished work. With all that done, I signed out a marked SUV and headed out.

Ross Kelly Farms had built Nuevo Pueblo on a rolling hundred-acre spread east of downtown St. Augustine. I drove out and parked beside a Catholic church on a bluff overlooking the rest of the community. Not a single cloud marred the blue sky. From my car, I had a clear view of the

Mississippi River and the chicken processing plant at which most of the town's residents worked. A rail line ran to the processing plant from the west, while cornfields surrounded the property.

It was a pretty piece of land marred by one unfortunate problem: When the wind stopped blowing, the whole place stunk like ammonia and animal shit left to rot in the summer sun. It wasn't pleasant.

I waited for about five minutes for Sasquatch to arrive. He smiled when he stepped out of the car, but then the breeze shifted and he caught a whiff of that foul country air and gagged.

"That's a powerful odor," he said, covering his mouth with his shirt sleeve. "How can people live around here?"

I looked around me. The houses near the church sat on pier-and-beam foundations, leaving them elevated above the soil. The piers prevented them from being flooded during heavy rains, but the wind would have whipped beneath them during the winter, making them cold inside. We were lucky the tornado hadn't turned toward here. It would have taken out everything. I looked at Sasquatch before nodding to the chicken processing plant down the hill.

"It's a company town. Room and board is probably part of their compensation," I said, reaching into my pocket for my list of names. I caught Sasquatch up on the case, double-checked an address, and walked to the first home on the list. The roads were gravel, and a thin layer of dust seemed to cover everything, including the grass.

Our first potential suspect lived in a narrow home with gray siding. The front porch looked like construction-grade pine that had turned gray in the summer sun, while the wooden steps sagged under their own weight. To avoid that sag, the builder should have installed a third stringer in the center to support the weight of everyone who walked up and down, but—if I had to guess—he probably cared more about turning a profit than following the modern building code.

I knocked on the front door and waited, but no one answered.

"It's Monday. You think he's at work?" asked Sasquatch.

"Maybe," I said, looking around. Sasquatch and I were alone amongst the buildings. Waterford College was still in session, but the public schools were out for the summer. Even if the town had its own daycare center, older kids should have been riding bicycles and running around. Something wasn't right. "We'll talk to the residents and then visit the front office."

Sasquatch nodded, so we visited the next house on our list. Like the first one, nobody answered. We tried the third house on the list next, but again, nobody answered. I looked around. In front of one nearby house, I found geraniums in a terra-cotta pot. They were healthy plants, so someone was caring for them. Clothes hung on a line in front of another house, and two children's bicycles leaned against the porch on another. People lived here. Someone should have been around. I looked at Sasquatch.

"You hear any air conditioners?"

He paused and shook his head. "No, why?"

"I don't, either. On a day like this, wouldn't you open your windows if you didn't own an air conditioner?"

He tilted his head to the side. "If they open the windows, they let in the stink."

It made sense, so I nodded even if it didn't convince me.

"That's true," I said, putting my hands on my hips.

"What are you thinking?" asked Sasquatch.

"I don't know, but something's wrong."

We knocked on one more door, but, again, no one answered. After striking out four times, we headed back toward our cars. About halfway to the church, a black SUV came down the road, trailing a long plume of dust. I covered my mouth so I wouldn't inhale dirt and squinted as it pulled to a stop near us. Mr. Molina sat in the front seat.

"Thought you'd be by, Detective," he said, rolling down his window. "I brought your suspects into my office. It's much more comfortable there."

I forced a smile to my lips. Having every suspect in one location saved me some walking-around time, but I much preferred talking to people inside their homes. It gave me an opportunity to see how they lived. Did they have pictures of their children on their mantels? Did they own a dog? Did the home smell like marijuana?

All those things gave me leverage, the most important commodity a police officer had during an interrogation. Molina had wasted a valuable opportunity.

"Where's everybody else?" I asked. "Place looks abandoned."

He looked around before shrugging. "Everybody must be inside for the day."

I shook my head. It was in the mid-eighties, which meant the interiors of those homes with their asphalt roofs were probably in the mid-nineties. No one would have stayed in there without air conditioning and with the windows shut without reason.

"You say the suspects are in your office, huh?" I asked.

Molina nodded and pointed a thumb toward the back of his SUV.

"Hop in. I'll give you a ride."

I glanced at Sasquatch before opening the rear door. The SUV had dark tinted windows, an anodized metal grill guard in front, and a light bar on the roof. It looked like something the Secret Service might have driven if they needed a menacing off-road vehicle. Sasquatch and I rode in silence in the back for about five minutes before we reached an office building near the main plant. Molina parked in a nearly empty parking lot and looked at the two of us.

"How's your Spanish, Detective?" asked Molina.

I tried the door, but it didn't open. It must have had a child lock.

"Nonexistent," I said. "You transport a lot of kids in here?"

Molina flashed me a smile before opening his own door.

"Give me a second. I'll get you right out."

He stepped out of the vehicle, closed his door, and pulled out his cell phone to make a call. The windows blocked his conversation, but I didn't like this. I glanced at Sasquatch.

"I've got a bad feeling about this place, and the longer we stay, the worse it gets," I said. "If Molina doesn't come back within a minute or two, I'm going to arrest him for interfering with a police investigation."

"Good," said Sasquatch. "I don't like being locked in the back of an SUV."

I nodded and dropped my hand to my firearm's grip. Molina opened my door a few seconds later and then hurried around the car to get Sasquatch. The lines demarcating one spot from another on the asphalt parking lot looked freshly painted, and the lawns and flower beds around the building were immaculate. The building itself had smoked glass windows and a modern, gray granite exterior. At least we knew where Ross Kelly Farms spent its money.

Molina looked at me and gestured toward the building.

"After you, Detective," he said. I nodded and walked toward the front door. Before we reached it, Molina hurried forward and waved his wallet in front of the key reader. The door buzzed and unlocked. The building's interior was clean and utilitarian. Thin gray carpet covered the floors, while light blue-gray paint covered the walls.

"This way, officers," he said, leading us toward an elevator up the hall. Molina accessed this, too, with his keycard.

"Your security is tight around here," I said. "It's almost like a prison."

Molina tilted his head to the side and chuckled. "Some days, it feels like a prison."

We took the elevator to the third floor before Molina led us to a small, nondescript office with two empty bookshelves, a big desk, and a pair of windows overlooking the parking lot.

"Will this office work for your interview?"

"Sure," I said, glancing toward the door, "but if you lock us in here, I'll arrest you."

"Don't worry," he said. "These doors lock from the inside. If you're tired of seeing me, you can even lock me out."

I nodded, although I didn't smile or acknowledge the joke.

"If I needed to use the restroom, where would I go?"

"If you need to go, I'll call a staff member to escort you to the ladies' room."

I crossed my arms. "I can't walk on my own?"

He shook his head. "Our company policy requires an escort for all guests. Would you like me to call my assistant? She'd be happy to escort you wherever you'd like to go."

"Just bring in Mr. Sanchez, our first guest."

"Sure," said Molina. The door shut behind him as he left, so I tried the handle to make sure he hadn't locked it. Molina turned down a hallway to the left and disappeared. I grabbed a lanyard from my purse to hang my badge from my neck. Then I looked at Sasquatch.

"Stay here. I'm going to take a walk."

He nodded. "I'll hold down the fort."

I grunted and left to explore. The floor held twelve offices, two restrooms, and a break room, but no people. There were emergency stairwells at either end of the building and an elevator in the center. Every exit required a keycard to enter, which meant Molina had locked Sasquatch and me on the floor.

I walked back to the office and found Mr. Molina and a second man inside with Sasquatch. Molina put a hand on the shoulder of his guest. He was short, maybe five-six, and he weighed about a hundred and fifty pounds. His barber had trimmed his hair close to his scalp. Wrinkles accentuated the roughness of his skin.

"This is Gabriel Sanchez," said Molina. I shook Mr. Sanchez's rough, calloused hand. "Find anything interesting outside?"

"Yeah, the elevator and stairs are both locked," I said. "You guys like locks around here, don't you?"

"Ahh," said Molina, nodding as if he had realized something. "This floor isn't in use, so the management keeps it locked. In an emergency, the electronic locks on the doors disengage. You were never in any danger."

"Great," I said, crossing the office. "Please tell Mr. Sanchez to sit."

Sasquatch opened his mouth to translate, but Mr. Molina barked an order before Sasquatch spoke. If Molina wanted to translate, that worked for me.

I started the conversation by introducing myself and asking Mr. Sanchez to confirm his name, occupation, and address. Then we got into things. I showed him a headshot of my victim and watched his face for any signs of recognition. Even though she was dead, he barely reacted.

"Is this woman familiar, Mr. Sanchez?"

Molina translated, and Sanchez shook his head.

"Please look again. Are you sure you've never seen her?"

Mr. Sanchez looked at my phone and nodded that he was sure. The worker clutched a baseball cap between his hands, and his foot tapped rhythmically on the carpet. He looked nervous and kept stealing glances at Molina, like a child hoping to get a read on his dad's mood.

"Do you ever go camping?" I asked.

Molina translated, and Mr. Sanchez furrowed his brow as if he didn't understand. Molina repeated the question. Mr. Sanchez shook his head.

"Do you know of a campsite on company grounds? And remember, camping isn't a crime—even if you get drunk.

No one's in trouble for that. I'm here about a homicide. I'm not interested in anything else."

Molina translated, but before Mr. Sanchez responded, Sasquatch cleared his throat.

"Detective Court, can I talk to you in private?"

I glanced at him.

Now? I mouthed. He nodded, so I looked to Molina.

"Can you step out into the hall, please?" I asked. "And take Mr. Sanchez with you."

Molina hesitated, but then he and Sanchez left the room. I looked at Sasquatch.

"What's going on?"

Sasquatch lowered his voice. "Molina didn't translate your question. He told Mr. Sanchez that if he doesn't stop complaining about the conditions at the plant, you'll take him to the woods and shoot him like you shot that woman in the picture."

I closed my eyes and ran a hand over my brow.

"Tell me you're kidding."

"I'm not kidding, boss. What do you want to do?"

"I want to do my job," I said. I swore under my breath, stood, and checked my firearm to make sure I had a round in the chamber. I saw Sasquatch do likewise. Mr. Molina and Mr. Sanchez were both in the hallway outside the office. Neither spoke, but Molina looked at us and smiled.

"Everything okay?" he asked.

I nodded. "Yep. Please turn around and put your hands on the wall. I'll pat you down, and then my partner will put cuffs on your wrists. You're under arrest for interfering with a police investigation. And because you're a dick."

Chapter 7

Sasquatch and I had to use Molina's keycard to get out of the building, which pissed me off. Outside in the sunlight, I jerked Molina's elbow without speaking, pulling him toward the road in front of the building. I tried to keep my expression neutral, but inside, I seethed. We had found our victim on the company's property. It wasn't far from Nuevo Pueblo. Someone in that town might have known her. Maybe someone even saw the murder.

They wouldn't help us now, though. And even if they wanted to, I couldn't trust them. Molina had told them we were part of a government-sanctioned kill squad sent to put down workers fighting for better conditions at the chicken processing plant. It sounded ridiculous, but the men and women in that town could have seen those sorts of squads firsthand in their home countries.

I wanted to kick Molina's ass up and down the road to show his workers they didn't need to fear him, but that would only make them even more scared of me. Molina and his security staff had poisoned this well so thoroughly the entire town was a lost cause. It'd take us years to earn their trust again.

At least I'd get to see Mr. Molina sit in jail for a while.

Instead of taking his SUV, we walked to our vehicles at the Catholic church with Mr. Molina's hands tied behind his back. Two people came out of their houses as we passed, but they turned away when Sasquatch shouted hello to them. In time, we might convince some of them to trust the local police, but my victim's murderers would have disappeared by then. We were on our own for now.

By the time we got to our cars, my stomach was rumbling. I helped Sasquatch put Molina in the backseat of his cruiser, and then I glanced at my cell phone. It was a little after noon.

"You had lunch yet?" I asked. He shook his head. "How about you drive this asshole back to the station, and I'll pick up sandwiches at Able's?"

"Meatball on Italian?"

"You got it. I'll meet you at the office," I said, walking toward my truck. As I climbed in and buckled up, Sasquatch got into his own car. We drove off together a moment later but separated when we reached the town.

Able's Diner was a greasy spoon about a block from Waterford College. At night, it filled with drunk college students looking for milkshakes, cheesy hash browns, and greasy hamburgers, but in the day it did a brisk business with sober men and women from the town.

I parked in one of the few open spots in the lot and ordered food at the counter. Able's didn't have the biggest kitchen around, but what it lacked in size, it more than made up for in efficiency. Within ten minutes of walking through the door, I left with one meatball sub, one cheesesteak sandwich, and one chocolate milkshake.

Trisha was behind the front desk as I pulled my station's front door open, so I smiled hello before looking around.

"Have you seen Sasquatch?"

"He's writing a report," she said. "He said you made an arrest this morning. You solve your case already?"

"Not even close," I said. "Unrelated matter. Your day going well?"

"Uneventful, so yeah."

"Good," I said. "I'll see you around."

She nodded and smiled, so I walked into the bullpen, where I found Sasquatch at my desk, typing on my computer. He glanced up at me before saving his written report.

"Didn't think you'd mind if I used your desk," he said. "Everybody else has stuff all over theirs. I feel like I'm typing in somebody's bedroom."

Where other people had family pictures and houseplants and mementos from family vacations on their desk, mine held an empty coffee mug and a computer monitor. It said something about my life choices that I didn't even have a picture of my mom and dad, but I didn't care. I liked my privacy and my life.

I put Sasquatch's sandwich on the desk beside him before digging into my own. For a few moments, I ate in silence, but then Harry walked toward my desk. He nodded to both of us.

"Detective Court," he said. "I was hoping I could talk to you for a few minutes in my office. Bring your lunch."

I hesitated.

"Can't we talk here?" I asked. "If you plan to swear, you can tell Sasquatch to put his hands over his ears. I don't think he'll mind."

Harry considered and put his hands on his hips. "I can talk to you here, but I planned to chew you out."

I rolled up my sandwich.

"Ahh, an uncomfortable conversation," I said, looking to Sasquatch. "Take your time. I'll write my report later."

Sasquatch looked at Harry before nodding. The boss and I left the bullpen a moment later and took the stairs to his office on the second floor. When we got there, he closed the door and gestured toward a seat in front of his desk.

"You get lunch from Able's?" he asked.

"Yep. Cheesesteak," I said. "Healthiest thing on the menu."

He grunted instead of laughing at my joke. Then he sat down on his side of the desk. "You made an arrest this morning."

"Lorenzo Molina," I said, nodding. "He was jerking us around. Sasquatch and I picked him up for interfering with a police investigation. I plan to release him tomorrow morning."

"I've already had two county councilors call me about your heavy-handed tactics at the plant this morning. They said multiple constituents had called to say you rolled on the town like jackbooted thugs ready to crack skulls."

"That sounds like me," I said, nodding as I opened my sandwich wrapper. "I love to crack skulls."

"This isn't a joke, Joe."

I took a bite of my lunch and tilted my head to the side.

"It's bullshit," I said. "The town was dead. Even if we had rolled in like jackbooted thugs, no one would have seen us."

"So you didn't talk to anybody but Lorenzo Molina?"

I put my sandwich down and wiped my mouth with a napkin. "We talked to a guy named Gabriel Sanchez. Molina told him that Sasquatch and I would kill him like we killed the girl in the woods if he didn't stop complaining about conditions in the plant. He was using us to scare his employees. You're getting phone calls because the County Council knows who butters their bread. The management at Ross Kelly Farms complained, and the council did their duty and bitched us out. That's all this is. We can all move on now."

Harry sighed and leaned back. "I hate this job."

I nodded and let him sit for a moment. Harry had only been sheriff for two weeks, but already he had bags under his eyes and a short temper. I liked working for him, but he had no business being the sheriff. Office politics went over his head, and he didn't care about statistics. He focused on fairness and justice, two guiding principles that had little bearing on his new position.

"On the plus side, assuming you don't stroke out or have a massive heart attack, you've only got four or five years left until your term is up. Then, you can retire. You might be a shriveled shell of a man, but you won't be a quitter. That doesn't sound so bad, does it, boss?"

He smiled but shook his head. "I appreciate your candor, but sometimes you can be a little too honest, Joe."

Harry and I got along pretty well, so I stayed up there for another twenty minutes to chat. After lunch, he kicked me out because he had a phone call to make, but I had stuff to do anyway. I walked downstairs to my desk to type my notes and plan the rest of my day. About halfway through that, my phone rang. I answered without looking at the caller ID.

"It's Dr. Sheridan at the coroner's office."

"Hey, Doc," I said, sliding back from my desk. "Haven't talked to you since the storm. How are you doing?"

He grunted. "Been better. A big tree hit the van. It's a total loss. I had to rent a hearse from Boone and Sons funeral home until we get a new one."

"I'm glad I pulled Sam out."

"So is he," said the doc. "Mrs. Rumora, the body I was transporting, didn't fare so well. Her family was not happy to hear what happened."

"I'm sorry. It was touch and go for a while, so I'm glad all the living pulled through," I said. "I don't imagine you called to chat, so what can I do for you?"

"I'm calling to let you know I ID'd your victim from her fingerprints. Her name is Laura Rojas, and she's an attorney licensed to practice in Missouri, Illinois, and Kansas. She was twenty-six at the time of her death, and she lived south of St. Louis. She had to submit her fingerprints as part of the character and fitness test when she applied to take the bar exam last year."

I grabbed my notepad from my purse and jotted down notes.

"Anything else you can tell me about her?"

"Gunshot wound killed her. I pulled a nine-millimeter round from her thoracic spinal column. It's pretty trashed, but I sent it to your forensic lab for analysis. Aside from the gunshot wound, her body lacked major trauma. She had minor cuts and scrapes, but they were postmortem. Her hands and forearms lacked bruising, and her body exhibited no signs of sexual trauma or recent sexual activity. She was, however, pregnant."

I winced and leaned back. Some of the energy I had felt earlier disappeared.

"That's sad. How far along was she?"

"Ten to eleven weeks. She wasn't showing yet, but she would have known."

I blinked and drew in a breath as I tried to fit that with everything else I knew.

"Can we tell who the father is?"

"I can pull DNA from the fetus, but I won't have anything to match it to."

"We'll get you something," I said, sitting upright and clearing my throat. "Why would someone take off her clothes if not to rape her?"

"I couldn't tell you," he said. "I hate what happened to this young woman, but she didn't suffer before she died at least. If you don't mind, I'll contact her parents and let them know what happened. They might take it better coming from a doctor than they would from the police officer who threw her body in the back of a police car."

"If you notify them, let them know I need to talk to them later."

"I will," said Sheridan. "Good luck, Detective."

Before hanging up, Dr. Sheridan gave me the victim's address. She lived in Mehlville, a suburb south of St. Louis. Given what had happened at Nuevo Pueblo, her occupation as an attorney was interesting. Ross Kelly Farms had problems with its workforce. If those workers hired Laura, and if she found significant safety or labor violations at the company's plant, she could cost them a lot of money.

It felt tenuous, but it was a start. I stood and walked toward the front door. Along the way, I stopped by the front desk. Trisha was typing something, but she looked up as I approached.

"Hey, Joe," she said, glancing down at the computer screen. "You look like you want to ask me something."

"I need a background check on a young woman named Laura Rojas. She lives in Mehlville."

Trisha nodded and typed before looking back at me. "She the victim you pulled out of the woods yesterday?"

"Yeah. Dr. Sheridan ID'd her, so I need everything you can get on her. Finances, immigration status, criminal records, social media accounts, everything you can get."

Trisha typed again before nodding. "I'll try to get it by the end of the shift."

"Great," I said, already heading toward the front door. "Type everything up and email it to me. And I'll see you tomorrow. I think I'll be working late."

Chapter 8

Nick slowed his rental car in front of a two-story Garrison Colonial with white siding and tasteful, minimalistic landscaping. A red plastic swing hung from a tree, and Tonka bulldozers in the front flower bed looked ready for some little boy or girl to play with. Woods ringed the property, providing privacy. That would make his job today much easier.

He parked in the driveway. Laura Rojas had given him the home's address. Nick hadn't enjoyed killing her, but she had threatened business deals already agreed upon by men who didn't take well to threats. She had brought her death on herself.

He stepped out of his car. The home's front door was shut, and none of its windows were open. The homeowner probably thought it was secure. It wasn't. Nick had never seen a truly secure residence.

If it were up to Nick, he'd burn Reid Chemical to the ground and never look back. His employers had made a sizable investment, though, and they intended to earn a return.

Nick worked for one of the most sophisticated logistics companies in the world. With forty-eight hours' notice, his employers could drop a thousand AKM assault rifles on a battlefield anywhere on the planet. With a few weeks' notice and a large enough advance payment, they could supply a militia in Syria or South Sudan with an entire air defense system capable of fending off the air forces of every two-bit despot and dictator on the planet.

He pulled out a portable cell jammer from the inside pocket of his jacket and hit the power button. Though he had never tested its range, the device was designed to block all cell signals within a ninety-foot radius. His employers sold them to police and military forces who used them to prevent adversaries from coordinating with one another via cell phones. They worked just as well to disrupt the radios in modern home alarms.

He put his jamming device on the ground and picked the lock on the walkout basement's door. The alarm blared upstairs, but he had a plan for it. He pocketed the jammer, and he checked out the home room by room.

According to Laura Rojas, the homeowner and several chemists with whom he worked had stolen hundreds of thousands of dollars' worth of equipment and chemicals from Reid Chemical's warehouse. It would have been a case for the local police, but the stolen chemicals were illegal to have without licenses Reid Chemical didn't have. An investigation would have hurt everyone. This was best handled in-house.

Once he had the house secured, Nick hurried back to his car for tarps and painter's tape. Then, he moved the basement furniture against the walls, leaving an open space, which he covered in clear plastic tarps. When he finished, it looked like something from a television crime show. That was the intent. Image mattered as much as actions.

With the room complete, Nick walked upstairs, placed a call to Austin Wright's cell phone from the house's landline, and waited through three rings before the man picked up. Wright made a good living for himself at Reid Chemical, but his wants exceeded his six-figure salary. He got greedy, and now he had to pay the price.

"Hi, Mr. Wright," said Nick, holding a hand over his left ear so the blaring alarm system wouldn't distract him. "This is Detective Chris Carter with the St. Augustine County Sheriff's Department. We got a call from your alarm company about ten minutes ago, so I'm at your house right now. I need you to come out here."

Wright hesitated. "Did somebody break into my house?"

"Nobody's hurt, but yes, there's been a break-in," said Nick. "I'm in your foyer right now. You think you can come out here?"

Wright swore. "Yeah. I'll be there as soon as I can."

"Thank you," said Nick. "I'm in an unmarked vehicle, so there will be a four-door car in your driveway."

"Okay. Thanks," he said. Nick hung up and waited on the front porch. A green Jeep Cherokee pulled into the driveway about fifteen minutes after Nick placed his call. The driver was about six feet tall and had a wiry build and black hair. His glasses were oversized but fashionable, and he wore a plaid button-down shirt and jeans. The moment Nick saw him, he stepped onto the grass.

"Mr. Wright?" he asked, holding his hand out. "I'm Detective Carter. Sorry to meet you under these circumstances."

Wright shook his hand but otherwise didn't slow as he hurried into the house.

"Were they after my guns?"

"That may have been the target. We'll go through the house room by room so you can show me what's missing," said Nick, already reaching into his own coat for his firearm. "You mind if we start in the basement? That's where they broke in."

"Fine," said Wright. They hurried to the basement. Once Wright turned the corner and saw the plastic taped to the walls and ceiling, he stopped midstep and drew in a breath.

"I've got a gun pointed at your back," said Nick. "If you make any sudden moves, I'll kill you. Are you armed?"

"What is this?" he asked.

"This is a conversation," said Nick. "Are you armed, Mr. Wright?"

He shook his head and put his hands into the air.

"No," he said, his voice shaky. "You can have whatever you want. Please don't hurt me."

"I'm not here to hurt or rob you," said Nick. "Now walk to the middle of the room and take off your clothes, please."

"Why do you want me to take off my clothes?"

Laura Rojas had balked when he asked her to do that, too, but she gave in when Logan agreed to leave. Apparently, she was squeamish about him seeing her nude.

"I need you to take off your clothes so you can't reach for a concealed cell phone or weapon. It also makes it less likely that you'll run. Naked people don't like going outside. I do this to everybody I interrogate. It's nothing personal. Fair enough?"

"I'm not taking off my clothes."

Nick lowered his weapon, aimed, and squeezed the trigger. Wright dropped to the ground, screaming as he clutched his leg. The round had hit him above the knee. Nick rarely had time to practice at the gun range, but that was a terrible shot. He slipped his firearm into his holster and sighed.

"I aimed for your knee. Sorry. I'm out of practice," he said, sliding his belt out of the loops. "I'll put this belt on your thigh and cinch it tight. That should keep you from bleeding out until we can get you to a hospital. Sound good to you?"

Wright stopped screaming. Nick dragged him to the center of the floor by the collar on his shirt and secured his belt on the guy's leg. Wright cried, but whether the tears came from pain or fear, Nick couldn't say. Either worked for him.

"Okay, Mr. Wright," said Nick. "You stole something from my employers. That's not a good idea."

Wright's lips moved, but no sound came out.

"Were you saying something?" asked Nick.

"You said you were a cop."

"I lied," said Nick.

"Fuck you. I'm not talking," said Wright, his voice soft and pained. Nick sighed and scratched his forehead. Then he took a step back, unholstered his firearm, and shot him again. This time, Nick's aim was true, and the round hit Wright in the knee. The beleaguered thief screamed again and clutched his other leg. Nick waited for the initial screams to turn to whimpers before speaking again.

"I don't have another belt to stop the bleeding this time, so you'd better talk fast if you want to live. You stole something from Reid Chemical. I'd like it back."

Wright curled into a fetal position, clutching both his legs and gnashing his teeth.

"This hurts."

"I know it hurts," said Nick. "It's supposed to hurt. The bleeding won't stop, either, so consider talking. You do that, I'll call 911 and get an ambulance out here for you. You refuse, I'll call your wife and tell her that somebody's broken into your house. I'll shoot her next. Do you want that?"

Wright seethed and clenched his teeth before speaking.

"What do you want?"

"The chemicals and equipment you stole," said Nick. "I'd also like to know why you stole them."

"I didn't steal anything," he said through clenched teeth.

Nick considered him and shook his head. "Your wife works at Structure's Salon, right?"

He closed his eyes. "Leave her alone."

"Not my call, buddy," he said. Wright trembled. It was the blood loss. A red puddle had grown beneath his left leg, so Nick pulled the belt tight again. "I'll go upstairs now and call Alyssa. I don't want to hurt her, but I will. Do you understand?"

"Leave her alone."

"That's your choice," said Nick, hooking his thumb toward the stairwell. "I'll call her upstairs. If you haven't talked by the time she gets here, I'll burn her with cigarettes until you tell me what I want to know. That sound okay to you?"

Wright thrashed on the floor, but Nick ignored him and walked upstairs. If he called Alyssa Wright at work and played the detective again, she'd come running. Wright might play hero when his own life was on the line, but not when his wife screamed in pain. If Nick brought Alyssa to the house, she'd have to die. He'd hate to do that, but he'd get over it.

Nick stayed upstairs long enough for Wright to believe he had made a phone call before returning to the basement. The injured man had crawled to the back door, leaving a trail of blood on the tarps. Tears streaked his cheeks. A cell phone lay in the middle of the floor.

"How'd your phone call go?" asked Nick. Wright sobbed but said nothing. "That well, huh? Mine went okay. Got a hold of your wife's salon, and she's on her way. How do you think she'd want to die?"

"I hate you," said Wright, his voice almost inaudible through his tears. "I fucking hate you."

Nick tilted his head to the side. "Alyssa doesn't have to die. Where are the chemicals you stole, and why did you steal them? Did you sell them to somebody? If you did, that's cool. I can work with that. Just tell me."

He clenched his teeth. Wright was hurting as much as possible with the tools Nick had available. Maybe he could find paint stripper in the garage. That on an open gunshot wound ought to do the trick. He turned to leave the room when Wright spoke again.

"Fentanyl," said Wright, his teeth clenched. "We were making fentanyl."

Nick stopped moving.

"Fentanyl," he said, surprised. "The narcotic?"

"We've been synthesizing it at night."

That was a problem. Nick's employers had the worldwide network to become major players in the narcotics world, but they had stayed away from the trade. It was too dangerous. The war on drugs may have been a symbolic fight to arrest users and dealers in the United States, but outside the country, it was a real battle with real weapons.

"Where are these drugs now?"

"We sold them."

Nick sighed and considered what to do. Wright's face was growing pale.

"You better hold that belt tighter, or you're going to bleed out," he said. Wright gripped the belt with white knuckles. "If you sold fentanyl, you've got money. Where is it?"

"I don't have any money."

"Okay," said Nick, scratching his brow. "I'll go upstairs and wait for your wife. Maybe she knows."

Wright thrashed on the floor, but Nick ignored him and walked upstairs. The garage was off the kitchen. Nick searched and found a hammer and a pair of needle-nose pliers in a pink basket on a shelf by the back door. When he got back to the basement, he found that Wright hadn't moved from his spot. His face was even paler, and his breath was shallow.

Nick held up both tools. "Found some tool. Do you want to watch as I pull out Alyssa's fingernails, or do you want me to take her upstairs?"

He narrowed his eyes but said nothing.

"Talk to me," said Nick. "Who do you work with? Where are the drugs? Where's the money? Tell me what I need to know, and I'll clean up your mess. Your wife and kids will move on with their lives."

Wright said nothing for at least half a minute. He stared at Nick, though, with black, hate-filled eyes.

"You'll hurt her even if I tell you."

"I promise I won't," he said. "You're dead no matter what, but if you give me the money, I'll shoot you in the heart. It won't even hurt. Then I'll rip down the plastic, roll you up, put you in my trunk, and get out of here before she arrives. So what's it going to be? You want to watch your wife die, or do you want to be a hero and let her live?"

He closed his eyes. "The money's gone. My partners took their share, and I bought a boat."

"How much did you spend on it?"

Wright opened his eyes, but he wouldn't meet Nick's gaze. "Almost three hundred grand."

"You didn't make fentanyl on your own," said Nick. "Who's in charge?"

Wright opened his mouth, but he said nothing. Nick repeated the question.

"I don't know," he said. "I'm a chemist, man. My bosses tell me what to make. If you want answers, talk to Ruby Laskey. She's in management."

Nick rubbed his eyes and thought. He had already tried to visit Ruby Laskey and Mike Brees—two other names Laura had given him—and found their homes empty. Someone had tipped them off. Nick would have to find them later.

"Okay. Here's what we'll do. You'll write your wife and kids a letter and tell them you're leaving the family for a girl you met on the internet. Tell her you've been unhappy for a long time, but this girl makes you whole. In that letter, you will tell Alyssa about the boat. Tell her you're sorry for your mistake. Then tell her to sell the boat."

Wright narrowed his eyes at Nick, confused.

"Why would I do that?"

"Because if you don't, I'll kill your wife and get rid of her body, too. If you write the letter, Alyssa will think you've run off. She won't call the police, and she'll have a nice boat to console herself with. Everybody wins. Except you. You're screwed, but I don't believe in punishing children for the sins of their father."

He blinked. "You'll leave them alone?"

"You have my word," said Nick.

Wright nodded, so Austin got him a pen and notepad from the kitchen. Over the next five minutes, Wright wrote his final letter to his wife. Then he signed it, and Nick put it in an envelope on the kitchen counter. When he came downstairs again, Wright was crying. Nick gave him a moment to compose himself.

"Any last words?" asked Nick.

"I'm sorry."

"Me, too," said Nick, raising his pistol. He shot Wright in the heart, just as he had said he would and just as he had done to Laura Rojas. Wright's body stilled, but blood spattered all the way to the ceiling. Nick holstered his weapon and tore away at the plastic. Poor Alyssa would never know what had happened at the house that day, but at least she'd live. Her husband's sacrifice had made that happen.

He tossed his burner phone onto Wright's body and then took out his primary phone to text his employer.

Subject down. Reid Chemical has a major problem.

And then he sighed, grabbed his cell jammer, and rolled up the plastic tarps. He hated cleaning up.

Chapter 9

I had just sat down in my SUV when Harry called. Part of me wanted to ignore him and pretend that I hadn't heard my phone ring over the sound of the road, but Harry was too good of a boss to do that to. As much as I needed to get to Laura Rojas's house, the boss wouldn't have called me without reason.

I pulled out my phone and swiped my finger across the screen to answer.

"Harry, yeah," I said. "I'm about to head north to Laura Rojas's house. What's going on?"

"Are you still in St. Augustine?"

"I haven't even left the parking lot," I said. "What's up?"

"A nurse at St. John's just called. A young woman from Waterford College came into the ER for a rape test. I can send Delgado, but the victim would probably be more comfortable talking to you."

My stomach tightened, and I drew in a slow breath. I hated rape cases more than any other. When one asshole killed a second asshole in a fight, the pain ended with the victim's death. A rape survivor, though, became a victim for life. She might move on, but she'd never forget.

I nodded and lowered my voice.

"Tell the hospital I'm on my way."

"I appreciate it," said Harry. "Good luck, Detective."

"Thanks, boss," I said before hanging up. For a moment, I sat in my giant SUV, preparing myself for the job ahead of me. Everybody was different, but I had been in this young woman's shoes, and I understood the courage it had taken for her to come forward. Even before I spoke to her, I hated what had happened to her and the person who hurt her. I also knew I couldn't help her one bit. Nothing would erase her memories of what had happened. My only consolation was that I might prevent her attacker from hurting anyone else.

St. John's Hospital was just off Lincoln Avenue on the outskirts of town. It was a good hospital for broken bones or minor illnesses, but for anything more serious, most people just drove to St. Louis. I parked in a spot reserved for police officers and walked into the ER's main entrance. The nurse working the front desk recognized me from previous visits and smiled.

"Are you here for Ms. Wellman?"

"Is she the young woman from Waterford?" I asked. The nurse nodded and led me to a private room inside the ER and knocked on the door.

"Ms. Wellman?" she asked, peeking her head inside. "A detective is here to see you."

An older woman's voice answered. "Please send her in."

The nurse stepped back and mouthed *get him* before pushing the door open. I nodded to her and then stepped inside the room. A young woman in pajamas sat on a hospital bed. She held her knees to her chest and looked at me with bloodshot eyes. Tear streaks stained her cheeks. Beside the bed, an older woman sat on a chair and held her hand.

I grabbed the doctor's rolling stool and pulled it toward the head of the bed so I could talk to everybody.

"Hey," I said, my voice soft. "I'm Detective Joe Court from the Sheriff's Department. The hospital called my office when you came in. Can we talk?"

Ms. Wellman, the girl, looked to her companion as if for permission.

"You're safe, honey," said the older woman. "You can talk to her."

Ms. Wellman looked at me and then nodded.

"Good," I said, keeping my voice soft. "Before we begin, do you feel comfortable and safe here, and would you like me to call anyone for you? I can call anybody you'd like. Mom, dad, big sister, grandma. Whoever you want. And if you're not comfortable, I can drive you somewhere else."

She blinked and looked away.

"I'm okay here."

Her voice was so soft I almost didn't hear it. That was okay, though. The important thing was that she spoke.

"I'm glad," I said, reaching into my purse for a pair of business cards. I scribbled my cell number on the back of both and handed them to Ms. Wellman and the older woman beside her. "Before we get into anything else, this is my business card. It has my desk number on the front. That's my cell phone number on the back. I work regular business hours, but you can reach me twenty-four hours a day on that cell number. If I don't answer my cell, leave a voicemail. Even if it's two or three in the morning, I'll call you back as soon as possible. I get cranky sometimes, but I'm always willing to listen. Does that sound okay with you?"

Ms. Wellman nodded. For the first few minutes of our interview, I let her talk. She was worried about what her mom and dad would think, but more than that, she was scared. She was a college student, and the boy who attacked her ran in her social circle. They had a lot of friends in common. She didn't want to lose them, and she didn't want them to think she was stupid or that she was lying about what had happened.

I hated to think it, but she had every reason to fear that. Nobody asked to be the victim of a crime, but too many people judged rape victims before knowing their complete stories.

We talked for about fifteen minutes. I couldn't allay her fears, but she seemed better after giving them voice. My victim's name was June Wellman, and she was nineteen years old. Her family lived on the Missouri side of Kansas City, and she hoped to become an elementary school teacher after college. The woman with her was Claudette Everly, and she was the house mother in June's sorority house. June seemed comfortable with her, so I was glad she was there.

"In just a few minutes, I will ask you some questions about what happened," I said. "Some of them will be uncomfortable. If you want me to stop, let me know. You're in charge of this interview. Before we talk, though, know that rape investigations take time to develop. We won't make an arrest today, and we probably won't make one tomorrow.

"No matter what happens, though, please don't think I didn't believe you. There's a long process we have to go through, and it takes time to collect the evidence we need to secure a conviction. Do you have any questions before I get started?"

She didn't, so we dove into things. The interview took almost two hours, including several breaks. June said her attacker was a young man named Chad Hamilton. The two of them had met during June's freshman year and became fast friends. She attended parties at Chad's fraternity house, and she had even taken him to her sorority's formal dance her freshman year. I suspected there was something more than friendship between them, but she didn't volunteer the information, and I didn't want to pry it out of her right away.

June said she'd visited Chad's fraternity house last night to hang out and watch TV. They had several drinks together and fooled around. June told him she didn't want to have sex and tried to leave. He refused to let her go. When she tried to leave anyway, he held her down and raped her. Then, he forced her to take a shower before kicking her out of the house. She was still drunk when she got back to her sorority, so her sorority sisters helped her to bed without realizing something had happened to her.

The next morning, she woke up crying and told a friend what Chad had done. June's friend told Claudette, who drove her to the hospital.

The story was heartbreaking but familiar to anyone who had ever worked sex crimes. It would also be hard to prove. Chad had forced her to take a shower, which told me he knew he had done something wrong. He was covering up the evidence. It made me wonder whether he had done it before.

The more June spoke and described the event, the hotter my skin became, and the tighter my muscles grew. FBI reports say eight percent of all rape claims are demonstrably false. In my career, I had investigated two false rape claims, and from the beginning, those claims had seemed...off. I didn't doubt June one bit, though.

At the end of my interview, I promised to do my best for her and asked whether she had any questions for me. She didn't, so I walked to the nurses' station. There, the same nurse who had greeted me when I walked into the hospital handed me a standardized sexual assault evidence collection kit. As I signed my name as the collecting officer, I glanced at her.

"Who conducted Ms. Wellman's exam?"

"Dr. Shah, but I assisted," she said.

"What do you think?"

The nurse blinked and then looked down at her desk. "Something happened to that young lady. She's not making this up."

"Yeah," I said, nodding my agreement. "Not going to be easy to prove."

"We included pictures," she said. "She has bruises on her inner thighs, wrists, triceps, and upper back. Dr. Shah found significant anal and vaginal bruising consistent with a rough sexual encounter, but I'm not hopeful we'll find DNA. Ms. Wellman said she took a shower before coming in."

She had only confirmed things I already suspected, but I squeezed my jaw tight and drew in a deep breath through clenched teeth, anyway. Drunk or not, she didn't deserve what had happened to her.

"Thank you for your help," I said. "June may not seem appreciative, but she might be one day."

"I'm just doing my job," said the nurse with a grim, resigned expression on her face.

I nodded my thanks and walked back to my car with the rape kit tucked under my arm.

The whole situation pissed me off, but the worst part was that even if we made an arrest, Chad would get a plea deal. He had given her a lifetime of nightmares, and he'd get six months of probation because that'd be easier and cheaper than taking him to trial. Some days, I loved my job. Some days, I hated it. Today was one of the latter.

I walked to my SUV and then climbed inside. Chad may not stay there long, but I would do everything I could to put him in jail. That was the least I could do.

This would be a long day.

Chapter 10

I took June's rape kit to the crime lab in my station's basement, but before I could leave again to drive to Laura Rojas's home, a voice called out. I was in the lobby. Trisha was behind the receptionist's desk, and my hand was on the front door.

"Detective Court."

I closed my eyes and squeezed my jaw shut. The voice belonged to Darren Rogers. He was probably a decent man in his private life, but at work he was a politician with an agenda. He owned two restaurants and several bars in town and thought St. Augustine should try to turn itself into some kind of tourist destination.

It wasn't a bad idea. The county was gorgeous and had plenty of lakes and trails to draw people in. Because of our Spring Fair—an enormous undertaking that brought in tens of thousands of people every spring—we even had the infrastructure set up for a tourist-based economy. I wished, though, that he would concede that some things were more important than making money.

I turned to him and smiled.

"Mr. Rogers, I didn't see you there," I said. "It's nice to see you, but I can't stay. I've got a murder to work."

"I understand, Detective," he said. "This will only take a minute."

In a larger department, we would have had a dedicated administrative staff to handle stuff like this. Here, we shoveled our own shit.

"I'm working on several important cases right now. How about you set up an appointment for later this week?"

"This is a delicate matter, and it's best if we go over it now," he said, grinning. "You're not getting out of here without talking."

"Okay," I said, sighing to myself. I led him through the bullpen to the conference room, where we sat on either side of the long conference table. He smiled at me.

"Thanks for taking time out of your schedule," he said. "You're a busy woman. You've got those missing kids, you got a murder, and just a moment ago I saw you come in here with a sexual assault kit. Did somebody get hurt?"

"Yeah," I said, drawing in a breath. "What can I help you with?"

He smiled. "You're a girl who gets right to the point, aren't you? That's admirable."

I considered telling him I was twenty-eight years old and preferred that people avoid calling me a girl, but that would start a conversation I didn't want to have.

"Glad to hear that. What can I do for you?"

"It's about this murder case you're working," he said, crossing his arms. "I understand you found this woman's body on property owned by Ross Kelly Farms."

"That's right," I said, nodding. "As soon as we learned that, Harry called the company. They sent out a representative. Harry can fill you in if you're looking for background information."

"I think I've got all the background I need, young lady," he said. His smile turned from something friendly to the look I would have expected from a high school principal. "I understand you have your own way of doing things, but we live in a world of rules. We can't go around doing whatever crazy thing pops into our heads. Do you understand what I'm saying?"

Already, my head started pounding. After spending two hours at the hospital with a rape victim, my temper had grown short. I closed my eyes and gritted my teeth.

"I think I understand what you're saying. Thanks for coming down."

"I'm not sure you get me," said Rogers, his voice growing sharper. "And I'd appreciate it if you would look at me when we're trying to talk. I'm a county councilor. I pay your salary. It's rude to roll your eyes or close your eyes or whatever you were doing."

I opened my eyes as wide as I could and focused on him without blinking. "Better?"

"Staring at me isn't any better."

I forced my expression to soften. Then I smiled.

"Okay," I said, nodding. "Let's try to start over. You're a county councilor. The good people of St. Augustine County elected you. I respect that. Please tell me what you need, and I will tell you if I can do it. If I can't do it, I'll try to tell you who can. Sound good?"

He crossed his arms. "You don't have to get snippy."

I cocked my head to the side and blinked. "That's not my intent. I'm tired, and I have a lot of work to do. I don't have a lot of time to sit and chat. Please tell me what you need, and I will do what I can to help. Okay?"

I flashed him a big grin.

"That's all you needed to do. A little smile. Young ladies ought to smile when men come calling."

"You're right," I said, not taking the fake grin from my face.

"I want to talk to you about your investigation. Several people have contacted me about the things you did at Ross Kelly Farms this morning. I can't say I approve of your methods."

"That's unfortunate," I said. He waited as if expecting me to say something else. I raised my eyebrows, unsure of what he wanted me to say.

"Do you understand what Ross Kelly Farms does for this community? They're one of our biggest employers, they contribute many hundreds of thousands of dollars a year in property and income taxes, and they ask very little from us in return. They even police their own employees. St. Augustine can't ask for more."

"I guess not when you put it like that," I said, hoping he'd either go away or get to his point.

"I'm glad you see it like that. And that's why I'm here. We all need to understand the situation. You can't harass your partners, and you can't arrest their head of security for doing his job."

"That's a fair point," I said, nodding. "We're all on the same page. I promise I won't arrest Mr. Molina for doing his job. Anything else?"

His bushy eyebrows formed a V shape, and his mouth opened in surprise.

"Well, I guess not, but I want to impress on you how important Ross Kelly Farms is to this community. They're an asset, and when dealing with assets like that, sometimes it's best not to rock the boat. I don't want to get another call from them."

I gave him a halfhearted salute. "Message received, Mr. Rogers. I'm on board, and I won't rock any more boats."

He hesitated.

"In that case, thank you for your time and discretion," he said. He started to leave but then stopped and cocked his head at me. "Detective Court, can I ask you something?"

"You just did," I said, smiling that fake smile he seemed to like.

"I guess I did," he said, taking a step toward me. His breath smelled like beef jerky. "Is there a Mr. Court, Ms. Court?"

He smiled at me, and I shuddered as if I had just passed a week-old dirty diaper on the sidewalk. He didn't seem to notice.

"There isn't, but I'm not looking for one, either."

"I understand, but you never know when Mr. Right's going to knock on your door. I've got a son. He's in his fourth year of medical school at St. Louis University, and he's as handsome as they come. You guys are about the same age. You two would be a real smart pair. How would you like to meet him?"

It wasn't what I had expected him to offer, but I shook my head anyway.

"I'm flattered, but I don't have time to meet anybody right now. I've got too much stuff on my plate."

"You're a career woman," he said, nodding. "I get it. That's admirable. One day, you'll be sheriff, I'm sure, but, in the meantime, it wouldn't hurt your career if you married a county councilor's son. Consider that, Detective. I'll talk to you later."

He winked and left the room, and I shook my head. At least he wasn't interested in dating me himself.

I waited in the conference room for a few moments, half expecting someone else to knock on the door and demand my time. Nobody did, so I walked back to the lobby and found Trisha at the front desk. She gave me a sympathetic smile.

"Sorry about Councilman Rogers," she said. "He likes to think he's the most important person in the world."

"So I should feel flattered that he offered me his son's hand in marriage?"

Trisha smiled from ear to ear. "Looks like that old dog learned a new trick. He must like you. I've never heard him offer his son to anyone before."

"I feel special. If anybody asks, I'm driving to Mehlville to visit Laura Rojas's house."

"I'll call ahead to let the locals know you're coming."

"I appreciate that," I said, heading out the front door to do the job I had intended to do hours ago.

The sun would set in two hours, which meant I wouldn't make it home until late. I hoped this would be worth it.

Chapter 11

Even though I'd grown up in St. Louis County, I knew little about Mehlville. The town didn't make the news often except for severe weather reports, but there were grocery stores, drug stores, hotels, and restaurants just off the main highway. If I looked hard enough, I was sure I'd find bars and movie theaters somewhere, too. It looked like a nice place to live.

I drove through town before turning into a neighborhood of small, single-story homes about ten minutes after leaving the interstate. Laura owned a brick ranch-style house with a bright yellow front door. An unmarked police cruiser had parked out front, while a red Honda occupied the driveway. A plainclothes detective sat on a rocking chair on the porch.

The detective was about my age—a rarity among detectives—and his shaggy jet-black hair framed his angular, thin face well. He wasn't a handsome man, but he held his head high and kept his shoulders back. A lot of women found confidence attractive, so I bet he did all right for himself in that department.

I parked on the street near the cruiser and held my hand out to him as I walked up.

"Joe Court," I said. "St. Augustine County Sheriff's Department."

"Mathias Blatch. County police. Nice to meet you."

I nodded my agreement and looked toward her house. "You knocked yet?"

"Yeah. Nobody's home," he said, reaching into the inside pocket of his navy jacket for a stack of papers. "Our prosecutor's office got a search warrant while you were driving up here. We're ready to go when you are."

"You get keys too, by chance?"

"Nope," he said, stepping onto the porch and lifting his leg as if he planned to kick the door down. I whistled before he could move. He turned and looked at me with his eyebrows raised.

"You got a better idea?" he asked.

"Yeah," I said, reaching into my purse. "I'll pick the lock. The victim's got family, but even if she didn't, I'm not into destroying property if I can help it."

He lowered his leg.

"My partner never lets me kick the door down, either."

I pulled out my lock pick kit and stepped past him to reach the door. The deadbolt took about two minutes. Blatch whistled as I stood straighter.

"Not bad, Detective Court," he said. "Still, we would have saved time kicking it down. Would have looked cooler, too."

I stood and slipped my lock pick set back in my purse before walking into the home's small entryway. Linoleum tile with a textured grip covered the floor. An odor of stale cigarette smoke hung in the air. I looked over my shoulder at Blatch.

"How about you get the kitchen and public rooms, and I'll get the bedrooms and bathrooms?" I said.

Blatch nodded. "Sounds good."

He reached into his pocket and pulled out a pair of blue polypropylene gloves before heading deeper into the house. The home was laid out like a double-wide trailer. Hallways branched left and right from a central family room. The kitchen was in the back.

I started my search in the guest bedrooms, and for twenty minutes, I didn't find a damn thing. Detective Blatch, however, found a small Ziploc bag of marijuana in a flour canister in the kitchen and some car keys on a hook beside the interior garage door. The drugs were a good find, but nobody had killed Laura for a quarter ounce of weed.

After striking out in the guest bedrooms, I turned my attention to Laura's master suite. She had a king-sized bed, a chest of drawers, a dresser, and two nightstands in a matching dark stain. Dirty clothes filled a hamper in the corner, while dresses, blouses, slacks, and other less formal clothing filled the walk-in closet. Several dozen pairs of shoes lay scattered on the floor throughout the room. Before I touched anything, I snapped pictures to give us a record of how the room looked before we entered.

Then, I got to work.

She kept a pack of condoms in an end table beside her bed, but she didn't keep men's clothes or toiletries anywhere in the room. If she had a boyfriend, he didn't live with her. Her other drawers held nothing but clean clothes.

Beneath her bed, she kept long shallow totes, two of which she had filled with sweaters. The third, though, held a digital scale that weighed to the hundredth of a gram. If I had found that in the kitchen, I would have assumed she used it for baking. Hidden in the bedroom, though, it gave me pause. A lot of drug dealers kept scales like that for weighing cocaine.

"Hey, Blatch," I called. "I've got a digital scale that weighs to the hundredth of a gram."

Detective Blatch banged pots and pans in the kitchen before coming into the bedroom to see what I had found.

"You find any drugs?" he asked.

"Not yet," I said. "Other bedrooms are clean."

He nodded and thought.

"I'll call my narcotics squad and get a dog to go through the house," he said. "We know she's got weed. If she's got something else, we'll find it."

"Sounds good," I said, standing. Blatch left a moment later, and I walked into the closet. Laura had stacked shoe boxes along the walls and hung her clothes from racks around the room. The first couple of shoe boxes held strappy black and white shoes that would have looked nice with cocktail dresses. Laura had good taste, but that didn't help my case.

In the fifth box, I found dozens of two-inch-by-three-inch mylar storage bags—the kind high-end drug dealers used to package weed. I took out my phone and snapped pictures before setting that box aside. In the next box, I found seven well-used cell phones. I tried to power one on, but the battery was dead.

I put that shoe box beside the one containing the mylar bags and opened the last four shoe boxes. One box held sealed mylar bags full of marijuana, while the other three held aluminum cylinders that looked like high-tech coffee thermoses. I unscrewed the top of one and heard the airtight seal break. Inside, I found a lot of weed. If the other containers held a similar amount, she was sitting on a couple thousand dollars' worth of marijuana.

"Detective Blatch. I need you in here."

He didn't answer, so I called again. He didn't answer me then, either, so I left the room and found him outside, searching Laura's Honda in the driveway.

"You find anything out here?" I asked, squinting in the sunlight.

"She left a briefcase with some documents in it on the front seat," he said. "Other than that, the car looks clean."

"Grab her briefcase. I've got stuff you need to see."

Blatch reached into the vehicle for a soft black leather briefcase with silver buckles. It looked like a nice bag. I led him to her master closet, where he saw the stash of drugs and opened his eyes wide.

"Good find."

"Yeah," I said. "She's got cell phones, mylar storage bags, airtight canisters full of marijuana, and about a dozen individual packets of marijuana in vacuum-sealed mylar bags."

He whistled again and put down her briefcase before snapping pictures with his cell phone. Then he looked at me.

"I'll call my narcotics squad and my crime lab. We'll get a proper search team down here to see what else we can find."

"Good idea," I said, nodding. "You mind if I look at her briefcase?"

"Go ahead," he said. "I'll call this in."

Blatch dialed, so I carried Laura's briefcase to the small breakfast table in her kitchen. Flour had spilled onto Laura's cheery yellow laminate countertops. Detective Blatch had left Laura's Ziploc bag of marijuana out in the open. Before opening the briefcase, I stared at the drugs, thinking and trying to put the scene together. It didn't add up.

The airtight, opaque containers in her closet would have protected her drugs from both mold and sunlight, guaranteeing that her weed would keep its potency for years to come. The Ziploc bag in her kitchen wouldn't even keep out flour. Already, light, fuzzy mold had grown on the drugs. If she had smoked that, she would have gotten sick. If Laura were a drug dealer—or even a frequent user—she would have stored her personal stash in a container that would keep it fresh.

Not only that, I'd found vacuum-sealed bags of dope but no vacuum sealer. The drugs brought more mystery than insight. Something wasn't right here.

I turned away from the drugs and focused on her briefcase. Blatch had already opened the latches, so I flipped the top over to give me access to the interior compartments. In one compartment, she stored a very thin laptop complete with a power cord. If we were in St. Augustine, I'd search the laptop myself, but Detective Blatch came from a department with at least two or three thousand officers and hundreds of support staff members. They'd have their own technical people with skill sets far beyond my own. They'd search the computer. In the other compartment, she kept manila file folders. Those, I could handle.

I pulled everything out and snapped pictures with my cell phone. The first folder held receipts and invoices from office supply stores, the phone company, and an accountant's office. Nothing helpful.

The second folder held two yellow legal notepads, both of which were full of handwritten notes. Laura was an attorney, so her conversations with clients were privileged. I wanted to flip those notes and see what she had written, but I couldn't.

I stacked them on top of each other and snapped pictures. The front page of the notepad showed nothing important, just a list of names. Aldon McKenzie, Austin Wright, Mike

Brees, and Ruby Laskey. I didn't recognize them, so my photograph alone shouldn't have violated any privilege.

The other folders held personal documents, including flyers from a realtor's office in St. Augustine. If the flyers she printed off were any sign, she was looking for a three- to four-hundred-thousand dollar detached house with several acres. It was a healthy budget for our area. It was also surprising. If Laura owned a thriving practice in Mehlville and St. Louis, why would she move to St. Augustine? We weren't the middle of nowhere, but we weren't Rome, either.

I left the briefcase and its contents on the kitchen table before returning to Laura's master bedroom, where I found Detective Blatch talking on his cell. He nodded at me and then took his phone away from his ear.

"I'll knock on some doors and see what the neighbors say about her," I whispered.

"Sounds good," he said before putting his phone back to his ear. He continued coordinating the rest of the search while I took my badge from my belt and hung it from a lanyard around my neck.

I spent the next two hours walking up and down the street and visiting Laura's neighbors. People weren't excited to have me interrupt their dinners, but most of the neighbors were cooperative. Most of them liked Laura. Her friends came over occasionally, but she didn't throw parties except on Halloween—and then, she invited everyone on the street. Few late-night visitors came by the house, and no one knew whether she dated. None of the neighbors knew she was considering moving to St. Augustine, either.

Importantly, no one mentioned anything about drugs. If she dealt drugs—and it looked like she did—she kept it quiet and didn't sell out of her house.

The evidence told me she was a drug-dealing lawyer. Her neighbors told me she was a personable but quiet young woman with few friends. The two sketches weren't incompatible, but neither gave me the complete picture of this young woman's life. We were missing something. There was a bigger story here, and I needed to find out what it was before her murderer dropped another body.

Chapter 12

Aldon McKenzie rocked on his front porch as his heart fluttered. He had bought his first firearm that afternoon, a Glock 19 nine-millimeter pistol. In an ideal world, he would have taken classes to learn how to care for the weapon and how to use it, but he didn't live in an ideal world. Besides, he didn't need to become an expert marksman. He only needed to stay alive long enough to protect his family until the threat passed.

Aldon and his wife lived in a beautiful house they had built on a five-acre spread in western St. Augustine County. Aldon loved that house, but more than that, he loved the memories he had made in that house. He had watched Daria take her first step in the living room; she had said her first word in the backyard as she ate a snack on their picnic table; and the family had spent their first Christmas huddled together around the fireplace in the living room. As much as he loved that house and his family, though, he wished it were empty.

As the sun set, Jennifer stepped outside, a concerned look on her face. She reached to his shoulder.

“What’s going on?” she asked.

He looked at her and reached for her hand. She was so gentle and good. She didn’t deserve this, and he didn’t deserve her.

“It’s nothing, sweetheart,” he said. “Work stuff. I still think you and Daria should head to your mom’s house until all this settles. Might be easier for a while.”

“We’ll do that as soon as you tell me what’s going on,” she said, crossing her arms. “You hate sitting outside, and now you’re sitting on the porch and watching that road closer than you watched me on our wedding night. Not only that, you’ve got a gun on your hip. You blew me off yesterday when you came home, but I’m not letting you do that now. What’s going on, Aldon?”

He looked to his wife. Jennifer had brown eyes and dimples. Her beautiful smile made his whole world stop, and her loving gaze made him feel wanted. As if her physical attributes weren’t enough, she treated everyone with such kindness and graciousness that she had friends everywhere. He was lucky to have her. Knowing that made lying to her much harder.

“The boss is changing things at work. We’re dumping most of our old contracts, and Mr. Stewart is hiring new hotshot chemists to develop our own chemical compounds. Everything’s changing at once. I’m worried about having a job.”

She squeezed his shoulder. "Every company needs accountants, and you're a good one. They need you."

"Yeah," he said, trying to muster strength into his voice. "I guess so."

She said nothing. His gut twisted.

"Mr. Stewart's bringing in new business partners," he said. "They've tightened security. Now there are biometric readers on the elevators, and I've got to give a retinal scan to log in to my computer. Our security guards carry guns now. It's like I'm working in the Pentagon or something."

"Is that why you're carrying a gun at home?"

He shifted as if that would hide the weapon.

"My dad kept guns in the house when I was a little girl," said Jennifer. "I don't mind them, but I wish you had consulted me before you bought one."

"It was an impulse buy," said Aldon, not looking at his wife. She may have said something, but he wasn't paying attention to her. In the distance, tires hummed as they rolled down the street. His body tensed as he held his breath. Jennifer squeezed his shoulder but said nothing until a minivan drove past the house. Then she relaxed her grip and patted him.

"Okay, mister," she said, nodding and stepping around so she faced him. "What's going on?"

Jennifer locked her brown eyes on his, but he said nothing for several moments. Then she raised her eyebrows. Still, he said nothing. She shook her head.

"Damn it, Aldon," she said. "Talk to me. I'm your wife. Your daughter's inside. What the hell is going on?"

He licked his lips and looked down. "I found a problem at work. Some dangerous chemicals were missing from our inventory. I brought it up with my boss, and he looked into it and told me not to worry about it. When I checked again, he had corrected the books like nothing happened."

Jennifer shrugged. "Okay. You found an error, you reported it, and Danny corrected it. What's the problem?"

"I've known Danny a long time. Something scared him. He told me I needed to forget what I'd found and destroy all my backups. The next day, IT came by and replaced my computer with another. They said it was an upgrade, but it was the same computer."

"Okay," said Jennifer. "You wouldn't be this upset if that was everything."

"Danny may not care about the numbers, but I could lose my license if I submit a false report. I didn't trust the numbers my computer was giving me, so I walked down to the warehouse and searched the stockpile. We were short almost a million dollars' worth of chemicals."

Jennifer covered her mouth. "And you think Danny's stealing?"

Aldon shrugged. "Might be Danny, might be somebody else. I contacted a lawyer and gave her what I had. She realized something shady was going on, so she looked into it.

Now she thinks somebody at that plant is making drugs, and somebody high in the company is covering it up."

Jennifer closed her eyes and nodded, her skin pale.

"Okay," she said. "I'll pack our bags. If you're this scared, you need to call your lawyer and tell her we're getting out of town."

"I can't get in touch with her," said Aldon. "I've been trying to call Laura for days, but she's not answering my calls. I even drove by her office, but her assistant said she hadn't been in for a while."

Jennifer raised her eyebrows. "Where is she?"

"I think she's dead," said Aldon, blinking and staring at the trees across the street. "I got coffee at Rise and Grind this afternoon. Somebody said the police found a body out by the chicken processing plant. It sounded like Laura."

"That's why you got the gun," said Jennifer, comprehension dawning on her.

Aldon nodded. "Yeah. Laura investigated, and they killed her."

Jennifer didn't even hesitate. "Call the police. I'll get Daria, and we'll go to my mom's house in Kentucky. You're coming with us."

Jennifer started walking into the house but stopped when he didn't move.

"What are you waiting for? If they killed your lawyer, they'll kill you as soon as they find out you're her client."

"Laura told me not to go to the local police," he said. "She was putting together a case. We planned to go to the US Attorney's Office in St. Louis."

"Your lawyer is dead," said Jennifer. "Call the police. If she's dead, you could be next."

He shook his head. "Mason Stewart's got at least one officer in his pocket. Laura told me. If we go to the police, we're dead."

Jennifer closed her eyes. "Fine. Then we're leaving now. I'll get Daria. Get the car ready."

He swallowed and nodded. "Okay. Get your bags together. I'll be inside in a minute."

Jennifer twisted around and ran into the house. Aldon stayed on the porch, watching the road. Then, he took out his cell phone and called Laura's number again. As before, it went to voicemail.

"Hey, Laura, it's Aldon McKenzie. I've called you half a dozen times. I need to talk. This is getting serious. Call me back because I'm getting scared. My family and I are leaving town. I hope you're not dead."

As soon as he finished speaking, he used the voicemail system's controls to replay his message. His voice trembled so much he sounded like a teenager who had found out his girlfriend was pregnant, so he hit the button to delete his message and stood. He had called Laura enough. If she was still alive, she'd call back. If she wasn't, one more message didn't matter. He had things to do.

He slipped his phone into his pocket and opened the door. Already, his wife's footsteps carried throughout the house as she hurried from room to room, packing their bags. Her mom's farm in Kentucky would be safe. If anybody came for them there, they'd find a trio of armed Marines—Jennifer's father and two brothers—waiting for them. Now they had to get out.

Aldon climbed the stairs. He and his wife could have packed an emergency bag for a typical kid in moments, but Daria had needs beyond the usual. At night, she slept with a special hypoallergenic pillow and a white noise machine. She also had two stuffed animals she loved and couldn't sleep without. Her autism had also made toilet training difficult, so she still wore diapers.

Leaving a familiar setting at home was hard enough for her, but leaving without her stuffed animals, her favorite clothes, or her favorite pillow would have been cruel. They could chance a few minutes. Once they got Daria's stuff together—a process that took about ten minutes—Aldon carried the bags to the hallway while his wife turned off the lights. His feet were lighter than they had been all day. They had a plan now. They'd run. Maybe it wasn't a perfect plan, but it'd keep them alive.

Then, their imperfect plan blew up when Daria opened the front door.

"Hi, honey. Is your daddy here?"

Aldon dropped the bags, and Jennifer gasped. Daria said nothing. Aldon held his breath.

Please, God, don't let him hurt her.

"I'm lookin' for your daddy," said the voice again., softly. "I work with him. Is he around?"

Jennifer shot her eyes to her husband. Aldon removed the weapon from his holster and crept toward the landing at the top of the steps.

"Hey, Daria, take a step back," said Aldon, turning the corner into the foyer. An unfamiliar man stood at the bottom of the steps. He was about fifty or fifty-five, and he had curly hair. He wore a beige linen sports coat, dark jeans, and a white shirt. Though the jacket partially concealed it, he had a black semiautomatic firearm in a holster against his chest. "Come upstairs, baby."

"She's fine here," said the man. "You and I need to talk in private, Mr. McKenzie. How about we go for a ride? My car's out front."

Aldon stopped walking and stood straighter. The man in the entryway didn't even react to the gun Aldon carried. From his vantage at the top of the steps, Aldon had a clear shot on him from about ten yards, but if Aldon missed, the man would have a clear, open shot on his little girl. Aldon's gut wrenched, and his knees threatened to buckle. He should have gotten his family out hours ago.

"Where do you want to go?" asked Aldon.

"Away from here," said the man, nodding. "It's a nice night. I'm not from around here, so I thought you could show me the sights. Please leave your sidearm at the house. Guns make me jumpy."

Aldon looked back to his wife and mouthed that he loved her before putting his firearm on the ground. She had tears on her cheeks as he climbed down the steps. Daria smiled at him from the entryway.

"Clownfish form symbiotic mutualisms with sea anemones in the wild," she said, repeating something she had heard on a documentary a few hours ago. She'd repeat the same sentence all night if Jennifer let her. Doctors called it echolalia. It was common among those with autism.

"I love you, sweetheart," he whispered. "You'll always be my baby."

She smiled and looked at him out of the corner of her eye before speaking again.

"Clownfish form symbiotic mutualisms with sea anemones in the wild."

He blew her a kiss and stepped onto the porch. The curly-haired man put a hand on his elbow and led him to a Toyota sedan in the driveway.

"Are you going to kill me?" asked Aldon.

The man hesitated before nodding. "Not in front of your family. If it's any consolation, your employer-provided life insurance will pay out no matter how you die. Your family will be taken care of."

"And if I don't cooperate, you'll kill them?"

"My partner will. If he has to do it, he'll make it quick," said the curly-haired man. "Please don't make us do that. I don't like killing innocent people."

"Did you kill Laura, too?"

Again, the curly-haired man nodded. "Yeah. She didn't suffer."

"Okay," he said. Aldon's legs trembled, and his lungs felt tight, but his mind was clear, and his heart was light. He opened the sedan's rear door and sat down, knowing he was about to take a ride to his death but also knowing Jennifer and Daria would live. They gave his life meaning and purpose. His death would keep them alive. That seemed fitting.

As the curly-haired man drove away, Aldon turned and looked out the rear window to see Daria standing on the front porch. She didn't wave or blink. She just watched. He memorized the way she looked standing there. She was perfect.

"For what it's worth, you don't deserve this. You were doing your job. Your co-workers screwed up. You got caught in the mess."

Aldon turned around.

"You can let me go," he said. "I won't talk. Let me go home. Jennifer and I will leave. You won't ever see us again."

The man looked in the rearview mirror. "I wish I could, but this isn't my call. If I let you go, I'll get visitors at my house. They'll kill my kids. I'm the nice one."

They drove for about ten minutes before pulling off on a side road in the woods. Aldon had driven by that side road dozens of times over the years, but he had never noticed the abandoned home in the woods. Vines covered the front porch and broke through the siding and windows. The curly-haired man led him inside. Clear plastic tarps covered the walls.

"You can stand, or you can kneel. Whichever you want. Once we're done here, I'll call my partner to let him know what happened. Your family will never even know he was nearby."

Aldon knelt in the center of the floor without saying a word. As he closed his eyes, he pictured Daria as she had been on his front porch. She and Jennifer would live because of him.

He never even heard the gunshot that ended his life. At the moment of his death, all he saw, all he knew, all he felt was love for his little girl and his wife, and that was fine with him.

Chapter 13

While Detective Blatch called in a team of dedicated forensic technicians to search Laura's house, I drove to her law office. It was in a strip mall about a quarter of a mile from I-55 on Telegraph Road. There was an old Waffle House restaurant in the parking lot and a pet shop at the end of the row of shops. Laura's office had a simple sign above it that said *Lawyer* in faded red letters.

I parked along the side of the building and walked to the front door. As expected, no one was inside. Through the dusty glass window, I saw desks and a waiting room. A hand-painted sign in the lobby advertised her services. Uncontested divorces started at $250, while simple wills started at $300. The sign was quick to note that all costs were negotiable.

Laura's practice was on the fringes of the legal profession, but that was the life she had chosen.

A sign on the door listed her hours, but it also gave a number to call in case of emergencies. I called it on my cell. A woman answered on the third ring.

"Rojas and Associates," she said. "What can I do for you?"

"Yeah, hi, my name is Joe Court," I said, looking around to make sure no one could hear me. "I'm outside your office right now. Who am I talking to?"

"Rojas and Associates, attorneys at law," she said. "What can I help you with?"

"Who is this?"

The woman paused. "Tina. What do you need?"

"I need to talk to you in person."

"Look, ma'am, we're not taking on clients right now. If you tell me what the problem is, I can refer you to an attorney who can help you out."

I paced in front of the office. The sun was setting, sending purple and orange streaks across the sky so that the horizon almost looked as if it were on fire.

"Has anyone called you about Laura Rojas in the past few days?"

"That's none of your concern."

"It is my concern," I said, "because I'm a detective from St. Augustine County and Laura Rojas is dead. We found her body two days ago. I'm trying to find out who killed her. Since you were Laura's assistant, you might know something. If you'd like, I can call the county police and ask for somebody to pick you up."

She drew in a sharp breath. "Laura's dead?"

"Yeah," I said. "I'm sorry to tell you."

"If you're a detective and you're calling me, you think someone murdered her."

"I'm positive someone murdered her."

"Oh, God," she said. She paused for a moment. Her voice was high, almost squeaky when she spoke. "I'm on my way. I'll be at the office as soon as I can."

She hung up before I said anything else. My stomach rumbled, so I walked over to the Waffle House, where I drank coffee and ate biscuits and gravy. It wasn't the healthiest dinner around, but everyone deserved an indulgence now and again.

By the time I finished eating, a white Kia Optima had parked beside my SUV. A woman stepped out. She was in her late forties or early fifties and had strawberry blond hair and a deep, even tan. I walked toward her and flashed her my badge. She nodded and lit a cigarette with trembling fingers.

"Are you Tina?" I asked, stepping close. She was smoking a menthol, and her face and neck had the bronzed patina of a long-term smoker. She nodded.

"Tina Babcock," she said, holding the cigarette to her lips. She didn't offer to shake my hand.

"I'm Detective Joe Court with the St. Augustine County Sheriff's Department. What kind of law do you guys practice?"

She shrugged and sucked on her cigarette so its tip burned orange.

"All kinds. Family law, DUI defense, things like that," she said. "Laura wasn't particular. She liked the work."

I nodded and took out a notepad.

"Like I told you on the phone, I'm investigating Ms. Rojas's murder. We found her body deep in the woods in St. Augustine County. Did she have clients in St. Augustine?"

Babcock looked at me and then drew on her cigarette. Her fingers had stopped trembling, and her expression had become calm and self-assured. We had stepped into her comfort zone now. I had the feeling she had given police officers that emotionless stare before.

"Do you have a warrant that would give you access to our client list?"

"Not yet."

"Then I can't answer that question," she said. "Get a warrant, and I will comply to the extent the law requires me."

"Okay," I said, nodding. "That's fair. I understand you're a law office and that you need to take care of your clients. Hypothetically, would she take on a client from St. Augustine?"

Ms. Babcock tilted her head to the side. "To answer that question, you'd have to get a hypothetical warrant."

I let the smile leave my face.

"Okay, how about this: I'm from St. Augustine. My neighbor keeps throwing his shit on my lawn. I'd like to hire a lawyer to draft a letter requesting that he refrain from doing that. Could your firm help me out?"

Ms. Babcock's expression didn't change.

"Is he throwing literal shit, or do you use that term to refer to household refuse?"

"Does it matter?" I asked, raising my eyebrows.

"One is a serious sanitation issue, while the other might give you cause for a civil action."

"Fine," I said, closing my eyes. "It's refuse. It's not literal feces."

She said nothing until I opened my eyes. Then she smiled and shrugged.

"My firm is no longer taking on any new clients. It seems our principal attorney has just died. If you'd like, I can give you the name of an excellent attorney who might help you out."

I almost told her off. Instead, I looked down at the ground.

"You liked Laura, didn't you?"

Tina drew on her cigarette. For a moment, her expression softened, but then she looked at me with hard, brown eyes.

"She signed my paycheck every week. I liked her fine."

"I don't believe you," I said, shaking my head. "You almost cried when I said she was dead. You liked her. The two of you were friends. Most people would help the police try to solve a friend's murder."

She drew on her cigarette again. "Laura believed in the law, Detective. Nobody's above it. If you get a warrant, I'll answer every question the warrant requires me to answer. That's what Laura would have wanted. It's the least I can do for a friend."

"As her friend, you can answer this, then: Was she considering moving to St. Augustine?"

She narrowed her eyes and jerked her head back.

"No. Why would she move there?"

"Friendly people, beautiful landscapes, good restaurants...the usual reasons people move to small towns."

She shook her head and tapped the end of her cigarette to knock off the ash. "If she moved anywhere, she'd move to Chicago. She liked it there and had a license to practice in Illinois."

"I found printouts from a realtor's website from St. Augustine at her house," I said. "Does that seem strange to you?"

She shrugged. "Maybe she was looking for a friend."

"That's possible," I said, nodding. "Did she tell you she was pregnant?"

Babcock raised an eye and lowered her cigarette. She stood straighter.

"No."

"Do you know who the father was?"

She blinked a few times and then shook her head.

"I may have bitched about my husband some, but Laura and I didn't talk about our love lives at work often. How far along was she?"

"Not far," I said. "Ten or eleven weeks."

She sighed and brought her cigarette to her lips again.

"That's sad," she said. "Laura was a nice woman. She would have made a good mom."

"You sure you don't want to talk about her?"

She shook her head. "I would if I could."

"All right," I said, reaching into my purse for a business card. "If you change your mind, call me."

She took the card.

"Thank you for considering Rojas and Associates, Detective Court," she said. "I'm sorry I couldn't be of more help."

"Me, too," I said. I walked to my car where I closed my eyes and took two deep breaths. Even if we got a warrant to search Laura's office, it would come with so many stipulations to protect her clients we wouldn't find a thing. The office was a dead end for the moment, so I took out my cell and called Dr. Sheridan. It took three rings for him to answer.

"Doc, it's Joe Court. Did you contact Laura Rojas's family?"

"I did," he said. "They cried a lot."

"I need to talk to them, so I need their address," I said, flipping through pages in my notepad. He gave me the information I needed and wished me luck before hanging up. At least that conversation had gone well. As I pulled out of my parking spot, Tina Babcock climbed into her car.

Part of me wanted to hate her, but an even bigger part of me liked her. Laura's death upset her, but she didn't break down, and she didn't stop doing her job. I liked that. I liked even more that Laura Rojas had seen that in her and hired her when she could have gone with someone from a temp agency or a legal staffing firm.

I had never met Laura when she was alive, but I was getting a picture of her in death. She may have been a drug dealer, but she had guts.

I put her parents' address into my GPS and drove. The Rojas family lived in a brick ranch home off Tesson Ferry Road. The home had mature trees in the front lawn and well-landscaped flower beds. An American flag hung near the front door, while boys played basketball in the driveway. As I parked, the boys took their ball and ran to the backyard of the home next door.

A woman with black hair and brown eyes opened the front door as I crossed the front lawn. She was the spitting image of her daughter. I gave her a tight, understanding smile but didn't receive one in return.

"Mrs. Rojas?" I asked. She nodded. "I'm Detective Joe Court. I'm trying to find out who killed your daughter, and to do that, I need information. Can we talk for a few minutes?"

She crossed her arms and leaned against the door frame. Her eyes looked as if she was close to tears, but she nodded.

"Who would kill my baby?"

"I don't know," I said. "From all I've found so far, Laura was a special person. It's always sad when someone like her dies."

"Don't use her name like you know her," she said, her voice sharp. I stepped back and nodded.

"You're right. I never met her," I said. "I apologize if I was presumptuous."

"Just ask your questions and leave us alone."

I took a notepad from my pocket. Interviews with the loved ones of a murder victim were always hard, so I started with open-ended questions that would get her comfortable talking. She told me Laura was the first person in her family to go to college, but after watching her succeed, three of her cousins had followed her footsteps and enrolled in the University of Missouri. Two more had enrolled in trade schools.

Laura's mom was proud of her, and she had every reason to be, but she saw her daughter through a mom's rose-colored glasses. In her view, Laura may have had flaws, but they weren't serious. She shut me down when I asked about drugs, and, when I asked about a potential boyfriend, she told me her daughter was a virgin who would remain so until her wedding night. She deserved to know Laura was pregnant at the time of her death, but she didn't need to hear that from me.

The conversation didn't waste my time, but it came close. Mrs. Rojas said Laura had a cell phone, though, which we had yet to find. Now that we knew the number, we could track it down.

Before leaving, I told Mrs. Rojas once more that I was sorry for her loss and promised that I would do my best to find out what had happened to her daughter. Back in my car, I flipped through my very sparse notes as waves of frustration washed over me.

Despite working all day, I hadn't accomplished a damn thing. Homicide investigations were like that sometimes, but it still disappointed me.

I sat in the car and rested my eyes for a moment before calling my station. Trisha had gone home for the evening, leaving me to talk to Jason Zuckerburg, our night dispatcher. He was a thirty-five-year veteran of the department. Now, he was coasting until the county forced him to retire. I liked having him around. People liked him, and he knew everybody in town. He was a nice guy. During the holidays, he dressed up as Santa and handed out presents to kids whose parents couldn't afford them otherwise. The world needed more people like that.

"Hey, Jason, it's Joe Court. How are you?"

"Can't complain," he said. "I heard you found a naked lady out in the woods."

"Something like that," I said. "Listen, I'm working a homicide, and I need you to work on a cell phone for me. It belonged to my victim. See whether you can get a list of incoming and outgoing calls. It'd be helpful if you could ping the GPS chip on it and track it down, too."

He paused for a moment. "Do I need a warrant?"

"The owner's dead, so you shouldn't," I said. "See what we can get without one. If her carrier won't cooperate without a warrant, we'll get one as soon as we can."

"Okay," he said, sighing. "What's the number?"

I gave him the information he needed and then thanked him before hanging up. When I hit the interstate, the city lights behind me almost looked like distant stars on the backdrop of the horizon. It was peaceful. As I drove closer to home, the night grew darker and traffic grew thinner until there were large stretches where I was the only car on the road. Jason called about ten miles from St. Augustine's exit.

"Hey, Joe, sorry it took so long," he said. "Right after you called, it got busy around here. Someone shot a woman in front of her kid. The daughter is here, but she's upset. We're trying to find her dad, but he's MIA."

My shoulders slumped.

"I've got too much on my plate already to pick up another murder."

"Don't worry about it," said Jason. "Delgado and Harry are working this one. Harry's at the woman's house now. Delgado is trying to talk to the little girl. She's crying, but she won't talk about anything but fish."

"Someone shot her mom right in front of her," I said. I paused. "That's rough."

"It is," he said. "You know the name Aldon McKenzie?"

The name sounded familiar, but it took a moment for me to remember why.

"Yeah. His name was on a notepad in my victim's car. Why?"

"He's the missing girl's father. He and your victim spoke on the phone eleven times in the past two weeks."

I gave myself a moment to process that. "Do we know where Laura's phone is?"

"No, but her last call went through a tower in south St. Louis County. Mr. McKenzie called her this evening, but he didn't leave a message."

I sighed. "Okay. Thanks for your work, Jason. Looks like my long day will turn into a long night."

Chapter 14

I reached St. Augustine at a little before nine. Jason was at the station's front desk, talking to somebody on the phone while typing. By the sounds of things, he was trying to route officers to Tommy B's, a dive bar on Main Street.

I did most of my drinking alone, but even if I wanted to get hammered in public, Tommy B's wasn't the place to do it. We broke up fights there three or four times a month and had arrested two of their bartenders for selling marijuana. Since Councilman Rogers owned the bar, though, it kept its business and liquor licenses despite the problems it caused. That was life in St. Augustine. Everything came with a price tag, sin and vice most of all.

Jason motioned me toward the desk, where he handed me a stack of papers listing Laura Rojas's most recent phone calls and told me Delgado was in the conference room. I thanked him and walked back. Delgado sat beside a little girl in the conference room. Brooke Ricci, a social worker from St. Augustine's Department of Children's Services, sat on the girl's other side. Brooke whispered encouragement into the girl's ear, but the little girl didn't seem to react.

I stood near the door until Delgado looked my way. He excused himself to talk with me in private outside the room.

"I'm in the middle of an interview, Detective. What do you want?"

Delgado and I had a history, so I had expected the hostility. It didn't bother me much.

"I'm working a homicide involving a woman named Laura Rojas," I said.

He crossed his arms. "Good for you. I'm working a homicide involving a woman named Jennifer McKenzie, so I'm sure you appreciate how busy I am at the moment."

I showed him the call logs Jason had printed. "Your victim's missing husband called my victim at least eleven times in the past two weeks. In addition, I found Mr. McKenzie's name on a notepad inside my victim's house."

Delgado looked at my printout, his mind processing that.

"You think they were bumping uglies?" he asked.

I wrinkled my nose at the crude comment but considered for a moment.

"Laura was pregnant at the time of her death, so it's a possibility."

He looked at the printout and then pointed to a highlighted entry near the bottom of the first page.

"If they weren't having an affair, why would Aldon McKenzie call your victim at two in the morning?"

"I have no idea," I said. "What's the little girl saying?"

"Something about clownfish and mutualisms," said Delgado, shaking his head. "She seems like a retard."

"I think she has autism," said Brooke, the social worker, walking toward us from the conference room. I looked past Delgado to see the little girl drawing at the table. "She's not retarded. In fact, she's very bright."

"Whatever," said Delgado. "Can she tell us who killed her mom or not?"

Brooke hesitated. Her gray hair was pulled into a bun behind her head, and she wore a white cardigan over an orange blouse. The skin around her neck was loose and wrinkled, but her mind was sharp. I had only met her a few times, but from all I had seen, she was a fierce advocate for the children in her charge. That made her okay in my book.

"She knows what happened," said Brooke, shaking her head, "but based on what I've seen so far, I'm not sure she can tell us anything."

"Terrific," said Delgado, shaking his head. "I'm wasting my time here when I should be out there hunting down the husband. Dollars to donuts, he killed Joe's victim when he found out she was pregnant, and then he killed his wife."

"Why would he do that?" I asked.

Delgado snorted. "Because he's a psychopath. They don't think like normal people. He knocked up his girlfriend but didn't want to have another kid, so he killed her. Maybe he killed his wife when she found out about the affair."

"It's weak," I said.

"Better than your theory," said Delgado.

"I don't have a theory yet," I said.

"Exactly," he said. "We'll pull DNA from Aldon McKenzie's toothbrush, and then we'll compare that to your victim's baby. I guarantee you there'll be a match. These two were getting it on. Trust me on that. You don't call a woman eleven times in two weeks unless you're putting the pole to her."

He wanted to get a rise out of me, so I forced myself not to react. It was better to disengage and leave him be.

"If that's where the evidence takes you, it's your case," I said, nodding. "Good luck finding him. I'll make sure you have access to my interview notes and evidence. If you have questions, you have my phone number."

I turned to walk away when he cleared his throat. I looked at him.

"Yeah?" I asked.

"You should thank me," he said. "I solved your case, too. Aldon's your killer, and I bet he's halfway to Mexico by now."

"That's a theory," I said, nodding. "Good luck finding evidence to support it."

I turned away, but before I could walk, Delgado once again cleared his throat.

"Are you quitting already?"

I wanted to give him the finger. Instead, I ignored him as he snickered. The guy was a jerk. I shouldn't let him upset me, but he knew where my buttons were, and he knew how to push them for maximal effect. I walked to my desk, where I pulled out my cell phone to call Harry. He answered after three or four rings.

"Harry, it's Joe," I said. "I'm at the office. I heard about Jennifer McKenzie. You at her house now?"

"I am," he said. "What do you need?"

"You have any clue where Aldon McKenzie is?"

"Not yet," he said. "Why?"

I filled him in on the phone calls and Delgado's theory that Laura and Aldon were having an affair. I didn't agree with Delgado's theory yet, but it fit the little evidence we had. Harry promised to bag any toothbrushes he might find.

Before he hung up, I cleared my throat.

"How are things with Paige Maxwell and Jude Lewis?"

He groaned. "Our missing teenagers are still missing. Highway Patrol has Paige's car in a garage. They found DNA on the backseat but no blood. The entire front of the car was wiped clean. No prints on the steering wheel, gear shifter, or radio."

"The lack of blood's a good sign," I said. "Maybe they ditched the car to escape their parents. I didn't think Paige's family approved of the relationship."

Harry drew in a breath. "Even without blood, somebody hid this car deep in the woods and wiped down the front seat. We weren't meant to find it. You don't hide a car that well for shits and giggles. We may never find their bodies, but these kids are dead. We might as well call it."

"Thanks for the uplifting pep talk, boss," I said. "You are a veritable bouquet of rainbows and sunshine."

"If you wanted rainbows and sunshine, you got into the wrong profession."

He was correct there, so I nodded.

"Unless you need me for anything, I'm going home. I feel like I've been up for days. I need sleep."

"Enjoy it while you can," he said.

"I will," I said. I thanked him, hung up, and left the building. When I got back to my truck, I found a clear, unbroken windshield with a bill for two hundred bucks tucked under one of the wiper blades. Considering the garage had driven to my station and replaced the windshield while I was at work, it wasn't a bad price. I tossed it on the seat beside me after climbing inside the cab and heading home.

My house was dark and almost foreboding when I arrived. The dog wasn't around, so I drove to my neighbor's house, where I found him on the front porch. Susanne was inside, but she came out when she saw my truck. She wore a pink bathrobe, and she carried a cup of hot tea.

"You look tired, sweetheart," she said, touching my elbow. "I can make you a cup of tea if you'd like."

"I'd love that, but I need to get home," I said. "I've had a long day. Tomorrow will be just as long."

"I don't envy your long hours. When you need me to feed Roger, just let me know."

I thanked her and gave her a hug before Roger and I climbed into my truck. At home, the dog jumped from the back of my truck and came trotting toward me as I walked toward the house. His pink tongue hung from his mouth, and he panted. I had always believed a tired dog was a happy dog. By that measure, Roger was ecstatic.

"It's good to see you, boy," I said, scratching his ear. His tail wagged hard as he leaned into my hand. "Feel good?"

He panted harder. I guessed that was a yes. Together, the two of us walked to the front porch, where I put down my purse and picked up a tennis ball from a terra-cotta planter beside the front door. His eyes locked on that yellow ball, and his body stiffened with anticipation. Roger had never been much of a retriever, but he loved tearing apart tennis balls with his powerful jaws.

I made sure the road was clear before throwing the ball as hard as I could. It ricocheted against a tree and landed in the front yard near my truck. Roger watched it sail away and then sauntered toward it. A year ago, nothing would have prevented him from sprinting after his ball like a man with his hair on fire. Now he didn't even run. At least he had still gone after it instead of lying down. That was something.

As Roger fetched the ball, I opened the front door and stepped inside. It was a little after ten. I needed to go to bed and sleep, but I needed a drink even more. I needed to relax. I put on some music—a Leonard Cohen album—and poured about half an inch of vodka into a rocks glass. Then, I reconsidered and poured another half an inch for good measure.

Roger came through the front door a moment later, clutching the tennis ball in his mouth. He dropped it at my feet and then walked to his bed. I put his ball with the others on the front porch before locking up for the night and sitting on the couch. As I drank and felt the vodka work its magic over me, the day melted away. Muscles all over my body relaxed, and my breath came easier.

I finished my drink and then had another before going to bed. My head was light and boozy as I drifted off to a drunken, dreamless sleep.

Chapter 15

It was pitch black when my phone rang. My mouth felt as if I had stuffed it full of cotton, and my head ached. Roger snored at my feet, his sleep still uninterrupted. I blinked and forced the world back into focus. My room was hot, and sweat stained my sheets. The air conditioner thrummed, but it did little to combat the day's heat.

The phone rang again, so I swung my legs off the bed and sighed before grabbing it from my end table. Before answering, I massaged my temples and looked at the caller ID.

STLCPD

St. Louis County Police Department. I cleared my throat and ran my finger across the screen to answer.

"Yeah?" I said, my voice scratchy.

"Detective Court, sorry to wake you up," said a familiar voice. "It's Mathias Blatch. I met you at Laura Rojas's house in Mehlville."

"That's all right, Detective," I said, standing. It was hot, so I had worn little to bed. Roger picked up his massive head and looked at me for a second before putting it back down again. He was snoring before I could even get clothes out of my dresser. "What's going on?"

"We caught a break with the drugs at Laura Rojas's house. I wanted to fill you in."

"Oh?" I asked, pinning my phone between my ear and shoulder as I pulled on a pair of shorts. "What'd you find?"

"Fingerprints on the baggie found in her flour container. They belong to a guy named Duke Trevino. That name familiar at all?"

I shook my head as I walked to the kitchen, where I had left my purse and notepad.

"Never heard of him."

"He's a midlevel weed dealer. Buys his stock from growers down south and sells it in bulk to other dealers around St. Louis County."

I yawned and grabbed my notepad, not as impressed by the find as Detective Blatch seemed.

"Okay. Great. You found who sold drugs to her. That's great information."

"We found more than that," said Blatch. "His prints were in the system, so we picked him up and searched his condo. We found a Taurus G2 beneath his mattress. Your coroner pull a round from your victim yet?"

"Yeah," I said, sitting straighter. "A nine-millimeter. Remind me what caliber round the Taurus G2 shoots."

"This one's chambered for a nine-millimeter."

My heart beat a little faster. Now we were getting somewhere.

"That's intriguing," I said, nodding and writing a few notes. "I'll have my forensics lab forward the round to your office. Dr. Sheridan pulled it out of her spinal column, so I'm not sure how usable it will be. Your ballistics lab might pull something from it, though."

"I'd appreciate that," he said. "And I'll keep you updated if there are further developments on my end."

"Me, too," I said, nodding and closing my notepad. "Thanks for your call."

"Hey, before you hang up, let me ask you something," he said. He sounded almost sheepish when he spoke. "When I saw you this afternoon, I noticed you didn't wear a wedding ring."

"You're very observant," I said.

"That's why they made me detective," he said. "Since you're not married, and since I made a huge break in your case, how about we get a drink to celebrate?"

By his tone of voice, I could tell he was smiling. I smiled as well and tucked a stray lock of hair behind my ear.

"I'm sorry, Detective, but I don't date."

He paused. "You don't date...other cops?"

"Period," I said. "It's a long story. You seem like a nice guy, but I'm not interested in men."

"Oh, okay," he said, sudden understanding flooding his voice. "Message received, Detective."

"It's not like that," I said. "I'm not gay. I don't date men or women. It's nothing personal. You seem like a nice man, so I'm sure any number of women would be thrilled to go out with you. It's not you. It's me."

I cringed even before I finished speaking. Blatch said nothing for almost twenty seconds.

"I don't ask many women out, so I don't have a lot of experience at this," he said, speaking slowly. "But it sounds like you just broke up with me."

"Sorry. I suck at this," I said. "I don't talk to men often, so I don't have a lot of practice with this. How about we compromise? I don't want to go out with you, but if you can convict Duke Trevino of Laura Rojas's murder, I'll buy you a drink. If not, then no drink. Does that sound fair?"

"Um, yeah, I guess that's a fair compromise," he said, his voice uncertain. He paused. I hoped he'd just hang up, but after a five count, he spoke again. "It'll be weird if I see you in the field again, won't it?"

"Yeah," I said.

"Then why don't we skip the date and stay friends? I don't take offense."

My shoulders relaxed, and I nodded. I breathed a little easier.

"Good, because I'm not interested at all," I said. After a few moments of awkward silence, I laughed to myself a little. "Believe it or not, this conversation is the closest I've had to a date in years."

"I believe that," said Blatch. "Good night, Detective. I'll talk to you later."

"Good night," I said. He hung up before I could even finish speaking. I sat in my kitchen until Roger sauntered inside. He looked at me, yawned, and then lay down on the linoleum with his head between his paws. "I think I made a fool out of myself."

Roger didn't react, so I glanced at the clock on my microwave. It was twenty to four in the morning. I looked at the dog, stood, and put my cell phone on the counter by the stove before yawning.

"You can stay up, dude, but I'm going back to bed. It's too early to wear pants."

As I lay down in bed again, I found sleep elusive. My mind kept drifting back to my brief conversation with Detective Blatch. I last went on a date nine years ago. Maybe it was time again. Then again, based on how I had botched a simple conversation, it was probably better if I stayed single. Life was less mortifying that way.

My love life could wait. For the moment, I wanted to sleep.

Chapter 16

Nick Sumner leaned against the side of his vehicle. It was ten to four in the morning, and the sun was still several hours away from rising. There were four tractor-trailers in the rest area's parking lot, but the men and women who drove the huge machines were asleep inside their vehicles. Nick's Toyota was the only car in the passenger-car side of the lot.

It wasn't the nicest interstate rest area Nick had ever been to, but it was far from the worst. The building smelled clean, and mature trees shaded the area near the picnic tables. The location afforded him little privacy, but he didn't need privacy. This was a meet and greet. It should be easy. Still, he had tucked a suppressed .22-caliber pistol into his waistband. The weapon didn't have a lot of stopping power, but it could still scramble someone's brain at close quarters. It would work well here.

Ten minutes later—right on time—a red pickup truck pulled into the lot. Two men sat inside. Both were in their late twenties, and they had the hard eyes common to professional killers and drug dealers. Nick had set up the meeting after finding their contact information in Austin Wright's cell phone.

Nick waved to them but didn't move from his vehicle. The two men stayed in their pickup for two or three minutes before he felt Wright's phone buzz.

That you?

Nick waved the phone like a torch over his head after reading the message. The men in the truck stepped out. They were tall and thin. One wore a pistol in a holster on his belt. The other likely had a gun somewhere, but Nick couldn't see it.

"Who the fuck are you?" one asked.

"Nick Sumner," he said, smiling. It was too dark to see much, but a smile didn't cost him anything. "I'm a friend of Austin Wright's. He gave me his phone and told me to call you."

"We're not interested in seeing Austin's friends," said the man who had spoken earlier. He wore a red sleeveless T-shirt and had tattoos over most of his arms. Despite the heat, the other man wore a black, long-sleeved T-shirt and dark shorts. They turned to leave simultaneously.

"Whoa, whoa, whoa," said Nick. "There's no reason to leave yet. You guys drove all the way out here to do business, and it so happens that I represent some very serious businessmen."

"What kind of serious businessmen?" asked the man in the black shirt.

"The kind who look out for their interests," said Nick. "You may not realize this, but Austin Wright was a thief. He sold you folks fentanyl, but he stole the chemicals used to make those drugs from my employers."

The man in the red shirt crossed his arms. "How is this our problem?"

"That's where things get tricky," said Nick. "Austin and his merry band of misfits stole from us and sold those products to you. You didn't understand what they did, so my people will forgive and forget on one condition."

"What condition?"

"I need information," said Nick. "My employers have a large organization overseas, but we don't dabble in domestic affairs. Here, we invest. We've sunk sixty million dollars into a company in Missouri, and we're afraid for our investment. Austin ripped us off, but he wasn't the only person involved. I'm guessing you know more than we do. We'll call it an information exchange. You tell us everything you know, and we'll forget that you're holding our property."

"Are you a cop?" asked the man in the red shirt.

"That's a good question," said Nick, reaching into his pocket. Both men tensed, but they didn't draw their weapons. They were skittish, but not jumpy. They seemed like professionals. He could work with that. He pulled out Austin's phone and sorted through the images until he found one of Austin's body. Then he tossed it underhand to the man in the red shirt.

"Did you shoot him?"

Nick nodded. "Yep."

The two men looked at the photo.

"I liked Austin," said the man in the black shirt. "He was a good guy."

"I'm sure he was," said Nick, "but he got his hand caught in the cookie jar. My people are strict, but we're fair. You stay out of our way, we'll stay out of yours. If someone steals from us, though, bad things happen. Life spans get shorter."

"If you say Austin stole from you, I believe you. We don't owe you shit, though. Lose our number."

"Okay," said Nick, reaching behind him for his pistol. "You have a boss or supervisor I can talk to?"

"Yeah, but he won't be happy you waxed Austin," said the man in the black shirt. "Like I said, we liked him. He sold us a quality product at a fair price."

"That he did," said Nick, nodding. "Does your boss think you came here to meet Austin?"

For a moment, neither man said anything. Then the man in the red shirt spoke.

"Yeah. Why?"

"No reason," said Nick. His weapon cleared his belt holster in a fraction of a second. He squeezed the trigger. The round hit the man in the red shirt square in the face. He went down fast. The man in the black shirt ducked and reached behind him for his weapon, but Nick aimed and fired smoothly and quickly. The round hit him in the forehead. He, too, fell to the ground.

In the silence that followed, a semi roared past on the highway. Nick walked to the men on the ground and put another round into each of their heads, ensuring that they were dead.

Then he picked up Austin's phone from the ground and slipped it into his pocket before walking to the pickup truck. He snapped on a pair of latex gloves taken from the inside pocket of his jacket and opened the door, where he found a duffel bag full of money in the passenger footwell.

He grabbed the bag and drove out of the rest area before anyone even saw him. He'd be just fine.

Nick had worked in this world for a long time, and in those years, he had learned an important lesson: Killing people and getting away with it was a lot easier if someone else pulled the trigger. Soon, some bad men would come to St. Augustine looking for their friends in the red and black shirts. When they found they were dead, they'd look for those responsible.

St. Augustine would have a lot of dead chemists soon, which meant Nick was almost done in town.

It was nice when things worked out.

Chapter 17

Roger woke me up by barking from the front room at about six the next morning. He must have seen a rabbit or squirrel near the house. Even this deep in his golden years, Roger remained vigilant against the ferocious threat posed by all rabbits, squirrels, and cats that stepped within a two-hundred-foot radius of our front door.

I groaned and swung my legs off the bed. My head didn't hurt, but my mouth was dry. The room felt cool and comfortable. Since it was still early, I dressed in a sports bra and shorts and took a jog through the woods behind my house. Roger didn't even follow me out the door.

The storm that had destroyed the campsite where we found Laura Rojas had knocked down almost a dozen trees in my woods, creating an obstacle course on my running trail. That was okay. It made my muscles work all the harder.

By the time I got back to the house, sweat, dried leaves, and a thin layer of dirt covered my skin, but I felt wide awake and energized. Even with a full day of grinding work ahead of me, I felt good. After my run, Roger sat with me in the kitchen as I scrambled eggs and toasted bread. It started earlier than I had expected, but it became a nice morning.

By eight, I had showered, dressed, and driven to work. The parking lot at the station was full, and the lobby buzzed as the evening and day shifts swapped places. I said hello to people as I passed and then attended the morning briefing in the conference room. Delgado and Harry had yet to find Aldon McKenzie; Paige Maxwell and Jude Lewis hadn't shown up; and no one had reported any other major crimes in St. Augustine overnight. Typical day.

After the briefing, I swapped my notepad with work on Laura Rojas's murder with the notepad I had taken to the hospital when I interviewed June Wellman. Her case was as important as anything else I had been doing, and it threatened to get lost in the shuffle. She deserved better than that.

I checked my cell phone to ensure it had a full charge and then walked to my truck, which I drove to Waterford College. Benedictine monks had founded the school almost two hundred years ago as a Catholic seminary, but over time, its mission had changed until it became a private, nondenominational liberal arts college for the sons and daughters of wealthy Midwesterners. It was a good school.

As I drove through Waterford's brick front entrance, I left the rural, poor streets of St. Augustine and entered an affluent world of privilege and power. Mature trees swayed in the morning breeze, and undergraduates walked to class, backpacks slung over their shoulders as their eyes remained glued to their cell phones. No leaves or weeds littered the sidewalk, and no cracks marred the roads. The Federalist-style academic buildings looked as imposing as any courthouse in the world.

The college employed its own police force, but they deferred to us on major felony investigations. I stopped by their office to tell them I was on campus to interview students, which they seemed to appreciate. A sleepy-looking uniformed officer offered to escort me around the school, but I told him I could manage on my own. Besides that, I carried a map and a gun. The world was my oyster.

I started at June's sorority. It was a little before nine when I arrived, and half the girls in the house—June included—were still asleep. The girls I spoke to seemed nice, but few of them had gone with June to the fraternity the night Chad had raped her, so few of them had firsthand accounts of what happened. Of those girls who went, none saw Chad slip anything into her drink or force her to drink more than she wanted.

Next, I walked to Chad's fraternity. Someone had locked the front door, so I rang the doorbell until an older woman in an apron opened.

"Can I help you?"

"Yeah," I said, flashing her my badge. "I'm Detective Joe Court. I'm looking for Chad Hamilton. Have you seen him this morning?"

The woman blinked. "I'm the cook. I don't see the boys until lunch."

"Please get someone who can help me."

She began to say something, but a tall, handsome young man stepped into the doorway before she could. His slick smile reminded me of a dead criminal defense lawyer I once knew. He wore jeans and a navy-blue T-shirt that hugged his chest and broad shoulders. College girls probably swooned over him. I could use that.

"I'm Jake, the chapter president. Molly's the cook. She doesn't know the brothers. Can I help you?"

I flashed my badge at him.

"I need to talk to Chad Hamilton."

He looked at my badge, but then his eyes strayed to my chest and hips. He wasn't leering, but he wasn't subtle, either. When he looked at my eyes again, he gave me a cheesy grin and held the door wide open.

"Beautiful women are always welcome in the Sigma Iota house."

"Terrific, thank you," I said, stepping inside. The fraternity's entry had carpeted stairs that led up to the first floor and down to the basement. The house smelled like bleach and stale beer with just a hint of vomit and body odor. It reminded me of my station's drunk tank.

I took the stairs to the lobby and found two guys in pajamas lounging in front of a giant television.

"Either of you two Chad Hamilton, by chance?"

The guys looked to Jake, their president.

"This is a detective," he said, the cheesy smile never leaving his face. "She's a police officer."

One guy sat up and held up his hands.

"I'm just a pledge."

Jake chuckled. "It's all right, Tony. She's here to talk to some brothers. Why don't you go home? You look like you haven't showered in days."

Tony nodded and left, barely taking the time to put on a pair of sandals. The other guy followed without saying a word, so I looked to Jake.

"Now that I'm in, I would appreciate it if you told me where Chad was."

A frown replaced Jake's smile. "I think he's upstairs in his room, but we only allow brothers and guests up there. It may be a while before he comes down. You're welcome to wait here."

"I'd like to talk to him. You think you could get him for me?"

He sucked in a deep breath through his teeth before shaking his head. "Chad can be grumpy when he wakes up, so I think it'd be better if we waited. Unless you have a warrant. If you have an arrest or search warrant, you're free to go up yourself and get him."

He smiled again. I returned it.

"So you're the fraternity's lawyer and its president. Good for you."

"I'm not a lawyer, but I am prelaw, and part of my job as the house president is to protect the brothers when appropriate."

"Well, you're doing a fine job, Jake," I said, looking around the lobby for the fire alarm. I found one near the front staircase, so I crossed the room and pulled it. An ear-piercing wail filled the air. Jake hurried after me and tried to push the handle up to turn the alarm off, but I wagged a finger at him and shook my head. "I wouldn't do that if I were you."

He took a step back. "What are you doing?"

"Fire drill!" I shouted. "It's important to conduct regular fire drills in communal living environments like this. As a sworn law enforcement officer, this is part of my community policing duties."

Footsteps pounded on the floor above me.

"Everybody, get the fuck up. This isn't a drill!" shouted a voice from upstairs. I looked at Jake and smiled.

"I'm glad to hear at least one of your brothers is taking this seriously."

Within moments, young men—and more than a few young women—streamed down the steps. I waited by the fire alarm for another few minutes until everybody left. Then I joined the men and women on the lawn in front of the house.

"Okay, guys!" I shouted, holding up my badge. "Thanks for cooperating with the drill. Everybody but Chad Hamilton is free to go back inside."

Several guys grumbled, but nobody complained aloud. A young man walked toward me. His pale skin and curly red hair spoke of Scandinavian ancestry. I must have gotten him right out of bed because he wasn't wearing a shirt. He looked at me and then to Jake, confused.

"I'm Chad," he said, looking at me up and down. "Who are you?"

"Detective Joe Court, St. Augustine County Sheriff's Department. I'm glad you're up. Let's talk."

"Can I get a shirt?"

I smiled and looked at Jake. "Be a dear, Jake, and get your brother a shirt. He's underdressed." I looked at Chad again. "We need to talk about June."

His chest and face turned red.

"Oh, shit."

"Good," I said, smiling. "It sounds like you know what we need to talk about. Let's go inside. I hope you've got good answers for me."

Chapter 18

I sat down in the lobby on a floral-print couch a few minutes later. Chad—who was now wearing a plain white T-shirt—and Jake sat across from me. Chad's right foot bounced, and he worked his hands together. Jake's face was almost emotionless. He'd be a good lawyer one day. Good for him. The world needed good lawyers. I reached into my jacket for my cell phone, opened a voice recording app, and put it on a coffee table between us.

"Okay, guys," I said, smiling at both men. "I'm Detective Joe Court with the St. Augustine County Sheriff's Department, and I'm sitting in the Sigma Iota fraternity house at a little after nine in the morning. With me is Chad Hamilton. Before I begin with my questions, this is an interview to gather information about an event that occurred in this fraternity house several days ago. Chad, you're not under arrest, and you're under no obligation to answer my questions. If you'd like, you can have an attorney with you. If my questions make you uncomfortable, you can leave. That clear?"

He looked to Jake.

"What happens if he leaves?" asked Jake.

"I have a credible report that Mr. Hamilton raped a young woman upstairs. If he refuses to talk about it, I will investigate the allegation to the best of my ability. That means people will know about it, including his professors and the university administration. If he talks, we might clear this up today. We can keep things quiet and save everybody some embarrassment."

"You should talk," said Jake. "The house doesn't need this kind of publicity."

Chad drew in a breath and nodded.

"Okay," he said. "Ask whatever you want to ask me."

I stayed with him for about an hour. I even let Jake stay because he shut up as soon as Chad talked. Chad claimed he and June had been dating for the better part of a year and that they'd had an active sex life. I didn't want details, but Jake broke his silence to voice his agreement and said every brother in the house had heard them having sex at least once.

Chad claimed he didn't rape June. He said they had broken up several weeks ago to see other people but couldn't stand to be apart from one another. They got back together that night. To celebrate, they got drunk. Drinking led to fooling around, which led to consensual sex.

Without prompting from me, he said June liked things a little rough. He claimed he pinned her arms down at her request and had both vaginal and anal sex with her. Afterwards, he helped her take a shower because she was drunk.

Then, she got dressed and walked home alone. He passed out in bed and woke up the next morning.

When Chad finished speaking, I looked up from my notepad.

"Since you were her concerned boyfriend, did you call her the next day?" I asked.

"Yeah, but she didn't answer," he said. "I saw her in the dining center. She seemed fine."

"Did you try to talk to her?"

Chad almost said something, but Jake interrupted him before he could.

"Don't answer that, Chad. This interview is over."

I looked at him. "Why don't you go take a walk, Jake?"

"This is my house," he said, pounding a finger on the coffee table. "You can't tell me what to do in my house."

I nodded and kept my lips thin and straight.

"To be clear, are you a licensed attorney in the state of Missouri, Jake?"

He shook his head. "No, but—"

"Is Chad Hamilton a minor in your care?"

"No, but this is my house," said Jake, shaking his head again. "You're our guest."

"To remind you, I'm a police officer investigating a rape. You're a kid who likes to play lawyer but who doesn't understand what he's doing. I've allowed you to stay here because you kept your mouth shut. Now you've interrupted my interview and told your friend not to answer my questions.

That means you've interfered with a police investigation. You can either walk away now, or I will call my station for help. A very burly, angry man we call Sasquatch will handcuff you and take you to our station, where you will spend the night in a cell pending arraignment tomorrow morning. Your choice. What do you want to do, Jake?"

Jake stood and opened his mouth. I cocked my head to the side and raised my eyebrow.

"Take a walk, kid," I said, smiling. "Let the adults work."

He muttered that I was a bitch as he walked away. People had called me worse, so I ignored it and turned back to Chad. His face was red once again.

"Are you going to answer my questions now?" I asked.

"I'm done talking."

"Okay," I said, nodding and reaching for my cell phone. I turned off the recording app and looked at him. "You want to listen for a minute?"

He sat back down and then shrugged.

"I guess."

"Good, thank you," I said. "Here's what's going on. June went to the hospital on Monday for a rather invasive exam. A nurse took swabs from all over her body, she took pictures, and then she boxed everything up for my crime lab. The exam sucks. Young women don't sit for it unless something happened to them. You've told me your story, and June has told me hers. I find her to be a compelling, credible witness. You, I don't."

His shoulders seemed to slump.

"You raped her, didn't you?"

He didn't respond. I had expected that.

"Did you tell Jake that you had raped June, or did he guess on his own from the way June reacted to you in the dining hall?"

"It wasn't like that," said Chad, staring at his hands. I waited for him to say something else, but he didn't. It wasn't quite an admission, but I was getting there.

"He sounds like a good friend," I said. He didn't look up. "It's kind of unfortunate he tried to help during the interview, though. I may have to charge him with conspiracy now. He seems like a smart guy. He'd make a hell of a lawyer one day. I'd hate to see that ruined. How many of your brothers know you raped her?"

He shook his head. "I don't know."

Again, it wasn't an admission, but it was closer still.

"June cried the entire night after she came home from your house. I know you care about her, and she cares about you. You didn't mean to hurt her, I'm sure. You were drunk. Things got out of hand. That doesn't make you a bad guy. You can still make this right."

Even as I spoke, I leaned forward and snaked my hand across the coffee table for my phone to turn on my recorder. My eyes never left his. I forced them to stay compassionate and kind, but inside, they burned.

Come on, asshole. Say it. Admit what you did.

He opened his mouth as if to say something. And then, it all went wrong.

The front door slammed open, and raucous laughter filled the lobby as three of Chad's fraternity brothers came home from class. Chad shot to his feet as his friends entered the room. All three gave curious glances to Chad, but then they focused on me. They didn't hide their leers.

"Hey," said one, casting his eyes down my torso. "Tell me you're applying to be our new house mother."

A second boy backhanded him on the shoulder and pointed at my hips.

"Dude, she's a cop," he said. "Look."

For a second, nobody said anything. Then the three looked at Chad.

"Don't say anything," said one newcomer, already hustling toward the stairs that led to the rooms on the second floor. "I'll call my dad. He's a lawyer."

"It's okay, Josh," said Chad, standing straighter. "I won't say anything. You need to go, Detective."

My lips threatened to curl into an annoyed grimace, and my fingernails bit into my palms.

"Are you sure?" I asked, knowing even as I spoke that it was pointless to keep pushing. Chad had shut down. "I can help you get ahead of this. If you face this on your own, you're likely to get hurt."

"Don't listen to her, Chad," said the boy whose father was an attorney. "She's just trying to get you to talk. You need a lawyer."

I wanted to tell him to shut up, but I kept my eyes focused on Chad. He opened his mouth to speak.

"I want to call my dad. I need a lawyer."

At once, the dam holding my anger in check broke. I had needed that confession. Without it, I had circumstantial evidence, but nothing that could even secure an indictment, let alone a conviction. It'd be June's word against Chad's. I clenched my teeth hard. I wanted to kick something. Chad hurried to the stairs. I scowled and shook my head.

I looked at the kid whose dad was a lawyer. He took a stutter step back as I glared.

"Chad raped a girl upstairs, and you persuaded him not to talk. Thanks. You're a real solid citizen. "

He said nothing, which I appreciated. I might have punched him if he had. Instead, I tightened my fists and stormed through the front door.

"Fuck."

I didn't say it to anyone in particular, but a pair of young coeds near me on the sidewalk jumped anyway. I didn't care. When I reached my truck again, I sat in the driver's seat and took deep breaths with my eyes closed, trying to calm down. My breath became more even, and the heat that had been rushing over my body cooled somewhat.

Then, somebody knocked on my window.

I opened my eyes and tilted my head to the right to see June Wellman staring at me from the passenger-side door. Her cheeks were rosier than they had been the last time I saw her, but her lips were just as thin and straight. I rolled the window down and forced myself to smile.

"Hey, June," I said. "I had planned to call you this afternoon."

"Miss Claudette said you were on campus," she said. "I thought I'd say hi."

My anger melted. This investigation wasn't about me. It was about June. I leaned over to the passenger side of my truck and unlocked the door.

"Why don't you have a seat?" I asked. "We'll talk."

She nodded and climbed into the cab beside me. With the windows cracked, a breeze blew through the truck's interior, carrying with it the sweet scent of cut grass and the occasional sound of laughter as undergraduates walked near the parking lot. It felt calm, almost peaceful. None of that made what I had to say easier, but I appreciated it.

"Chad raped you," I said, once June sat down. "I talked to him this morning."

She sat straighter. "He admitted it?"

I looked down and sighed before shaking my head. "I came at him hard, but no. He would have confessed, I think, but someone interrupted us."

She nodded and shifted the backpack on her lap. "What now?"

"With your permission, I'll contact the school and tell them what happened. As I understand it, Waterford has an honor code. He'll face sanctions there. If you'd like, I can also file a restraining order on your behalf. I know a lot of therapists who have worked with rape victims, too, so I can—"

"You're not going to arrest him?" she asked, interrupting me, her voice sharp and angry. "You're going to let him go?"

I had been in June's shoes, so I understood how helpless, angry, hurt, disappointed, sick, and defeated she felt. A sour, heavy pit formed in my gut. I wanted to take those feelings from her, but I couldn't.

"You deserve better than this, and I'm sorry," I said, my voice low. "I did my best, but I can't arrest him based on what we have."

"No," said June, throwing open her door. It hit the car beside us, leaving a dent in its black paint. As she got out of the car, she glared at me. "I don't accept that. If this is your best, it's not good enough."

Then she slammed the door shut. I stayed still and swallowed hard.

"I'm sorry," I whispered to no one in particular. My chest felt heavy, and there was a bitter taste in the back of my mouth. After a few moments, I wrote my name and phone number on a piece of paper from my notepad and slid it beneath the windshield wiper of the Honda Accord June had hit with my door.

When I got back in my truck, I didn't want to go anywhere, so I sat for a few minutes. I had become a cop so I could help women like June. Most days, I loved my job, but days like this left me wondering whether, maybe, I should have gone to medical school instead. My grades in college were strong enough, and I had a degree in biology. I would have made a good doctor. I could have been a pediatrician.

Before I could sink any lower, my phone rang. I cleared my throat before answering.

"Yeah?" I said.

"Detective Court, it's Mathias Blatch. I wanted to update you on my investigation. You got a minute?"

I sucked in a deep breath so he wouldn't hear the catch in my throat.

"Sure. Go ahead."

"Our lab ran the ballistics on the round your coroner pulled from Laura Rojas. It matches rounds fired by the gun we found in Duke Trevino's apartment. You want to talk to him?"

June was still on my mind, but I sat straighter and tried to focus on my other case.

"Have you got him in custody now?"

"We do."

I reached into my purse for my keys and turned on my car.

"I'm in St. Augustine. Are you in South County, or are you in Clayton?"

"South County, Fourth Precinct."

"I'm on my way," I said. I hung up and tossed my phone to the seat beside me before buckling my seatbelt. Nailing a murderer wouldn't make up for failing to arrest Chad Hamilton, but it would make me feel a lot better. I put my car in gear and headed out. It was time to do my job.

Chapter 19

The Fourth Precinct station in southern St. Louis County was a modern, clean building well suited for a professional police organization. My mom—a retired captain in the St. Louis County Police Department—and I had attended the ribbon-cutting eight months ago when they opened the building, but I had yet to go inside. The instant I stepped through the front doors, though, jealousy spiked throughout my body. Everything was clean and open, and all the overhead lights worked. It didn't even smell like vomit or mold.

The officer manning the front desk smiled upon seeing me, so I showed him my badge and introduced myself. He handed me a sign-in sheet.

"Mathias knows you're coming, so he should be down any moment."

"Great," I said, writing my name and contact information in the squares on the paper. Detective Blatch walked into the waiting room a few moments later with a smile on his face.

"Come on back, Detective," he said. "We've got Trevino in an interrogation booth now."

I followed him through the station to a row of interrogation rooms at the back of the building. Two rooms were free, but the third had a sign on its door that showed someone was inside.

"Have you told him about the ballistics match yet?"

Blatch shook his head. "That's your case, so I thought you could break the news to him. At the moment, we're holding him on a lot of drug charges. He's looking for a deal on those because he knows we've got him dead to rights."

I lowered my chin. "Has he asked for a lawyer?"

"Not yet," said Blatch, "but he knows the system. He's already signed a rights waiver form, so we're good to go as far as the interrogation."

I nodded.

"What kind of record does he have?"

Blatch drew in a breath and raised his eyebrows. "We've picked him up four times for the distribution of a controlled substance but nothing violent."

I slowed and furrowed my brow. "We found over a pound of marijuana in Laura Rojas's home. If Trevino is selling in that quantity to other dealers, he must be a big player. Why was he still on the streets?"

"You'd have to ask the prosecutors," said Blatch, a bemused smile on his face. "Are you questioning our police work?"

"Not at all," I said, softening my tone. "I'm trying to get the facts straight before we go in there. Are you ready?"

Blatch nodded and held the door for me, and I stepped inside a small, windowless room with rough gray fabric on the walls and ceiling and matching Berber carpet on the floor. In the center of the room, thick bolts held a metal table to the floor. There were wooden chairs around it. On one sat Duke Trevino. Blatch had said he was in his mid-twenties, but he looked forty. He had a jagged scar on his cheek and cold, brown eyes. The harsh overhead light gleamed on his dark skin. He was bald and looked pissed off.

Had I been alone in a dark alley with him and had he looked at me with the malevolence I saw in his eyes now, I might have drawn my weapon. As it was, he wore an orange jumpsuit and thick shackles that kept him rooted to his chair. He could have lunged across the table at me, but there were dozens of officers not ten feet away. If he touched me, he'd be beaten down hard, and then he'd spend the next twenty to thirty years in prison.

I pulled a chair from beneath the table and sat across from him. Blatch did likewise, sitting beside me.

"Duke Trevino?" I asked. He nodded.

"Yeah. Who are you?"

"I'm Detective Joe Court from the St. Augustine County Sheriff's Department. I imagine you've already met Detective Blatch."

He looked at my face and then to my chest. "Your momma want a boy or something?"

I cocked my head to the side. "Excuse me?"

"You're a lady. What kind of name is Joe?"

I smiled. "My full name is Mary Joe. My mom was a big fan of Joe Montana, the football player. He was NFL MVP the same year I was born. She claims she named me after him. You like football?"

Duke looked confused by the question.

"You bring me all the way down here to talk football?"

"No," I said, shaking my head, "but sometimes it's easier to start an interview if you know something about the person sitting across from you. I was trying to be nice."

He grunted. "You want to be nice, you'll take these chains off me. You keep a man in chains too long, he's liable to snap."

"They'll come off you soon enough," I said. "We won't let you snap."

"Why the hell am I here?" he asked, throwing up his shackled hands and looking at me. "I'm missing lunch."

"I'm sorry to hear about your lunch," said Blatch, tossing a manila envelope in front of me. When Trevino looked away, Blatch winked at me and nodded to the envelope. "Tell you what. I'm hungry, too. How about we get through this interview, and I'll get us some tacos? There's a food truck up the street."

Trevino considered but then nodded.

"I want mine with cheese and beans and shit."

"You answer our questions, you can have anything you want on it," said Blatch.

Trevino leaned back and nodded. “Fire away, boss.”

Blatch looked at me, so I reached into my purse for my cell phone, which I used to record the conversation.

“For the record, this is Detective Mary Joe Court. I’m sitting with Detective Mathias Blatch and Duke Trevino in the St. Louis County Fourth Precinct station. Do you agree to talk to us today, Mr. Trevino?”

“Like I got a choice?” he asked, rattling his shackles.

“Detective Blatch has placed you under arrest, but you can remain silent. If you talk to us, we can use what you tell us in court against you. If you want a lawyer here, we can get you one. If you can’t afford a lawyer, the court will appoint one for you. So. You want to talk to us or go back to your cell?”

He paused for a moment and focused on me. “View’s better here.”

“Is that a yes?” I asked.

He looked at Blatch. “I know my rights. Yeah, we’re cool.”

“You want a lawyer here?” I asked.

“Nah,” he said, shaking his head. “I can’t pay one, and those public defenders ain’t worth shit. They screw up more than they help.”

“Okay,” I said. “I’m here to talk to you about Laura Rojas.”

He gave me a blank stare. Then he shrugged.

“Don’t know her.”

“You sure about that?” asked Blatch.

Trevino focused on the young detective and leaned forward.

"I ain't ever heard the bitch's name."

Blatch didn't respond, but I leaned back. "Okay. Let's take a step back. What do you do for a living, Mr. Trevino?"

He looked at me. "Whatever I gotta do."

"Does that include selling drugs?" I asked.

He jangled his chains and looked at Blatch. "Ding, ding, ding. Get the lady a prize. That's why you folks arrested me, isn't it? You say I'm slinging dope or something."

"We found four ounces of marijuana in your apartment," said Blatch. "That's good evidence."

He smirked. "Four ounces? That's nothing."

I sat back, surprised. He was right. Possession of more than an ounce and a quarter was a felony, but if we sent everybody with that much weed to prison, our college campuses would go empty, and our prison population would swell tenfold. Not only that, he had supposedly sold Laura a pound of product. If he moved that much dope, I doubted he'd only have a quarter pound in his apartment.

"Who do you get your product from?" I asked.

"That ain't none of your business," he said, looking at me.

"My badge says it is my business," I said, "but we'll get back to that. Can you tell me about the gun you hid under your mattress?"

He sat straighter and shook his head. "Ah, hell no. I didn't hide no gun under no mattress."

"Are you sure?" asked Blatch. "Because we found one there. Three officers witnessed the search."

"They're liars," he said. "I've got kids. I don't keep guns around the house."

"But you keep drugs around the house," said Blatch.

"It's weed, man. God made it grow in the ground," he said, shrugging. "That means it's okay, right?"

I doubted that reasoning would hold up in court, but I nodded as if it made sense.

"If it wasn't your gun, how'd it get under your mattress?" I asked.

He nodded to Blatch. "Mr. Suit-and-Tie put it there."

Blatch chuckled. "Sorry, buddy, but no. It's your gun. And it's Detective Suit-and-Tie."

"You find my fingerprints on it?" he asked.

"Someone wiped it clean," said Blatch. "They also wiped the magazine and every round inside. If you had thrown it away after killing Laura Rojas, we wouldn't have been able to tie it to you. Why did you keep it? You want a souvenir?"

"Whoa, whoa, whoa," he said, holding his hands up, palms toward us. "I ain't even heard of Laura Rojas."

"And yet we found her murder weapon under your mattress," said Blatch, "and we found a bag of marijuana in her closet with your fingerprints on it. How do you explain that?"

"I didn't kill nobody, and that's the truth," he said, pounding his index finger on the table. "I ain't even heard of this chick."

I picked up my phone and flipped through pictures until I found one of Laura's face. I turned it around and showed it to him.

"You didn't kill this girl?" I asked. His eyes shifted to the picture.

"Nah. Never seen her."

"Look again," I said. "And consider your answer well. We've got enough evidence to put you away for her murder. Are you sure you've never met her?"

He looked at me and spoke so that every word became its own sentence.

"I. Don't. Know. Her."

"If you don't know her, let's clear this whole thing up right away," I said. "It's Tuesday today. She died on Saturday night. We found her Sunday afternoon. Where were you?"

"Saturday?" he asked, his eyebrows raised. I nodded. "I was in fucking Jeff City with my baby's momma."

Blatch leaned forward.

"Can anybody verify that?" he asked.

Trevino held up his fingers and counted them off as he spoke.

"My baby momma, my kids, my baby momma's momma, her dad, her grandma, the minister at her church, and everybody in church. We went to a church picnic."

"Even if you were there earlier, that doesn't mean you were in Jefferson City when Laura died," said Blatch.

"What time did she die?"

"Late," I said.

"I spent the night in jail. Got drunk and pissed on a fire hydrant. Cop took exception."

Neither Blatch nor I said anything for a moment. Then Blatch took a notepad from his pocket and tossed it to Trevino before standing up.

"Detective Court and I will step outside for a minute. Do me a favor and write down the names of everybody who saw you in Jefferson City on Sunday."

"I'll need a pencil," he said. I tossed him a pen from my purse and left the room with Detective Blatch. He shut the door and gave me a tight smile.

"How certain is your coroner of Laura Rojas's time of death?"

"Not very," I said. "Laura's body went through an ordeal when she died."

"Do you have evidence that could tie him to the scene?"

I sighed and rubbed my eyes. "Maybe if we're lucky. We got hit by a tornado right after finding her body. My team did what they could, but the storm wrecked the scene and destroyed the coroner's van. We're lucky nobody died."

He raised his eyebrows. "Jeez."

"Yeah. It was a mess. Once we saw the tornado coming, we evacuated the scene but had to leave most of the evidence behind. We picked up a handful of beer bottles, I think. They might have prints on them, but I doubt they'll match."

Blatch looked at the door. "You believe our intrepid drug dealer in there?"

"I don't know what I believe right now. You think it's strange that you'd pick up a drug dealer who sold over a pound of marijuana to Laura but who only had four ounces in his apartment?"

"Maybe he made a big deal and sold most of his supply," said Blatch, shrugging.

"That's possible," I said, nodding more to myself than to him. "Did you find any canisters like the ones we found in Laura's house in Trevino's place?"

Blatch hesitated and shook his head.

"No," he said. "He kept his weed in Ziploc bags."

"Laura kept her drugs in sealed canisters and mylar bags. Those would keep her weed safe and potent for a long time. Her dealer kept them in Ziploc bags that would allow the cannabinoids to break down within months."

Blatch looked to the closed door. "Maybe he gets the drugs, keeps them for a while, and moves them on before they can break down."

"It's possible, but I'm not feeling this. He whipped out his alibi right away, and it's not just his girlfriend. It's his girlfriend's family, it's her minister at church, it's the church congregation. If he's lying, it won't be hard to find out."

"Don't tell me you believe his story," said Blatch, crossing his arms. "We didn't hide a gun on him."

"He's lying," I said, my voice soft, "but that doesn't mean he's a killer. He deals drugs, but I don't think he killed Laura."

"Who did?"

I hesitated and then shook my head. "I wish I had a clue."

Chapter 20

Since Trevino wasn't my killer, I left the station after the interview. It had been a week since I last saw my parents, so I figured I might as well visit them while I was in town. I sent my mom a text message and drove to Kirkwood, their upper-middle-class suburb west of the city.

When I was a little girl, I lived out of a car with my biological mother. After Erin overdosed on heroin, the county's Department of Children's Services took me in and put me in foster care. I bounced around for years, but I never had a permanent place to live until I met Julia and Doug Green. They gave a broken young woman a home and a family without asking for anything in return. I could never thank them enough.

Dad must have seen me park because he opened the door before I knocked.

"Hey, old man," I said, smiling. "I was in the neighborhood, so I thought I'd stop by."

"Your mom told me you were coming," he said, taking a step back. "Come on in, sweetheart."

As I stepped inside, Dad hesitated and then put a hand on my shoulder. I reached my arms around his back and squeezed tight. He did the same.

When Doug and Julia took me in, I was a young woman whose previous foster father had raped her. Even the thought of anyone touching me had made me ill. It had taken years, but I liked hugs from other women now. Dad was still one of the very few men allowed to touch me. He made me feel safe.

"It's good to see you," I whispered.

"You, too, sweetheart," he said, stepping back. "Your mom's in the kitchen, but I've been tinkering in the garage. I'm building a Shaker end table. I've been watching woodworking videos on YouTube."

I looked at his hands. "You haven't cut off your thumbs yet, so it looks like you're doing okay."

"I don't know what I'd do without the support of my children."

I squeezed his arm. "Speaking of kids, where's my little brother?"

"At work. He's a lifeguard at the Ladue Country Club's pool. I'm pretty sure he's just there to pick up girls."

"So I've heard," I said, nodding. "How do you like knowing you'll be a grandpa soon?"

Dad flashed me a coy smile.

"You telling me something?"

"About me? No," I said, smiling. "Based on what Audrey tells me, though, Dylan should have at least half a dozen kids on the way."

He patted me on the shoulder and nodded down the hallway toward the kitchen.

"You're hilarious," he said. "Now go see your mom. I'll be in soon."

As Dad went to finish his project in the garage, I walked into the kitchen and hugged my mom. Mom had retired from the St. Louis County Police Department four weeks ago. She was in her late fifties, so she hadn't planned to retire for several years, but sometimes life gets in the way. Mom had been an excellent cop, but she and her former partner had lost their ways over the years. Retirement was for the best.

I stayed at my parents' house for an hour and had sandwiches and a few laughs. For that hour, I didn't have to think about murder, or rape, or abductions. I could just be me. I had a home, and it was wonderful.

Even wonderful visits home had to end, though.

After lunch, I hugged my parents one last time and got back in my pickup for the drive to St. Augustine. The moment I sat in the cab, the weight of my cases pressed down on me.

Laura Rojas had died on Saturday night, and last night, someone murdered Jennifer McKenzie. Aldon McKenzie, Jennifer's husband, was the key to all this. We needed to find him.

I drove to St. Augustine, parked in the lot outside the station, and walked to the front desk, where Tricia greeted me with a subdued smile.

"Has Detective Delgado found Aldon McKenzie yet?" I asked.

Tricia shook her head. "If George has found him, he hasn't brought him by my desk. You need to go to Harry's office, though. He's meeting with Shaun Deveraux and Councilman Rogers to talk about you."

A mild headache spread from the front of my skull to the back.

"I'm assuming they're not talking about giving me a medal for outstanding police work."

"Fair assumption," said Trisha. "Councilman Rogers looked ticked."

I sighed. "All right. Thanks, Trisha."

She smiled and wished me luck, so I climbed the stairs to the sheriff's office. Harry worked out of one of the bigger rooms in the building, but that didn't make it nice. Water stains dotted the ceiling, while wind and rain passed through his aging but enormous front window as if the glass didn't exist. His desk, conference table, and chairs all came from secondhand stores in town. The room smelled like a wet dog. As much as I would have enjoyed having a private office, I didn't envy Harry one bit.

When I opened his door, three pairs of eyes turned. Harry sat behind his desk, while Councilman Rogers and

Shaun Deveraux, the St. Augustine county prosecutor, sat in wooden chairs in front. Nobody looked happy to see me, but at least Harry stood up.

"Joe, I was hoping to talk to you," he said. He looked to his guests. "If you don't mind, let's move this to the conference table where we can all sit."

Rogers and Deveraux agreed, so Harry and I sat down opposite from them at Harry's small conference table. For a few moments, nobody said anything. Then Councilman Rogers leaned forward and smiled a fake grin at me.

"I'm glad you stopped by, Detective. I hear you drove to St. Louis this morning."

"Yeah," I said. "I interviewed a murder suspect at the Fourth Precinct's headquarters."

"We'll get to your interview in a moment," said Rogers, folding his hands together at the table. "Before we do, though, I'd like to ask you a question: What vehicle did you drive to St. Louis?"

I hesitated. "My truck. Why?"

Rogers sighed. "The county provides a wide range of vehicles for our law enforcement officers. The vehicles we provide are fine, modern cars that get excellent gas mileage. I'm guessing that your old truck gets, what, ten miles to the gallon?"

"Better than that," I said, eyeing him. "Why?"

"It's just that gas is expensive, young lady, and your truck isn't the most economical of vehicles. We'd prefer if you took one of our cruisers. It'd save us all some money. I understand you were driving your truck the day of the tornado, too."

I hesitated again. "Yeah."

"I bet you want the county to pay for your broken window, too."

I glanced at Harry out of the corner of my eye and then to Councilman Rogers.

"Since I was on official police business, yes," I said. "The department doesn't have enough vehicles for everyone who needs one, so I drove my truck because it was available. I made the best out of a lousy situation. If the County Council gave us the budget they promised us every year, we wouldn't have half the problems we do."

Rogers held up his hands and nodded.

"Mr. Deveraux and I didn't come here to talk about the council. We're not even here to talk about your questionable expenses. We came to talk about Laura Rojas."

"Sounds good," I said. "As this is an active investigation, Councilman Rogers should step out, though."

Rogers lowered his chin. "Watch yourself, Detective. Don't forget that I pay your salary."

I matched his posture and lowered my voice. "You're on the board that allocates my department's budget. From that budget, I get a salary. That's quite a big step from paying me."

Rogers opened his mouth to retort, but Harry cleared his throat. "If the councilman would like to stay, he's welcome.

This is an active case, though. I trust that everyone will be discreet about the things they hear."

"Of course," said Rogers, smiling at Harry. "You have my word, Sheriff Grainger."

Harry opened his mouth to speak, but Deveraux cut him off before he got a word out.

"I got a phone call from a colleague in the St. Louis County Prosecutor's Office this afternoon. Why is Duke Trevino sitting in a holding cell in St. Louis instead of here?"

"Because he had illegal drugs in St. Louis County," I said.

"But he killed a woman here. He had the murder weapon in his possession, and detectives found his fingerprints in the victim's home," said Deveraux. "I understand you lost evidence that might have tied him to your crime scene during the tornado, but you've got enough for an arrest."

"I might agree if he didn't have an alibi," I said. "Not only that, we don't know where Laura died. Someone could have shot her in Chicago for all we know."

Deveraux shook his head.

"We've got the body, the gun, and his prints. That's enough to charge him. Pick him up, let him sit in a cell for a few days, and then we'll see whether we can get him to talk about a plea deal."

"I won't arrest somebody for a crime he didn't commit," I said. "At the very least, we need to wait until Detective Blatch checks Trevino's alibi."

Councilman Rogers spoke before Deveraux responded.

"I understand your trepidation, Detective," he said, nodding. "It speaks well of you that you want to withhold judgment until you have all the facts, but you've got to understand something: St. Augustine is a tourist town. We can't let a murder go unsolved."

"I'm not letting a murder—"

"Let me finish," said Rogers, interrupting me before I could tell him off. "I understand you're not comfortable making an arrest, but you're not the only detective in town. I've already spoken to George Delgado. He's ready to move on this."

"George is a good detective," said Deveraux. "He's good on the witness stand, too. If he's comfortable making an arrest, I am, too."

"I don't care if George is comfortable," I said, shaking my head. "This is my case, and it's premature to make a move against Trevino. Not only that, he's sitting in a jail cell right now on felony possession charges. He's not going anywhere. If we arrest him now, we're all going to look stupid when it blows up in our faces."

Rogers sighed and then closed his eyes.

"This story is all over the news, Detective," he said. "The *St. Louis Post-Dispatch* had it above the fold on the second page this morning. People don't want to visit a town where naked ladies turn up dead in the woods. We've got to do something now before our businesses get hurt."

I narrowed my eyes at him. "You think they'd rather visit a town where the village idiot might arrest them on shitty evidence and half-cocked theories?"

"George Delgado is far from the village idiot, and he doesn't think the evidence is shitty," said Rogers. He looked at Harry. "You need to weigh in here and control your officer, Harry."

Harry looked at me, his expression a mix of sympathy and annoyance.

"Detective Court, if you continued working this case, could you find Laura Rojas's killer?"

"I don't know. The tornado tore apart our crime scene, we've got no eyewitnesses, and there's little forensic evidence to work with."

"We appreciate your honest answer," said Councilman Rogers, nodding. He turned to Harry. "You've got to put George Delgado on this. He's got the experience, and he's willing to put St. Augustine first."

I didn't understand what it meant to put the county first, so I said nothing.

"What more do you need to make an arrest?" asked Dev-eraux.

I looked at him. "Better evidence than I have."

"How do you plan to get it?"

"For a start, I'd love to look at Laura Rojas's office. She was a practicing attorney. It's possible a client killed her, but I can't get a peek at her client list without a warrant.

I'd also like to talk to Aldon McKenzie. He and Laura have exchanged dozens of phone calls over the past two weeks. Not only that, someone murdered Aldon's wife yesterday."

Deveraux drew in a breath and then nodded.

"I'll call the prosecutor's office in St. Louis County and see about putting together a warrant for Laura Rojas's office, but it won't be easy. The court will appoint an attorney to examine her files so we don't see anything protected by attorney-client privilege. It'll take time, and I can't guarantee you'll find anything helpful."

"It's a start," I said.

"I think George Delgado could handle this case better," said Rogers. "He's an experienced man."

"Detective Delgado is busy on a case already," said Harry, his voice sharper than it had been a moment earlier. "If we had more detectives, I might move him around, but since we're already shorthanded, Detective Court will do. Repeated questioning won't change my mind. Is that clear, Councilman?"

It wasn't a ringing endorsement, but at least Harry had shut him down. The civilians bickered for ten more minutes but left when they ran out of complaints. Harry asked me to stay. When we were alone, he looked at me and sighed.

"Sorry about that," he said. "Small-town politics. It's nothing personal. You know how it is."

Actually, the previous sheriff had kept me pretty well insulated from it in the past, so I didn't know.

"What do you want me to do?"

"Your job. Close this case," he said, standing. I stood and walked toward the door. Harry followed a few feet behind me. "Councilman Rogers is an asshole, but people listen to him. You don't close this thing soon, we might both lose our jobs."

"So no pressure," I said.

He smiled. "Good luck, Detective."

I probably needed it.

Chapter 21

As much as I wanted to find Laura Rojas's murderer, I had little to do on the case until George Delgado found Aldon McKenzie, or until Shaun Deveraux got my warrant for Laura's office. Even apart from Laura's case, though, I had enough work for three detectives, which meant I had little difficulty finding a project.

I left the building and drove home at three in the afternoon. At this time of year, the sun would be up for at least another four hours, and I didn't plan to waste the time. Once I reached my house, I changed into clothes appropriate for walking in the woods, filled up my canteen, gave Roger a couple scoops of food, and then got back in my truck. Roger whined at me, clearly wanting to go. A year ago, I would have taken him, but now, he'd slow me down too much.

I waved to him from my truck's cab and backed out of the driveway. When Paige Maxwell's parents had come and said their little girl was missing, I hadn't been too worried. I figured she might show up pregnant, but I thought she'd come home when she ran out of money. Harry had convinced me otherwise, though. This wasn't a missing-person case anymore. It had become a homicide investigation in all but name.

I drove to the area in which we had found her car and parked on the side of the road. Dozens of sworn officers and volunteer searchers had scoured the surrounding countryside, so I didn't expect to find anything. Still, Paige and Jude might have died there. Maybe their killer had even buried their bodies nearby. The tornado that had ripped through the area might have unearthed them or even scattered their bones across the landscape. Almost anything was possible.

I stepped out of my truck and onto soil still wet from a recent rain shower. Thick woods surrounded me. The Highway Patrol's wrecker had left deep furrows in the mud when it picked up Paige's car. Rainwater had filled those furrows, creating a perfect breeding ground for mosquitoes. The air was still. Even the birds were quiet. It was both eerie and beautiful.

I walked through those woods for two hours, wondering whether Paige and Jude had ever seen them. Their killer could have dumped Paige's car anywhere. Why did he choose here? Ross Kelly Farms was about four miles to the west. The interstate was at least five miles away. I didn't even know where the nearest home was.

This place was special to our killer. It meant something to him. The steep hills and jagged limestone outcroppings didn't make for great farmland, but hikers and campers should have loved it. If I hadn't been making so much noise, there'd be deer and other wildlife, too. Hunters should have been all over this place. Despite that, I hadn't passed a single trail, campground, cabin, or deer blind. I made a mental note to stop by the library and read up on the history of the property.

Birch, box elder, and black gum trees swayed in the warm breeze around me as shafts of light cascaded down through the forest canopy and struck the ground at my feet.

"You were here," I said, my voice almost a whisper. "You know this place. Who are you?"

Nobody answered. I continued walking—and stumbling—until the sun set. I found nothing, but I felt an ominous presence while walking those hills.

When I got back in my truck, I downed the last of my canteen of water and wiggled my toes inside my hiking boots. So far, my hiking boots had held up well considering I had purchased them at a secondhand store for five bucks. Already, though, the padding beneath my heel had grown stiff, and the arch support had disappeared. A pair of inserts would make them more comfortable, but these boots had served their purpose. I could raid my home-improvement fund and buy some decent ones. Until we found Paige and Jude, I figured I'd be spending a lot of time outside.

I drove back to St. Augustine and hit the town proper in about fifteen minutes. My fridge at home held little food, so I stopped by Able's Diner for a tuna melt sandwich and a cup of soup. It wasn't even nine yet, and already there were several intoxicated undergraduates from Waterford College inside the restaurant. If they had acted rowdy, I would have called the college's security office to have them picked up, but they were behaving themselves.

I walked by their table and showed them my badge. They smiled. One girl fluttered her eyes at me. I didn't understand what she was trying to do, so I ignored her and focused on the others at the table.

"You guys have a sober driver tonight?"

"We're not drunk, officer," said a boy. He didn't slur his words, but he smelled like alcohol. "We're just having dinner."

"Dude, people lie to me every day of my life," I said, shaking my head. "You suck at it."

He didn't seem to know how to respond, but a girl in the corner held up her hand.

"I'm the driver. I don't drink."

"Good," I said. "Just checking. You all look like you're over twenty-one, so I won't ask for ID. Have fun, but don't be stupid. Okay?"

They nodded, one of them so effusively he almost butted heads with the man in the booth behind him.

"You guys be careful," I said, stepping away from the table. The girl at the register handed me a paper sack with my sandwich and soup a moment later, and I got back in my truck. My drive home took me right by Waterford College's main entrance. Outside, a young woman sat on a bench as if she were waiting for the bus. She held a paper sack from which she took drinks.

I pulled off the road and parked near her. She didn't even glance at me as I shut my door.

"June?" I called. She looked at me with eyes muddled by booze.

"Yeah?"

"It's Joe Court," I said.

She grunted and took another swig.

"What do you want?"

I said nothing. Instead, I sat beside her and held out my hand for the bag. I didn't drink anything, but I took a big whiff once she handed it to me.

"Peach schnapps, huh?" I said, handing it back. "I'm more of a straight vodka drinker."

She reached into her purse for a plastic pint of vodka.

"That's next. I wanted something that tasted good first."

"Not a bad plan," I said, nodding. "Any reason you're out here getting drunk?"

She shrugged. "Roommate's fucking her chemistry lab partner in our room. Figured it'd be awkward if I stayed to get drunk while that was going on."

"I can see that," I said, nodding.

She took another sip of her peach schnapps. Neither of us spoke for two or three minutes. Then she looked at me.

"Are you going to arrest me for public intoxication?"

"You don't look that intoxicated," I said, tilting my head to the side. "I could arrest you for minor consumption, but I don't want to fill out the paperwork."

"Why are you here then?"

I shrugged and leaned forward so my elbows rested on my knees. "I saw somebody who looked like she needed a friend."

She looked at me. By the way her lip curled, I thought she was going to puke, but then she snorted and took another sip of her cheap booze.

"You're not my friend."

"No, I'm not," I said. "But I'm here. Are you getting drunk tonight for a reason, or is this how you spend your nights?"

"None of your business," she said.

"All right," I said, taking out my phone from my purse. "I'll call Waterford's campus police and have them pick you up."

She looked at me with genuine hurt in her eyes. "Bitch."

"You've stung me to the core," I said, thumbing through my address book for their number. June stood up. She wobbled for a second, but she didn't fall down.

"I got it, okay?" she said. "I'm going home."

"Stay and talk to me instead. Most people think I'm a nice person."

"I'm fine."

"If you say so," I said.

She hesitated and then walked away. Her footsteps were plodding, and her head and torso leaned to the left, drawing her off course. Before she fell over, I jogged toward her and put an arm around her shoulder to lead her back to the bench. Her shoulders were thin, and the stink of cheap alcohol came off her in waves.

She didn't fight me, so I helped her sit before taking the bottle of peach schnapps from her and dumping it out on the street. Then, I reached into her purse for her vodka. That, too, I opened and poured onto the street.

Once she realized what I was doing, she sat straighter and reached for my arm.

"That's mine," she said. "Give it back."

"You're underage, and you've had enough to drink for your entire sorority," I said, fending her off with my right hand while I poured with my left. Once both bottles were empty, she crossed her arms.

"You're such a cunt."

I narrowed my eyes at her. "That's not a nice word."

She didn't respond, not that I expected her to.

"Have you eaten anything today?" I asked.

She said nothing, so I repeated the question.

"I've got a meal card," she said.

"That doesn't answer my question, June."

She closed her eyes and shook her head. "I'm fine."

"You're drinking cheap booze alone on a bench by the side of the road," I said. "Does that sound like healthy behavior to you?"

She said nothing for a time. Then she looked down.

"I'm fine."

"You want half a tuna melt sandwich?" I asked. "I've got potato soup, too, but that's mine."

She seemed to think for a moment. "Would it matter if I said no?"

"It always matters if you say no."

"Not to Chad," she said. "And he's still out there."

"He is," I said, softening my voice. "We can talk about that over dinner if you want."

Neither of us said anything for at least five minutes. Finally, she looked at me and sighed.

"I could eat," she said.

"Good," I said, standing. "Let's talk and eat."

Chapter 22

June and I walked to my truck for its comfortable, padded seats, but the moment we got inside, she wrinkled her nose.

"It stinks in here."

"I've been searching the woods for evidence in a double homicide. Give me a break," I said, glancing at her and then reaching into the paper sack between us for the sandwich. I gave her half. "You're not a Georgia peach, either, honey."

She took a bite of her sandwich but said nothing. I ate my soup with a plastic spoon. The Styrofoam container had kept it warm, but I would have preferred an actual bowl. It would have felt like dinner instead of diner fare. When June finished her half of the sandwich, I glanced at her.

"You can eat the rest of the sandwich, but if you puke in my truck, I'll make you clean it up tomorrow when you're sober."

"I won't puke," she said.

I nodded and ate. "You drink alone often, or is this a new thing?"

"New thing. I wanted to try it out," she said, shrugging and reaching into the bag for the other half of the sandwich. She paused and looked at the dashboard. "I hate him, you know. He walked past me today and smiled at me like we were old friends or something. I wanted to scratch his eyes out."

"I assume you didn't attack him," I said, finishing my soup and putting the empty container back in the bag.

"No, but I wanted to."

I nodded and shifted in my seat to get comfortable.

"I appreciate your restraint."

"So what happens now?" she asked. "I pretend that I'm fine?"

I shook my head.

"The next step is up to you. There are therapists if you want to talk to someone. I can give you some names."

"Talking won't help," she said, looking out the window. "I'll remember what he did for the rest of my life, and he gets to move on like nothing happened."

I looked at the steering wheel and considered how to respond.

"You won't forget what he did, but it will get better. You can heal."

She shook her head and reached for her door. "I don't need this shit from you. I hear it all day from my sorority sisters. They don't know what I'm going through, and neither do you."

She opened her door and stepped out, but I spoke before she could take more than a step.

"My foster father drugged and raped me on the living room sofa of his house in Chesterfield when I was sixteen."

She stopped trying to leave, but she didn't close her door. "What happened to him?"

"Prosecutors sent him to prison for murdering one of his other foster daughters. He raped her, too."

"Whoa," she said. She got back in the car. "That's for real? You're not just saying that?"

"It's for real," I said. "It's a long, old story, but it made the news a few weeks ago. You can look it up."

"I'm sorry," she said, her voice low. Neither of us said anything. Then she looked at me. "You seem so normal."

I smiled just a little. "Aside from drinking cheap schnapps alone on a bench, so do you."

We lapsed into silence. She mulled things over.

"How did you get over it?"

I looked at my steering wheel so I didn't have to see her.

"I didn't. My anger isn't as bad as it used to be, but I still hate him. I still have nightmares, but they're not as bad as they used to be. I don't like my hate, but I don't want to let it go, either. Some days, it's the only emotion I can feel."

"I hate Chad, too," said June. "I want him to die."

I said nothing.

"Does it get easier?" she asked.

I looked at her and tried to smile but found it was harder than expected.

"Depends on what you mean by easier."

She blinked and looked at the dashboard in front of her.

"Like when you're walking around," she said. "I used to have a lot of friends who were guys. Now, I see them on the sidewalk, and it's like I've got a weight on my chest. I can't breathe. I just turn around and run to my sorority house."

I nodded and tilted my head to the side.

"That got easier after a month. I'm still uncomfortable being alone with a man, but I'm okay talking on the street or at work."

"Are you married?"

"No," I said, not looking at her.

"Do you have a boyfriend?"

I shook my head. "I had a boyfriend once. He was a nice guy. He's a fourth-grade teacher in Glendale now. He married another teacher. I see him on Facebook sometimes. He had a daughter about three months ago. He looks happy."

"What happened?"

I didn't want to answer her, but she deserved an answer. I drew in a slow breath.

"You really want to know?" I asked.

"If you think it would help," she said.

I kept my eyes on the dashboard so I wouldn't have to look at her.

"Sex. I was a junior in college. My boyfriend and I had been dating for three months. He wanted to do it. I thought I did, too, so I got drunk and pretended the situation didn't terrify me. Afterward, I cried so hard he wanted to take me to the hospital. He thought he had hurt me."

"Oh."

I pushed a lock of hair behind my ear and then blinked.

"It's not like that for everybody. You'll probably be different. I hope you are."

We said nothing for a few minutes.

"Are you happy?" she asked.

As soon as the words left her mouth, I remembered the pint of vodka I had poured onto the street earlier. Booze would have made that question easier to answer.

"I don't know," I said, blinking. "I pretend to be."

June's voice was soft. "Your life doesn't seem so bad from where I'm sitting."

"I'm a borderline alcoholic who drinks alone most nights of the week, and I push away everybody in my life but my parents and my dog. I'm trying to be happy, but I'm not great at it yet. Let's talk about something else."

We said nothing for another minute. When we spoke again, the conversation was lighter. We talked about television—she liked *The Bachelor*—and about books and music. June hadn't told her parents about what had happened to her yet, but she promised she would. Her mom and dad would help her through this. I had no advice to give her, but I hoped she'd be okay.

At a little after ten, she got out of my truck and walked to her sorority. She wasn't sober yet, but she was close. I put my car in gear and drove home, where I found Roger waiting on the porch for me. He lifted his head but didn't get up. His bowl of food lay beside him untouched.

"Hey, sweetheart," I said. "Not hungry?"

His eyebrows moved, and his tail thumped once against the ground. I scratched him behind the ears and then unlocked my front door. The two of us walked inside, where he lay down on his bed beside the fireplace. I poured myself a glass of straight vodka and sat on the couch without bothering to turn on the light. The moon outside was bright enough. Besides, some things are best done in the dark.

I sipped the drink and felt it slide down my throat. Then I opened my laptop and visited Facebook. Mark, my college boyfriend, and I were friends on Facebook, but we never spoke. I looked him up and found dozens of pictures of him with his wife and daughter. In every single picture, they looked happier than I'd ever felt.

I tried to pretend that was me standing beside him, that I was smiling and holding a beautiful little girl, but even my fantasy rang hollow and false. I didn't have a husband or a baby. I'd liked Mark when we were dating, but even then I'd had no illusions about our relationship. He was a sweet guy who had made me laugh, but I had never dreamed of spending my life with him. My life didn't have room for dreams.

When Christopher Hughes raped me, he stole my naiveté and what remained of my childhood. He showed me how cruel the world could be. I hated him. He made me stronger than I might have otherwise been, but the cost was too high for what I got.

I finished my drink and thought back to my conversation with June. My answer had been honest. I wasn't happy, but if I kept trying, maybe I would be one day. For now, that hope kept me going. Some days, it was all I had.

Chapter 23

Roger was at the end of the bed, still snoring, when my alarm clock went off the next morning. I rolled over, turned it off, and blinked to let my eyes adjust to the morning light. All things considered, I didn't feel too bad. I had a lot of work ahead of me, but I could do it. As I swung my legs off the bed a moment later, Roger lifted his head and put it back down.

"Don't get up on my account, bud," I said. He blinked but didn't get up. I patted his side as I walked by and felt his ribs expand and contract as he breathed. At his age and with his health, he deserved to sleep in. "You're a good boy. Mommy loves you."

It was still early, so I didn't shower yet. Instead, I did yoga in my living room. Since I had never put in fancy window shades and I was just wearing my pajamas, I flashed the wildlife when my T-shirt bunched around my neck while doing the downward dog pose. The squirrels didn't seem to mind.

Afterwards, I showered and poured Roger's breakfast into his bowl in the living room. The kibble hit with a familiar rattling noise, and Roger came sauntering in to smell what I had given him. Just as he had last night, he didn't touch the food. This morning, though, he didn't touch his water, either. It looked like clean water, but he had a better nose than I did. I dumped the water out in case he smelled something off in it and replaced it with fresh stuff. Still, he didn't touch it.

I knelt beside him. He lifted his face to look at me with sad eyes. His torso trembled.

"You okay, buddy?"

He put his head down, and I ran a hand across his chest and back. He licked his lips but didn't otherwise move.

"You didn't eat dinner or breakfast, dude. How about a treat? You want a treat?"

He perked up a little, so I smiled and patted his haunches before going back to the kitchen. Dog treats from the store were expensive, so I made Roger my own treats by drying slices of sweet potatoes in the oven. He liked them, they were healthy for him, and they were cheap. Everybody won. I got the bag from the freezer. The sound of crinkling plastic usually made him come running with his mouth open, but he stayed in the living room. I got him a treat anyway. The moment he saw me, Roger raised his head but didn't move.

I stayed in the opening that led to my kitchen.

"Come here, buddy," I said. "I've got a treat."

Roger lumbered to his feet and came. I handed him the sweet potato, which he put into his mouth but didn't chew.

"Come on, dude," I said, feeling a catch in my throat. "You've got to eat it."

Instead, he carried it back to his bed and put it beside him as he lay down again. My shoulders dropped, and I sighed without thinking.

The vet's office didn't open until eight, but I called the office line anyway hoping someone had come in early. Nobody had, so I left a voicemail letting them know I planned to bring Roger in. Then I called my boss.

"Harry, it's Joe. I get you at home, or are you at work?"

"In the car," he said. "What can I do for you?"

"I'll be late coming in. Roger's sick, and I need to take him by the vet's office. You know if Shaun Deveraux has made any progress on my search warrant?"

"He's in Clayton right now with the St. Louis County Prosecutor's Office. They've got a hearing this morning. Shouldn't be too much longer."

At least I had something productive to do today.

"Good. And I assume Aldon McKenzie hasn't showed up to confess to his wife's murder in the night or I would have gotten a phone call."

Harry paused. "Mr. McKenzie is dead. His body got snagged on some debris in the Mississippi River near Cape Girardeau. Barge captain saw the body this morning and called it in. George Delgado's already on his way down."

Cape Girardeau was a college town on the Mississippi River about sixty miles south of St. Augustine. I rarely visited, but it seemed like a nice place.

"Cause of death?" I asked.

"Gunshot wound."

I nodded to myself, thinking. "Laura Rojas had a list of people in her briefcase. Aldon was on top of the list. If he's dead, we should check the other names on that list, too, to make sure they're still alive."

Harry paused again. "What kind of list was this?"

"A bad one to be on."

I gave Harry the names and hung up. I had been working Laura's murder for days now, and I knew little more than I had when I started. That needed to change soon. We had three bodies already—Laura Rojas, Jennifer McKenzie, and Aldon McKenzie—and I didn't want to get a fourth. That was a worry for later.

I put the phone down on an end table and sat beside my dog.

"Please eat, buddy," I said, stroking his fur. He put his head between his front paws and looked at me. He almost looked like he was pleading with me. "I'm taking you to the doctor. You'll feel better soon. He'll put you on some medicine, and you'll be good again. Don't worry."

He raised his eyebrows, which was a good sign, I thought. He had moved, at least. At ten to eight, I grabbed a leash and led Roger to the truck. He got in and sat down in the cab beside me. The vet's office wasn't far, so I got there as the vet was opening for the day. He held the door for me as I led Roger inside.

"I'm glad you brought him in," he said, kneeling in front of Roger in the lobby. He petted Roger's cheek and lifted his jowls to see his gums and teeth. Afterwards, Dr. Johnson tried to hand him a treat, but Roger wasn't interested. The vet scratched Roger's cheek and focused on me. "So he's not eating, huh?"

"He hasn't been eating well for a while, but last night, he stopped," I said, shaking my head. "He's been a little slower than usual, so I thought he was tired. The total lack of eating is scary."

"Has he been drinking?"

"A little," I said. "I've been at work in the day, but I put out water for him while I'm gone. On most days, he visits my neighbor when I'm at work. She gives him water, too. Today, he wouldn't drink anything."

"Any vomiting?"

I shook my head.

"No."

"Does he go to the bathroom okay?"

I hesitated. "Yeah. I think so, at least. I usually consider that his business. He goes in the woods."

Dr. Johnson nodded and considered.

"When you are home with him, does he ever seem confused?"

"No. He's more tired than anything else," I said. "When I get home, I try to play with him, but he's not into it. I throw him tennis balls, but he doesn't want to chase them. Then I gave him a new rawhide bone, but he doesn't want to chew that. He's a good boy, and he walks around the yard, but he doesn't even like walking to Susanne's house anymore, and he loves Susanne."

"We'll run tests to see what we've got going on," said the vet, nodding. His voice was low and almost somber. "If you don't mind, I'll keep Roger for the day. You okay with that?"

I shifted my weight from one foot to the other, unable to find a position that felt comfortable.

"He's okay, isn't he?" I asked. "I mean, he looks healthy. He's happy, I think."

"He looks happy," said Dr. Johnson, his voice gentle. "I've got food for him here. He's allergic to chicken, right?"

"Yeah," I said. "It makes him fart so much I have to leave the house."

"I remember," said the vet, smiling at me. "Don't worry. My staff and I will take good care of him. And I'll call you this evening."

"Okay," I said, kneeling down in front of Roger. He lifted his head to look at me. "Buddy, I have to leave you here. Okay? You be a good boy. Mommy loves you."

He didn't understand what that meant, but he thumped his tail on the ground before lowering his head again. I patted him on the cheek.

"Thank you, Doctor," I said. "I'll have my cell phone on. If you need anything, call me."

He said he would, and I stepped outside into the morning light. A steady stream of cars passed on the road in front of the office as commuters made their way toward the interstate. A heavy pit weighed down my stomach, and my throat had tightened so that I could barely breathe.

As I walked back to my truck, my cell phone rang. It was Harry, but he could wait a minute. The muscles of my jaw ached from my clenched teeth, and heat radiated from my skin. I turned on my car and blasted the air conditioning to high. Then I forced myself to take deep breaths before I answered.

"Hey, Joe, it's Harry. Listen, Shaun Deveraux came through with the warrant. He's negotiating to have an attorney to go through Laura Rojas's files now. In the meantime, you should be able to get into her office."

I nodded. "Thanks, boss."

Harry paused. "You okay?"

I swallowed the thick lump in my throat and nodded, grateful he couldn't see me.

"Yeah, I'm fine. Councilman Rogers warned me against using my personal vehicle for official business. We have any cruisers free at the station?"

"If we don't, I'll find something for you."

"Okay," I said, drawing in a breath. "I'll be in."

After hanging up, I took a couple more deep breaths and stayed put until my truck's aging air conditioner put out cold air. It didn't make me feel better, but at least I felt as if I were in better control of myself. I closed my eyes.

"Everything's fine, Joe. Everything's just fine."

Before putting my truck in gear, I looked back over my shoulder at Dr. Johnson's office.

"See you tonight, Roger."

I drove to work after that, but I left my heart in my vet's office. I hoped I hadn't seen my best friend for the last time.

Chapter 24

True to Harry's word, the department had a marked police cruiser waiting for me when I got to the office. I signed it out and headed north toward Mehlville. When I got to Laura's office, Detective Blatch was already outside waiting for me. He had a couple days' worth of growth on his chin and bags under his eyes. His mouth opened in a wide yawn as I opened my door.

"Morning, Detective," I said. "You look like you pulled an all-nighter."

He grunted. "I did. Duke Trevino's alibi checked out. He was drunk in a holding cell in Jefferson City at the time your victim died."

Councilman Rogers and his cronies wouldn't like hearing that, so I looked forward to telling them.

"Did you find Laura's fingerprints on any of the weed we found in her closet?"

He shook his head.

"No."

"And you didn't find fingerprints on the murder weapon, either."

Blatch lowered his chin. "He's a convicted drug dealer, and the weapon was beneath his mattress. He was a good suspect. I had good reason to pick him up."

"I agree," I said, nodding. "Laura's actual killer probably thought the same thing when he framed him."

Blatch looked to the office. "It's elaborate for a frame."

"It is, but it's a good explanation for the evidence we have."

Blatch considered and then swore under his breath.

"I hate that you're probably right."

"I get that a lot," I said. I walked to the office. It was closed, so I took out my cell phone and called Tina Babcock, Laura's former assistant.

"Rojas and Associates," she said. "We're closed at the moment, but if you tell me what you need, I can refer you to another attorney."

I furrowed my brow and looked down at the shadow cast on the sidewalk by the overhead awning.

"Do you get a referral fee for sending clients to other attorneys?" I asked. "Is that why you're still answering the phone for Rojas and Associates, Ms. Babcock?"

Babcock sighed. "It's you again. Like I told you before, I'm not interested in answering any of your questions unless you've got a search warrant. Good day, Detective."

"I've got a warrant."

Babcock hesitated. "I need to see it before I can talk."

"That's fine," I said. "I'm outside your office with Detective Mathias Blatch of the St. Louis County Police Department right now. I'll give you ten minutes before I pick the lock and go inside. Sound good to you?"

I didn't wait for her to respond before hanging up. Blatch whistled and then chuckled.

"You're mean in the morning."

"It's been a long morning," I said. "I'll get coffee at the Waffle House. You want anything?"

He shook his head, so I left him in front of the office and walked to the restaurant, where I ordered a large cup of coffee to go. The caffeine would do me some good. Since it was hot outside, I stayed in the restaurant and watched the parking lot. Tina Babcock's white Kia Optima pulled in about ten minutes later, so I walked out to meet her. She read through the warrant.

"This says the court will appoint a special master to search our files."

I nodded. "That's the plan. In the meantime, I need to search her desk. We won't read Laura's files, but she'll have personal items, I'm sure. If you're comfortable with it, I'd like to ask you a few questions, too."

She hesitated. "I'll answer what I can, but I'm still limited by attorney-client privilege."

"I understand," I said. "Now please open the door. It's hot as hell out here."

Babcock nodded and let us in. The office had a musty aroma, and the wooden furniture looked well used. There were file boxes stacked along the rear wall and three desks inside. Babcock sat at the desk nearest the front window and crossed her arms while I looked around.

"There are three desks," I said. "You have one, and Laura has one. Who has the third?"

She swung around on her chair and nodded to a desk adorned with a dead houseplant.

"It came with the office," she said. "Laura talked about hiring a partner, but we never got around to it."

I nodded. "Was she a good lawyer?"

Babcock paused, but then she nodded. "She was learning the ropes, and she had talent. She was an idealist, though. That makes the job hard."

"What kind of idealistic things did she believe in?" asked Detective Blatch.

Babcock shrugged. "The shit they fill your head with in law school. She wanted to change the world. Instead, she helped couples file for divorce for three hundred bucks each."

"Let's talk about her caseload," I said. "What was she working on?"

Babcock opened a drawer on her desk and pulled out a planner.

"Laura liked to keep a lot of balls in the air," she said, flipping through pages. "The day before she died, she met a client about setting up a trust for his daughters. Before that, she helped a couple file for divorce."

"Did she do any criminal law?" asked Blatch.

"Some. DUI defense and the occasional drug charge," said Babcock, crossing her arms. "Is that a problem?"

"Only if it got her killed," said Blatch. "Any of her clients give you the creeps?"

She snickered. "Plenty of them gave me the creeps, but none were murderers. She took whatever work came through the door, but we're not high-profile here. We've got a slick website that makes us look fancier than we are, but Laura didn't get many big cases."

"Did she win her DUI and drug cases?" I asked.

Babcock turned. "She pled out a lot. When her clients didn't plea, she won more trials than she lost."

Blatch seemed to lose interest in the conversation because he moved around the room. I focused on Babcock still.

"Do you recognize the name Aldon McKenzie? He and Laura were in contact."

Babcock sat straighter and blinked. "I've heard the name."

Blatch looked at me and raised an eyebrow.

"What can you tell us about him?"

She looked at Detective Blatch out of the corner of her eye. "Before I say anything, I'd like to talk to an attorney."

"That's fine, but let me talk first. Someone shot him in the head and then dumped his body in the Mississippi River," I said. "A barge captain found his corpse near Cape Girardeau last night. Someone murdered his wife in her home in front of their daughter. If you know anything about that, you should talk to me now."

Babcock covered her mouth. "Oh, my God."

Detective Blatch walked toward Babcock's desk and sat on the edge, his arms crossed.

"Praying's not a bad idea, either," said Blatch. "These are dangerous fellows your boss got involved with."

"Mr. McKenzie was a client," said Babcock. "Laura didn't have a personal relationship with him."

"Good," I said. "What kind of case did he hire Laura for?"

Babcock's eyes fluttered, and she shook her head. "Laura never told me. It was something big, though. Laura was working on it all the time before she disappeared. She was down in St. Augustine a lot. That was where Aldon was from."

"Are you sure they weren't having an affair?" asked Blatch.

"Laura was discreet about the men in her life," said Babcock, screwing up her face, "but I have a hard time imagining she'd date a client. She was a professional."

"You can't tell us anything about the case itself?"

"Laura didn't tell me details about her cases," she said, turning toward the back of the room. "Those files are all his, though."

I followed her gaze to a stack of white cardboard banker boxes. There must have been ten. If they were all full of legal documents, it'd take us days to go through everything. I didn't have that much time. Not only that, my warrant only allowed me to read her client files after an impartial attorney first saw them.

"Those won't help," I said. "I need something concrete. Even if you can't tell me the details, you've got to tell me something. What was his case about? Remember, I've got three bodies down so far. If you know something, you might be our killer's next target."

"If I knew anything, I'd tell you," she said, shaking her head. "Aldon came in about six weeks ago. He said he found us from our website. He and Laura talked while I was at lunch. After their meeting, he gave Laura a check for ten thousand dollars, and she got to work."

"What did she do?" asked Blatch.

She sighed. "She was researching a pharmaceutical company called Reid Chemical. They're in St. Augustine, and Aldon worked for them. He was a whistleblower. That's all I know."

Reid Chemical employed almost five hundred people in St. Augustine, making it the county's second-largest employer after Waterford College. As I understood the company's business model, they made drugs for private-label brands. Generic-drug makers rarely employed professional hitmen, but if Aldon threatened their business somehow, I could see him pissing people off.

"How about the names Austin Wright, Mike Brees, and Ruby Laskey? Laura had them written on a notepad in her briefcase at home."

Babcock considered for a moment before nodding.

"They're familiar," she said before walking to her desk at the front of the office. She turned on her computer and typed a few minutes later. Then she looked up. "Laura interviewed each of them and billed the time to Aldon McKenzie."

The tornado had destroyed all the forensic evidence at the campsite where Laura's body was dumped, but I was getting somewhere. Motive, means, opportunity. If we found the person—or persons—with all three, we might have our killer, and at the moment, all my evidence pointed toward Reid Chemical. That was where I needed to go.

"Thank you for your time, Ms. Babcock," I said, reaching into my purse. I pulled out a business card and handed it to her. "If you remember anything that can help me find out who killed Laura, you've got my number."

She looked at the card. "What if somebody comes after me? Should I call you?"

"No. I'll be too far away," I said, shaking my head. "Call 911."

She nodded and stuck the card in her purse. "Thank you."

I told her it was no problem. Detective Blatch and I left a few moments after that. In the parking lot, he looked at me.

"You think calling 911 will help if these guys are after her?"

I considered and shook my head. "Based on what we've seen? No. If they're after her, she's better off calling a priest."

"It's good you kept that one to yourself," he said. "You going to stay here?"

"No," I said, shaking my head. "There's nothing we can do here until the lawyers clear the office of privileged material. I'm not wasting my time babysitting. I'm going to Reid Chemical and throwing some shit at the fan."

Chapter 25

Nick Sumner sipped his coffee and flipped through the newspaper. It had been a relaxing morning so far. At home, his kids kept him so busy he never got the chance to sit and read the newspaper. He felt as if he were on vacation.

Then, his phone vibrated, signaling an incoming call. He looked at the screen and found Logan Reid's name. Nick swore under his breath before answering.

"Yeah?"

"It's Logan. Where are you?"

Nick blinked a few times and sipped his coffee. "Having breakfast. What do you want?"

"My stepdad needs you at the plant. There's a cop here asking about Aldon McKenzie."

Nick nodded and lowered his voice. "I'm at Able's Diner. Can you pick me up?"

"I'm on my way."

Logan hung up, and Nick sighed once more before taking two big bites of his pancakes. Before leaving, he tossed a twenty on the counter. A familiar black BMW pulled into the lot a few minutes later and parked beside Nick's rental car.

"Get in," said Logan, rolling down his window. Nick raised his eyebrows.

"You ruined my breakfast," said Nick. "The least you can do is apologize and wish me a good morning."

Logan closed his eyes and shook his head. "Sorry for ruining your breakfast, Mr. Sumner. Please get in the car. My stepdad needs you at the plant."

"All right," said Nick. "You think I'm okay leaving my car here?"

"It's fine. If they tow it, my stepdad will get it out. He owns this town."

Nick opened the door. "Must be nice."

They drove for about twenty minutes in silence before coming to the plant. A chain-link fence topped with barbed wire surrounded the property, while security cameras filmed the parking lots. The property had only one entrance, and it ran beside a brick guardhouse with its own small parking lot. It was tight security for a company that specialized in making cough drops.

Logan opened his window as they approached the front gate, but the guard waved him through. Someone had parked a white St. Augustine County Sheriff's Department SUV in the guardhouse's small lot, but Nick saw no signs of a sheriff's deputy.

"What are we walking into?" asked Nick, shifting his weight on the seat.

"What do you mean?"

"Is this deputy going to arrest us the minute we step foot inside the building, or is he here to ask questions? I'd rather know now so I can prepare."

"She's not here to arrest anybody," said Logan, his voice sounding confident. "My stepdad owns this town."

"If you believe that, you don't understand what ownership means," said Nick, shaking his head. There was only one police car. They would have brought at least two to arrest a murderer—one car to transport the suspect, and another to transport backup in case the suspect resisted arrest. Still, he didn't like this. The local police were too close for comfort.

They parked and walked to the office of Mason Stewart, Reid Chemical's CEO. The room was bigger than many apartments. It had an enormous desk, an area with a conference table, and two separate seating areas, one of which had a full bar. A woman with blond hair and cold, intelligent eyes sat on a sofa in the center of the room. She wore a badge on a lanyard around her neck and a firearm on her hip. Nick had met a lot of cops over the years. She was the most attractive by far.

He straightened and smiled at her and Stewart. Reid Chemical's CEO had a thin face and an angular jaw. He wasn't a large man, but he was tall, at least six two or six three, and he had big hands. Today, he wore a navy suit, a quilted red and blue striped tie, and a white shirt. Nick rubbed his hands together and walked to the sofa beside Stewart.

"What did I miss?" he asked, smiling from Stewart to the officer. She stood up.

"Detective Court, this is my security consultant, Nick Sumner," said Stewart. Nick shook the detective's hand. "He understands our security arrangements well, so I thought it would be helpful if he sat in on our meeting."

"Who's the young man near the door?" she asked.

"My stepson, Logan," said Stewart. "He gave Mr. Sumner a ride. He can go now."

Logan hesitated but then withered under his stepfather's glare and left the room. Nick turned his attention to the police officer once again. She smiled at him, but it didn't reach her eyes.

"Are you armed today, Mr. Sumner?" she asked.

Nick nodded. "I am. It's legal under Missouri law."

She nodded. "Please take your weapon out and unload it for me. I get nervous around guns. Call it a courtesy."

"If you don't like guns, you chose the wrong profession," said Nick, reaching to his holster for his pistol. He removed the magazine and cleared the chamber before putting his now unloaded weapon on the coffee table. "Hope you don't mind me saying that."

"You can say whatever you want. I don't have to listen," she said, smiling as she turned her attention to Mr. Stewart.

"I'm here to talk about Aldon McKenzie. He's dead, and I hear he worked for you. What can you tell me about him?"

"Several hundred people work for me," said Stewart. "I don't know them all by name."

"Mr. McKenzie was an accountant. He was murdered. His attorney, Laura Rojas, was murdered, too."

"It's a tragedy whenever an employee dies, but it happens," said Stewart. "Our company carries a generous life insurance policy for the men and women who work for us. We'll take care of Mr. McKenzie's family."

She smiled. "I'm sure his daughter will appreciate that."

Stewart didn't respond. The detective had guts walking into the belly of the beast and confronting Stewart, Nick thought. If she didn't watch out, though, that courage could get her killed.

"I didn't realize how big this operation was until I got here," she said. "What do you do?"

Stewart drew in a bored breath before crossing his arms. "We manufacture pharmaceuticals. Our website can give you all the background information you need."

"You have a lot of guards. Is pharmaceutical manufacturing a dangerous business?"

"I appreciate that you came all the way down here, but I'm a busy person," said Stewart, standing. "Unless I'm under arrest, this meeting is over. Please direct all your future questions to my general counsel's office. They will give you the information you need."

The detective didn't move. "Do you own any firearms, Mr. Stewart?"

"I own many firearms. Why do you ask?"

"Someone shot Mr. McKenzie with a .22-caliber round. We found a nine-millimeter round in his wife, though. Do you own a .22 or a nine-millimeter pistol, by chance?"

Nick opened his mouth, surprised. "Mrs. McKenzie is dead, too?"

Detective Court looked at him and nodded, her eyes cool and impassive. "Yep. What do you carry, Mr. Sumner?"

Nick tried to keep his face neutral, but muscles all over his body quivered, and his skin grew hot as his temper built. No one should have hurt Jennifer McKenzie. That wasn't part of the plan.

"It's a Remington R1 chambered for a .45 ACP round," said Nick. "Good luck finding your murderer, Detective. Anyone who'd kill an entire family deserves to spend the rest of his life in prison."

"If you want to know about my firearms, get a warrant, Detective Court. I take my Second Amendment rights seriously," said Stewart, walking around his desk. He hit a button on his phone. Almost immediately, a security guard knocked on the door. "Anthony will escort you out of the building. Have a nice day."

The detective stood and nodded. "Thank you both for your time. It's been a pleasure."

Nick ground his teeth as the detective left the room. She knew more than she should. He wondered whether he should call his employers and suggest they cut their losses. They'd lose a lot of money, but at least they wouldn't be here when Reid Chemical imploded.

Logan stepped into the room a few seconds later.

"Shut the door," said Nick, his voice sharp. Logan looked to his stepfather, who nodded and turned his gaze to Nick.

"She's a problem," said Stewart.

"Yeah, she is," said Nick, nodding and looking at Logan. "She's not our biggest problem, though. You killed Jennifer McKenzie."

"She was a threat," said Logan. "For all we knew, her husband told her everything."

"That's possible," said Nick, his voice rising. "But that wasn't our deal. If she became a threat, I would have taken care of her, and I would have done it in a way that deflected blame from us. You brought the police right here."

"They found Aldon," said Stewart. "They would have come here, anyway."

"Maybe, but you don't kill families if you can help it. If you knock off a drug dealer, the police don't care. They'll investigate, but they won't put in overtime. You knock off a family, they bring out the knives. You understand that? Jennifer McKenzie was a schoolteacher. She had an autistic daughter. People are going to fight for her. We could have made her disappear. A million bucks. That's all it would have taken. No one would have seen her again."

"A nine-millimeter parabellum costs less than a dollar," said Stewart. "You don't get to my place in life by wasting money."

Nick walked around the sofa and picked up his firearm and ammunition from the coffee table. Once he had the weapon put back together, he slid it into the holster on his belt.

"It's a business expense, and it might prevent you from going to prison for the rest of your life," said Nick, shaking his head. "You guys are both fucking amateurs."

"What do you suggest for handling this situation?" asked Stewart.

"We've got to kill that cop," said Logan. "She's coming after us. We've got to get in front of the problem. I could do it."

Nick sighed and closed his eyes. "What would happen if you killed her?"

Logan hesitated. "They'd investigate, but my fraternity brothers would cover for me. They'd give me all the alibi I needed."

Nick brought his hands to his face and shook his head.

"This isn't a gangster movie, kid. If you shoot a cop who's investigating you, you will go to prison, and they will put a needle in your arm that pumps poison straight to your heart.

If you kill her, you might as well kill everybody in this room and save the state of Missouri the expense of a trial."

"What should we do?" asked Stewart.

"For now, you slow her down. Logan says you own this town. Prove it. Call the sheriff or the chief of police or whoever tells her what to do and throw up roadblocks. I'll do what I can to point her in another direction."

"And what if that doesn't work?" asked Stewart, crossing his arms.

"Then I call my employers, and they'll send a cleanup team."

Logan shifted his weight from one foot to the other. When he spoke, his voice quavered. "What does that mean?"

Nick looked him in the eye. "It means Detective Court won't be a problem anymore. And neither will you."

Chapter 26

I knew little about the pharmaceutical industry, but I knew assholes, and all three men in Mason Stewart's office were major assholes. More than that, I didn't trust them one bit. Something was going on at Reid Chemical. If I had to guess, I'd say Nick Sumner, the security consultant, had killed Aldon McKenzie and Laura Rojas. He hadn't killed Jennifer McKenzie, though. Her death had surprised him. I didn't know what that meant.

A security guard escorted me back to my SUV. Reid Chemical was about fifteen miles outside town, so I took out my cell phone on the way and called my boss.

"Harry, it's Joe. I've had a busy morning. Want to hear about it?"

Harry warned me he was in an area with poor cell reception but told me to talk anyway. I filled him in on my search of Laura Rojas's office and the meeting at Reid Chemical. Harry was quiet, but he asked questions where appropriate. When I finished, he paused for a few moments.

"What's your plan?"

"Mason Stewart is dirty, Reid Chemical's security consultant is dirty, and I don't trust the kid, either," I said. "The kid's the weak link. I don't know what's going on at that plant, but I think Logan Reid does, and I think I can break him."

"If you go after him, be careful," said Harry. "Mason Stewart will have an army of lawyers, but I'll do what I can to keep them from you."

"Thank you," I said. "I'm on my way to the office to run a background check, so I'll talk to you later."

"Good luck, Detective."

I thanked him and hung up. It was midday, so few cars crowded the roads. When I got to my station, I parked in the lot and walked inside, where Trisha flagged me down at the front desk. She had a plastic Tupperware container in front of her and a flimsy plastic fork in her hand.

"I was hoping to catch you," she said, wiping her mouth with a napkin. "Sheryl over at Rise and Grind called about half an hour ago. She's got two guys there that are creeping her out."

I raised an eyebrow. "Any reason they're creeping her out?"

"They've been there since eight this morning. Sheryl said she doesn't recognize them, and they're not too interested in talking."

"Okay," I said, nodding. "Have they acted inappropriately toward anybody?"

"No, but they've been there for almost four hours, and neither has said a word except to order more coffee," she said, before lowering her voice. "We've had three murders this week. When two creepy strangers show up at the town coffee shop, I thought you might be interested. Sheryl said there'd be free coffee in it for you if you chase them off."

With three bodies on the ground so far, any break from the normal routine was notable. I nodded and reached into my purse for my keys.

"You should have led with the free coffee. Call Sheryl and tell her I'm on my way. Put two or three uniformed officers on standby, too, in case these creepy strangers decide they don't like me."

"Will do, Detective," she said, already calling up the patrol map on her computer. "Alicia Maycock is nearby. You want me to have her meet you?"

"No, but have her stay in the area," I said. "I might need a hand."

Trisha nodded and picked up her radio to call it in. I left the building and jogged to the SUV I had signed out. Rise and Grind was one of St. Augustine's hidden gems. Their coffee was always good, but their house-made pecan rolls were better than anything I had ever eaten at any bakery in any big city. Sheryl, the lady who owned it, was an attorney who had decided the law wasn't for her and had retired early to open a coffee shop. I'd never met her when she was practicing law, but every time I saw her now, she had a smile on her face. I'd say she had found her calling.

Rise and Grind took up the bottom floor of a brick three-story Italianate building downtown. There were antique stores, restaurants, and bars all around. An old-fashioned candy shop up the street made its own fudge, hard candy, and chocolates. Tourists loved this stretch of downtown. During our Spring Fair, the crowds became so thick you could hardly walk down the street. The area was lively in the summer, but, thankfully, I didn't have to worry about bumping into anyone.

I parked about a block away and checked my firearm before climbing out of my SUV. A pair of squirrels chased one another down the sidewalk in front of me, while trees overhead provided a little relief from the hot midday sun.

From the street, Rise and Grind looked almost empty, but even if people had sat at every table, I would have known which guys had given Sheryl the creeps. They were sitting at the front window. One of them had a tattoo of a spider's web on his neck, while abstract tattoos ran up and down the wrists and arms of the other man. Neither looked happy to see me.

I pulled the door open and walked to the counter. A teenager worked the register, but as soon as she saw me, she walked to the kitchen for Sheryl. She came out momentarily.

"Hi, Joe," she said, smiling as she walked toward me. Sheryl was in her mid-forties, but she could have passed for thirty. She had black hair past her ears and bright green eyes that lit up every time she saw someone she liked. I didn't know her well, but she was almost always jovial and happy. Today, though, she gave me a nervous grin as her eyes flicked toward the men near the front window.

"Trisha told me what was going on," I said, leaning against the counter, my voice low. "They're just drinking coffee, right?"

She nodded. "They bought two pecan rolls, too. The one on the right has a gun on his waistband on his lower back. I feel silly for calling the police, but I don't like them in my shop. They're scaring Molly. When my employees get nervous, I get nervous."

I nodded again and smiled at her, hoping I looked confident. "Don't worry. I'll talk to them and see what's going on. You never know. Maybe they got a flat tire, and they're waiting around for a tow."

"Maybe," she said. She hesitated. "Did you see a car with a flat tire outside?"

"No," I said, shaking my head. "You go back to work. I'll talk to them."

She nodded and walked to the kitchen but didn't send Molly out front again. I crossed the room, pulled a chair from a table near the two men, and sat down. Up close, the two men were ugly, and at least one of them smelled like body odor. I didn't want to talk to them, but I put a smile on my face anyway.

"Hi, guys," I said, pulling on the lanyard around my neck so they could see my badge. "I'm Detective Joe Court with the St. Augustine County Sheriff's Department. You two new in town?"

The man on the left raised his eyebrows as he checked me out. Cigarette smoke had stained his teeth a light brown, and his nose swept to the left—likely because he had broken it in a fight and left it to heal on its own. The other guy had straight teeth, shaggy hair, and a beard like a threadbare quilt on his chin. He smelled like he had recently left the gym.

"Have we done something wrong, Officer?" asked the bar fighter.

"Nope," I said. "I'm here to chat. We're a tourist town, and we like to welcome newcomers. This time of the year, our bed and breakfasts are full of couples on romantic weekends. Are you guys having a good time?"

"We're not a couple," said Stinky. I couldn't quite place his accent.

"Is that a Bosnian accent?" I asked, furrowing my brow.

The two looked at one another. Then the bar fighter sighed.

"He's Ukrainian. What do you want?"

"How do you like the coffee?" I asked. Neither had made a move toward me, but both men had at least fifty pounds on me each. I wouldn't win a fight if it came down to that, so I kept my hand near my firearm. "You must like it. You've been here for hours."

The bar fighter locked his eyes on mine while Stinky looked toward the register.

"Don't look over there," I said. "We're talking. It's rude to look away."

Stinky stood. He was bigger than me, but he was slow. I could get to my feet faster than him and use my chair as a club, but I couldn't do much damage to a man his size. Not only that, I'd still have to deal with his friend. I put my hand on my firearm but didn't pull it out yet.

"Have a seat," I said. "And put your hands flat on the table. That goes for both of you."

Stinky looked to his partner. The older guy nodded—having seen my firearm—so Stinky sat down.

"I'm here to talk, boys. I can't ask you to leave town, but I can make you miserable. So why are you here?"

"Camping," said the bar fighter.

"You're going camping, great," I said, nodding. "This is a good area for that. Where are you pitching your tent?"

The bar fighter shrugged. "Haven't decided yet."

"That's unfortunate. Every campsite in town is booked right now. I think you boys might have better luck going home."

The bar fighter smirked and turned his head. I followed his gaze to see Molly at the register again. She had blond hair with brown roots and freckles on her cheeks. She was seventeen or eighteen, and the lecherous look the bar fighter gave her made my stomach churn.

"We'd rather stay," he said. "I like the view."

I didn't turn my head. "Molly, go back in the kitchen."

A moment later, I heard a door open and close. My throat tightened, and my heart pounded in my chest. I should have brought backup.

"Now why'd you do that?" asked the bar fighter. "I think she liked me. What's the age of consent in Missouri?"

"This is a private establishment," I said. "It's time you two moved on."

"No," said Stinky, lacing his fingers behind his head. "I like it here."

"Okay," I said, nodding. "Then you won't mind staying here a moment longer while I call for backup. I've asked you to leave on behalf of the establishment's owner, but you've refused. You're under arrest for trespassing. I plan to disarm you and call for backup. We will place you in custody and take you to my station. From there, we'll work things out. That sound okay with you?"

"We're not armed," said Stinky.

"I saw your weapon when I walked in, dumbass. It's tucked into the waistband of your pants," I said. "I'm guessing your partner has one, too. One at a time, I want you both to unholster your firearms, unload them, and put them on the table. This doesn't need to escalate. If you cooperate, everyone will be fine."

Though I tried to convey a sense of calm confidence, every muscle in my body felt tight. Neither man moved.

"You first," I said, looking to Stinky. "Reach behind your back and remove your firearm from its holster. Remove the magazine and any round in the chamber and put it on the table. If you fail to comply, we're all going to have a bad day."

He stared into my eyes as he complied. I thought he would spit at me, but he did what I wanted. The older guy did likewise.

I picked up the firearms and moved them to another table.

"Both of you, keep your hands flat on the table," I said, reaching to my purse for my phone. Trisha answered at the station and called in my backup. Officer Maycock was there within a minute. She wasn't much bigger than me, but she was armed, and she wore a uniform. Sasquatch—Officer Preston Cain—arrived a minute or two after that, allowing me to breathe a little easier.

Sasquatch led the two men outside and put them in the back of two separate cruisers, while Alicia collected their firearms. Once we had everything secure, Sasquatch handed me their IDs. According to their driver's licenses, both came from Chicago. The older guy was named Kurt Wilkinson, while the other guy was Stephan Kushnir. Neither had an open warrant against him, but Stephan Kushnir had a felony conviction for assault.

In Missouri, trespassing in the first degree was a class-B misdemeanor. If I charged them, they'd pay a fine and go on with their lives. Meanwhile, I'd have an hour or two of paperwork and more headache than the arrest was worth. I didn't plan to take them in. Now that I had seen their driver's licenses, I had everything I needed.

Sasquatch let both men out of their respective squad cars and removed their handcuffs.

"Okay, gentlemen," I said. "We've decided not to press charges. Mr. Wilkinson, we'll be returning your firearm, but we will keep Mr. Kushnir's. Since Mr. Kushnir has a violent felony conviction, he's ineligible to own a weapon in the state of Missouri. If you've got an attorney, he or she can contact my office. We'll return the weapon to you once you've left the state. Does that sound good with you two?"

Kushnir grumbled, but Wilkinson nodded. Sasquatch gave Wilkinson his firearm back, and then the two of them climbed into a red sedan and drove off. I walked to Officer Maycock.

"Alicia, have you got the firearms we confiscated?"

She nodded.

"Good. Take them to Darlene and ask her to run ballistics on them. We'll see whether they match the rounds pulled from Jennifer McKenzie or Laura Rojas," I said. I turned to Sasquatch. "Preston, get in your cruiser. Follow our new friends. If they leave the county, great. If they don't, keep on them. Don't bother hiding. Let them see you."

"On it, boss," he said, hurrying back to his car.

I didn't know who those guys were, but we needed to watch them all the same. I watched Sasquatch drive off before heading back to the coffee shop. Sheryl and Molly had returned from the kitchen. Both looked shaken, but they'd be okay.

"They're gone," I said. "I've got one of my officers following them, so they shouldn't bother you anymore. If they come back, call us. We'll send somebody to pick them up."

"Thank you, Joe," said Sheryl, drawing in a breath. "I feel silly for calling you, but they scared me."

"Calling me wasn't silly. They were scary dudes," I said, nodding and looking around. I hesitated and smiled. "Before coming, I heard something about free coffee."

Sheryl smiled. "For you, it's on the house."

"I knew there was a reason this is my favorite coffee shop in town," I said, smiling.

"This is the only coffee shop in town," said Molly.

"Just adds to the air of exclusivity," I said. Sheryl came back a moment later with a tall paper cup full of steaming black coffee. I thanked her and put a dollar in the tip jar despite her protests. "You deserve a tip. Your coffee and pecan rolls are the only reason I get up in the morning."

"I'm both glad and sad to hear that, Detective," said Sheryl, winking.

I thanked them again and headed out. It was already midafternoon, and the work kept piling on. I yawned and sipped my coffee before heading to my car. No rest for the weary. I had a murder to solve.

Chapter 27

As much as I liked my truck, my department's marked SUVs were faster and more comfortable, and they could transport far more gear to a crime scene. More than that, the department's SUVs had their own laptops complete with 4G internet access. My connection at the station was faster, but it was hard to beat the convenience of a laptop on the road.

I sat in the front seat and used the laptop to look up the number for the Chicago Police Department's liaison office. After I told the liaison officer the situation with Kushnir and Wilkinson, he transferred me to a lieutenant in the organized-crime division. I sipped my coffee and hummed along to terrible electronic music as I waited. After a few minutes, the lieutenant grunted and answered.

"Lieutenant Jim Cornell," he said. "What do you need?"

"Lieutenant, this is Detective Joe Court with the St. Augustine County Sheriff's Department in St. Augustine, Missouri. You got a minute to talk?"

"I might. What do you want?"

"I'm hoping you can fill in some gaps for me," I said, allowing myself to sink into the warm, black upholstery of my SUV. "I've got three bodies on the ground here, and I ran into two guys from your area. Both carried firearms. They seemed shady. I thought you might have heard of them."

He grunted. It was midafternoon, but he almost sounded as if he were hung over.

"Give me some names."

I read him the names and waited while he typed. After a moment, he made a deep, throaty growl.

"We've got files on both gentlemen," he said. "Are they still in town right now?"

"I've got an officer following them," I said. "I assume so."

"Tell your officer to back off," said the lieutenant. "Dumb and Dumber are both hitters for a Ukrainian gang in town. They didn't earn their nicknames for their sparkling judgment, and I doubt they're in your area to see the sights."

"Do they work in the pharmaceuticals industry?"

"They're into anything that can make them money. Drugs, guns, girls, you name it. They don't discriminate."

"Is the name Reid Chemical familiar?"

He paused. "No. Not at all. Why?"

"Two of my victims worked there," I said. "Anything else you can tell me about the bad guys?"

"If they're in town, it's not for their health."

I snickered a little. "Somehow, I didn't think they were here to go hiking. Thanks for your time."

He grunted again, and I hung up. The moment I did, I called Trisha and asked her to warn Sasquatch about our bad guys. I wanted to assign an additional officer to sit in a car with him, but we didn't have the manpower to allow that. As long as he kept his eyes open, he'd be okay. After that, I focused my attention on the laptop again.

Even with Kushnir and Wilkinson in town, Logan Reid was my primary suspect. According to the license bureau's information, he was twenty-one, and he lived six miles outside the town of St. Augustine. If I had to guess, he lived with his parents.

I looked him up on Facebook, but the privacy settings on his profile were so tight I couldn't see anything but his profile picture. A quick Google search, though, gave me what I needed. He was a member of the Sigma Iota fraternity at Waterford College. I knew the house well, having interviewed Chad Hamilton—June Wellman's rapist—there. The fraternity's recruitment board must have liked assholes.

I put my car in gear and headed out. As I had on my previous visit, I first stopped by the college's Public Safety Office to let them know I was in the area. While there, I also showed them a picture of Laura Rojas on my phone. The officer at the front desk looked at her face and nodded.

"She's familiar, but I'm not sure from where. I might have seen her around town. St. Augustine isn't a big place."

"Have you ever seen her with a student?"

He shook his head. "Couldn't say. Our door is always open, but we don't get to know many students."

"How about Logan Reid? Did you get to know him?"

The officer cracked a smile and nodded. "We've picked him up three or four times for public intoxication. He's over twenty-one, so we took him home and made sure he was safe."

I nodded. "Have you ever found any weapons on him when you've picked him up?"

The officer hesitated. "Do you know something we don't?"

"He's a person of interest in a homicide I'm working."

The officer raised his eyebrows and drew in a breath. "We catch students with guns occasionally, but nine times out of ten they're hunting rifles. We don't get too many handguns on campus, and if we find one on a student, he's expelled. It doesn't matter how much money his family gives to the school."

"Has Logan ever gotten violent on campus?"

The officer shook his head. "No. He's on alcohol probation, so if he had gotten into fights, too, we would have moved to have him expelled. We can't have an angry drunk on campus."

It was a big step from public intoxication to a triple homicide, but he had the motive. His mom owned Reid Chemical, and if Laura had found something incriminating about the company, his family stood to lose a lot of money. Still, I had a hard time pegging him as a murderer.

"Thank you for the background. I'll talk to his fraternity brothers and see what I can find."

"You want to search his room while you're there?"

I hesitated and cocked my head to the side. "It's a communal living environment, but I'd still need a search warrant for his room."

"The university owns the building, and everyone who lives inside it signs a code of conduct before moving in. Since Logan's on alcohol probation, we can search for alcohol. If we see something else during those searches, it should be admissible in court."

I wasn't a lawyer, but I already knew a competent defense lawyer would tear that community code of conduct apart. At the same time, my lack of a law degree might benefit me. The court couldn't hold me to the same standard as an attorney. As long as I believed my search was legal, the prosecutors could argue I had searched in good faith.

"Let's go find his booze."

The officer—his name was Corey Sutton, I found out—and I walked to the Sigma Iota house. Unlike my previous visit, I didn't need to ring the bell and hope someone would come out. As a university employee, Sutton had a key. He opened the door, and we walked into the lobby. We found a shirtless young man asleep on the couch with his hand inside his pants and a wisp of a smile on his face. As I shut the front door, the kid's eyes fluttered open and landed on me. For a second, his smile broadened, but then he saw Officer Sutton and fell off the couch. I covered a snicker by coughing into my hand. "Don't mind us," said Sutton. "We're visiting one of your buddies."

He pushed himself up and jogged toward the stairwell, shouting that the police were in the lobby. Sutton looked at me.

"Something I said?"

I knew he meant it as a joke, but my shoulders tensed up, and my fingers and toes tingled with nerves. I hadn't been upstairs yet, but I could imagine what the place would look like. Narrow corridors, doorways everywhere, debris on the floor.

In the police academy, we had trained to clear entire floors of apartment buildings, and every time, at least one person in the unit "died." Only in a real situation, it wouldn't be instructors hiding behind fire doors with paintball guns. In the field, death was permanent.

Sutton looked at me up and down. He wasn't checking me out; instead, he looked curious.

"You okay, Detective?"

I nodded. "I'm annoyed that they know we're coming, but there's nothing we could have done about that. We should call in some backup in case somebody's armed. I'd rather not get ambushed up there."

He considered me and shook his head. "You ever been in a fraternity house?"

I glanced at him and then looked to the stairwell. "It's been a while."

Sutton looked toward the stairs. "He went up to tell his friends to hide their beer and weed. He's not looking to start a fight."

"True, but we're going upstairs to search the room of a murder suspect. I'm not interested in getting shot in the back."

"What do you propose?" he asked.

"Clear everybody out of the building and search for stragglers. Once we've cleared the house, we'll search Logan's room. Last time, I pulled the fire alarm to get everybody out. I'm not sure they'll fall for that again."

Sutton sighed and swore under his breath before getting on his radio to call for backup. It took almost fifteen minutes, but three more uniformed campus police officers arrived. When Officer Sutton told them what was going on, they looked at me as if I had suggested they climb Mount Everest in their underwear. One officer screwed up his face.

"You understand you're asking us to eat a shit sandwich, right?" he asked. "If we go in there and clear them out, we'll deal with the fallout for a week."

"Then I'd suggest you get ready to eat shit, Officer," I said. "This isn't up for debate. You guys can help me out, or I'll call my station and get my people here. I'll warn you now, though: My team won't be gentle. It's your choice, but you'll eat shit either way."

Nobody said anything. Then Sutton looked at me.

"Is everybody at your station this vulgar?"

"I'm a little above average," I said. The room plunged into silence once more. Sutton looked to his fellow officers.

"The detective is working a homicide, and there's potential evidence in the building. Janet and I will take the second floor. Shelby and Bart can get the third. We will funnel the residents down the west stairwell to the ground floor, where they can assemble on the grass. We're only interested in Logan Reid's room, so make sure the boys know that."

They nodded, although they still didn't seem too enthusiastic about the job. I stayed in the lobby while they worked. The ceiling didn't have a lot of soundproofing, so I heard every word the officers on the second floor said. They were cordial, but they were also firm. Nobody argued with them, which was nice to see.

After about fifteen minutes, Sutton came down the stairs to tell me the house was empty. I thanked him, and the two of us walked to the third floor to search. Logan Reid had a case of beer in his minifridge, and several bottles of vodka, rum, and gin in his closet. Officer Sutton had everything he needed to charge Logan with violating the school's alcohol policy. Evidence for my case was scarcer.

The room was small, but Logan had stuffed three ratty couches and an enormous TV inside. I sat down in front of that TV after finding nothing in the entire room. That was when I felt the hard edge of a cell phone wedged between the couch cushions. I fished it out and found a Samsung Galaxy S9 cell phone.

I took my phone from my purse. Laura Rojas had received calls from dozens of numbers, most of which we had identified. A few, though, had gone to prepaid phones without subscriber information. I had called them but didn't get an answer on any of them. Now, I wondered. I searched through my phone's history until I found the block of numbers I needed. Then I dialed. On my third number, the phone I had found buzzed.

"Did you find something, Detective?" asked Sutton.

No judge in the world would let me look at that phone without a search warrant, but I might be able to get one now.

"Yeah. I found something good."

A smile cracked Sutton's lips.

"This wasn't a waste, then."

"Not at all," I said. "Congratulations, Mr. Sutton. You brought me one step closer to bringing down a murderer."

Chapter 28

I drove to my station after searching Logan Reid's room, but Trisha stopped me in the lobby before I could reach my desk.

"Shaun Deveraux came by with file boxes," she said. "He said they're from Laura Rojas's office."

I furrowed my brow. "Already? I wasn't expecting anything from there for several days at least."

Trisha shrugged. "Looks like you pushed the right buttons. They're in the conference room."

I thanked her and then walked. Shaun Deveraux might have found a speedy attorney to review Laura's files, but I doubted it. More than likely, he had found boxes of files so disconnected from any cases or clients they didn't need a thorough vetting.

Before going to the conference room, I dropped off Logan Reid's phone with our forensics lab and then sat at my desk for half an hour to write a search warrant affidavit for the phone's contents. I felt good about our chances of securing a warrant, but I was less sanguine about our chances of recovering any information on it.

Nobody in my department had the expertise to crack a modern cell phone's security, which meant we'd have to turn it over to the Highway Patrol. They had more resources than we did, but even with their help, our chances of recovering anything useful were slim. I'd worry about that later, though.

I sent the affidavit to the prosecutor's office for review and then walked to the conference room, where I found four brown file boxes stacked along the far wall. The first held documents with Reid Chemical's logo splashed across the top. It looked like Laura had printed off the company's website and every financial document the company had filed with the SEC for the past decade. The second box held contracts and invoices, all of which had Reid Chemical's logo at the top. The third and fourth boxes held even more invoices and receipts, some of which dated back years. To learn anything from them, we'd need to hire an accountant.

As I returned the documents to the boxes, somebody knocked on the door. I looked up as my boss walked inside.

"Hey, Harry," I said.

"Evening, Joe," he said, crossing his arms and leaning against the doorframe. "Tell me you didn't march a bunch of college kids out of their dorm in their underwear."

I considered before answering. "I didn't march a bunch of college kids out of their dorm in their underwear."

"Did you order someone else to do that?"

Again, I considered my answer before speaking. "I conducted a legal search of Logan Reid's room in the Sigma Iota fraternity house at Waterford College. Before conducting that search, I requested that officers from the school's Office of Public Safety clear the house of inhabitants. If those idiots walked out in their underwear, that's their own damn fault."

Harry ran a hand across his face and sighed.

"I've already gotten a call from the president at Waterford College. He wasn't happy. Neither is Mason Stewart, who's sitting in my office with his lawyer and his stepson. In a week, you've alienated the administration at Waterford College, the CEO of Reid Chemical, and the entire workforce at Ross Kelly Farms. Whose Corn Flakes are you going to take a dump in next?"

I sighed and shook my head. "I'm following the evidence. What else would you have me do?"

"You can follow the evidence and be diplomatic."

"My methods are legal and appropriate," I said. "I'm working a murder, Harry. I'm not planning a church picnic. If I step on someone's toes, that means I'm doing something right. That's what you taught me."

"All I'm asking is that you be a little more careful," he said. "There are considerations here beyond the law."

"You sound like a politician."

He shook his head and sighed. "I am a politician, Joe. Logan Reid's in my office. You searched his room and confiscated his cell phone. He wants it back, and I'm inclined to give it to him to avoid a lawsuit. The school had a right to search his room for alcohol, but you had no right to collect his phone. What'd you hope to get from it, anyway?"

"I don't know, but it clearly links Logan to Laura," I said. "I've seen Laura's call logs. They talked several times a day. There's no telling what he's got on there. I've already filled out a search warrant affidavit so we can look at its contents."

"That won't happen," said Harry. "Find what you need another way."

I balled my hands into fists and held my breath for a ten count so I wouldn't snap at him.

"Fine. You said Logan Reid's up there with his attorneys?"

Harry nodded.

"Can I talk to him?"

"About?" asked Harry, crossing arms and lowering his chin.

"I want to offer him an apology."

Harry cocked his head to the side. "I don't believe you."

"You didn't use to be this cynical."

"And you didn't use to lie," he said. "Seems we've both picked up character flaws over the years."

I forced myself to smile. I respected him, so it was easier than it might have been with other people.

"The County Council has you by the balls," I said. "I get it, and I'm sorry, but I've got a murder to solve. Logan Reid and Mason Stewart are both suspects, and they're both sitting upstairs with an attorney. I need to talk to them. Are you going to let me do my job or not?"

Harry swore under his breath and then took a step back. "Fine. Do your job, but don't expect me to keep sweeping your messes under the rug."

"I've never expected that," I said, lowering my chin. "And if that's what you think you're doing here, do us both a favor and quit. You're not cut out to be the sheriff."

I regretted the comment almost the moment the words left my mouth.

"That was out of line," I said, lowering my voice and dropping my chin to my chest. "I shouldn't have said that. I'm sorry."

Harry drew in a slow breath but said nothing. When I looked up to meet his gaze, he looked away and nodded.

"I hate this job. I should have known better when the County Council offered me the position. They're not competent enough to offer it to someone qualified."

I smiled. "You can still get back at them for making you sheriff. Let me work my case. I can almost guarantee I'll piss off somebody important."

He chuckled but then considered me before responding.

"You think there's something to find at Reid Chemical?"

"Laura Rojas did. I'm following her lead."

He looked away and then covered his mouth before nodding.

"Have at it," he said. "Reid and Stewart are in my office. Good luck."

"Thanks, boss," I said, walking toward the door. "You want to supervise my interview?"

"No," he said, shaking his head. "I'd rather have some plausible deniability in case you do something stupid."

"That's a good idea," I said, nodding to him as I left the room. Even with all the work I had done, I didn't know why Laura Rojas was dead, but I was getting closer to finding her killer with every step I made. I hoped that'd be enough. We had enough victims already.

I walked to Harry's office, where I found Logan Reid, Mason Stewart, and a man in a suit I didn't recognize. They sat around Harry's small conference table. As I walked toward them, the man in the suit stood and positioned himself between me and his clients.

"Kevin Rasmussen," he said, holding out his hand. He was middle aged, and he wore a well-cut charcoal gray suit, white shirt, and gray tie. I shook his hand and nodded.

"Detective Joe Court. I understand my search of the Sigma Iota fraternity at Waterford College has ruffled a few feathers."

"Your search was illegal," said Rasmussen, walking back to the table. "We'd like the phone you stole. If you return it to us, we'll consider not filing theft charges against you."

"That's tempting," I said, nodding. "But I'm not sure the search was illegal. Your client was on alcohol probation with the school. The school's personal conduct policy allows the school's Office of Public Safety to search his room for alcoholic beverages. If, during that search, they find evidence of other crimes, that should be admissible in court, don't you think?"

The attorney humored me with a smile.

"Are you an attorney or a detective, Detective Court?"

"A detective. Since I'm not a lawyer, I can't say whether a judge will side with me, but I'm willing to roll the dice. How about you guys?"

"What do you expect to find on the phone?" asked Rasmussen.

"Evidence of contact with a murder victim."

"There's nothing on it," said Logan. "Just some pictures."

"Shut up, Logan," said Stewart.

I looked past the lawyer to his young client.

"What pictures?" I asked. Logan wouldn't meet my gaze, so I looked at his lawyer and raised my eyebrows. "I guess we'll find out, huh?"

"The photographs on that phone would embarrass Mr. Reid," said Rasmussen. "They have no evidentiary value."

"I'd like to assess that for myself," I said.

The lawyer leaned forward.

"If my client unlocks his phone and shows you the pictures, would you agree to release it back to him?"

"Will he answer questions, too?"

Rasmussen blinked. "My client will sit for a voluntary interview if he can leave when he chooses, and if he can refuse to answer whatever questions he'd like."

"Sure," I said. "That's fine. The phone's downstairs. Give me a minute, and I'll get it."

The lawyer agreed, so I walked downstairs to the crime lab, where one of our technicians gave me Logan's phone. When I returned, Rasmussen sat beside his clients on the far side of the table. I sat on the other side and slid the phone toward Logan.

He picked it up and looked to his lawyer. "So I unlock it and give it to her?"

Rasmussen looked to him. "Just show her the pictures. She can get everything else with a search warrant from your phone company."

Logan slid his thumb across the screen and then tapped a few times before he slid the phone toward me to show me a picture of a naked young woman.

"Friend of yours?" I asked, looking to Logan and raising my eyebrows.

"She goes to Waterford with me. We hook up sometimes."

I nodded and used my thumb to open the next picture. It, too, was a photograph of a nude woman in her late teens to early twenties. She had sent Logan at least three pictures. A third woman sent half a dozen.

"I assume these young ladies are all over eighteen," I said.

"They are," said Rasmussen. "I hope you understand why my client was reluctant to give up his phone now. Laura Rojas sent him pictures, too. There's nothing illegal there."

I thumbed through a couple dozen more nude photographs until I came to a set of pictures of a young woman with Laura Rojas's skin tone. The pictured woman wore no clothes, but someone had cropped out her face, leaving only her body.

"This is Laura Rojas?" I asked, holding the phone toward Logan.

"Yeah."

"The pictures don't show her face."

"It's her," said Logan. "Trust me. Her body's hard to forget."

Only it wasn't her. This young woman—whoever she was—had a tattoo along her rib cage. Laura didn't. If Laura had sent him these pictures, she was playing him. I put the phone on the table and focused on Logan.

"Okay. I get it. You knew Laura Rojas. Did she tell you she was an attorney?"

He looked to his stepfather before speaking.

"No," he said, his voice low. "She told me she was a librarian."

"How'd you meet her?"

"At the library," he said. "Not the college one, but in town. I was looking for an audiobook. I listen to them when I work out."

"What did you two talk about?"

Mason Stewart scoffed and then shook his head, but Rasmussen cleared his throat before Logan could say anything.

"Can we please stick to the matters at hand, Detective?" he asked. "My clients are busy people. We don't have time to waste."

I forced myself to smile at the attorney, but I didn't allow it to reach my eyes.

"I am sticking to the matters at hand," I said. "Ms. Rojas was a beautiful, successful attorney who was investigating Reid Chemical. I'm wondering whether she ever told Logan about her practice."

"No," he said.

"Then what did you talk about?"

He blinked and then tilted his head to the side.

"We didn't have that kind of relationship," he said. "We got together to have sex. That's it."

It was a lie, but I didn't know what he hoped to get from it. I paused.

"Since we've been investigating Ms. Rojas's murder, we've pulled a list of her incoming and outgoing phone calls. You guys spoke often. If the primary focus of your relationship was sexual, what'd you talk about?"

"Positions and stuff," he said, his voice meek.

Stewart rubbed his eyes and then cleared his throat.

"We've heard enough about my stepson's sex life," he said. "Can we move along?"

"One more question," I said, not taking my eyes from Logan's. "She was pregnant when she died. Is it yours?"

Logan drew in a sharp breath and covered his chin with his hand.

"My client can't answer that," said Rasmussen. "He had a sexual relationship with Ms. Rojas, but that doesn't mean he was the only person."

"That's true, I suppose," I said, nodding. "Did you suspect that Ms. Rojas was more than she seemed to be?"

Logan shook his head. "No."

"Did she ever ask you about your family's company?"

Again, he shook his head. "No."

I thought back to the pile of invoices and receipts I had sitting in the conference room.

"Did you ever give her access to company files?"

Logan looked to his stepfather. Stewart answered.

"If she had company files, they didn't come from my stepson," he said. "As those company files contain trade secrets, we expect you to return them."

"Talk to the prosecutors about that," I said, focusing on Logan again and speaking before his stepfather could throw off the rhythm I was developing. "To reiterate, your story is that you happened to meet Laura Rojas in the county library. This beautiful, successful attorney lied to you about her identity, but she was so taken with lust that you two slept together immediately. During this relationship, you spoke on the phone two to three times a day to talk about sexual positions. Even though Laura was investigating your family's company, she never once asked you about Reid Chemical, and you never once gave her access to company files or information. Is that correct?"

Logan leaned forward and nodded. "Yeah."

I looked around.

"Huh," I said, a moment later.

"Something wrong?" asked Rasmussen.

"I was looking for the turnip truck you guys think I fell off."

Stewart's lips curled into a tight smile, and his predatory eyes locked on mine. I almost shuddered.

"I've always had a thing for clever women."

"Is that right?" I asked. "I've never had a thing for creepy murder suspects twice my age. Sorry."

Stewart leaned forward. Even though he was several feet from me, I almost pushed away from the table.

"From what I hear, you don't date at all," he said. "You live alone in that old house with your dog, your only friend is the old lady who lives next door, and you don't even know who your father was. Does that sound right?"

I forced a smile to my face. "For future reference, when you and your stepson are suspects in a murder investigation, it's not a good idea to investigate the investigating officer. It makes you look guilty and creepy. Kind of expected your attorney to have told you that."

As if on cue, Rasmussen pushed back from the table. “This interview is over. Can we have Mr. Reid’s phone now?”

“Sure thing,” I said, sliding the phone across the table toward them. Everybody glared at me as they shuffled out of the office, but I didn’t care. I had learned what I needed to know. Laura Rojas wasn’t just after Reid Chemicals. She was investigating Mason Stewart and his family, and Mason Stewart killed her for it.

Now I had to prove it.

Chapter 29

Harry returned to his office about two minutes after Stewart and his entourage left. His face looked drawn and pale. When he saw me, he ran a hand across his scalp and crossed the room to plop down on the chair behind his desk.

"You okay, boss?"

He nodded before sighing. "Long day. I've been considering what you said. Once you close your case, I'm putting in my letter of resignation."

I sat straighter and shook my head. "Don't listen to me. My advice is terrible. You're a good boss, and if you think I was mean to you, you should have heard the things I said to Travis before he retired. They were brutal."

Harry smiled but focused on the desk in front of him instead of my eyes.

"I'm tired, Joe," he said. "I was a good detective, but this isn't my world anymore."

"At least wait until the County Council lines up somebody else. If you quit now, they'll promote Delgado. He'll fire me. You know he will."

"You're too big for this pond as it is, Joe," he said. "Time to get out while you can."

"I like this pond. It's my home."

"I know you like St. Augustine," he said, nodding and smiling. "But it doesn't like you back."

I couldn't fault him for his honesty, but it didn't make me feel good, either.

"I don't even know where I'd go."

He shrugged. "Your family's done pretty well in St. Louis, but any police department in the state would be lucky to have you. You'd have to start at the bottom, but you'd move up. Since you're young, you could take your time and do things right. Hell, you're bright enough you could even go to law school and leave us all behind."

I tossed up my hands. "If we're throwing things out, maybe I should just become a drug dealer. I hear there's good money in that."

He smiled, but it didn't reach his eyes.

"Just think about your future," he said. "St. Augustine is going to get worse before it gets better."

I stood and paced the room by the front window. "I appreciate the uplifting pep talk, Harry, but this is my home. You're not getting rid of me."

He grunted and then sighed. "Okay."

"That's all you've got for me?" I said, standing still. "Okay?"

"You're an adult, and I respect your judgment. I warned you that things will get ugly, but I can't make you listen to me."

I shook my head again and looked through his window. People ambled about on the sidewalks as they walked to restaurants and bars. From my vantage, the world looked idyllic. St. Augustine wasn't perfect, but I liked my life here. I felt safe here, and I didn't plan on leaving.

I looked at Harry.

"Thanks for being a friend," I said, "but I'm not leaving without a fight."

He grunted and then nodded. "I thought you'd say that."

I smiled but said nothing. Then I cleared my throat.

"So I'm working a murder involving some very wealthy people."

"Yeah," said Harry, nodding. "I've heard."

"I need to hire an accountant to look over Laura Rojas's files."

Harry thought for a moment and then crossed his arms.

"What have you got?"

"Four boxes full of inventories, spreadsheets, ledgers, and receipts," I said. "Laura was on to something. We need to find out what."

Harry considered and then nodded. "Call Darius Adams. He's a CPA now, but he worked for the IRS when he was younger. He's the best forensic accountant in the county."

I lowered my chin. "Is he the only forensic accountant in the county?"

"Yeah, but he'll get the job done," said Harry. "His office is on Second Avenue in the basement. Tell him to bill the department."

"Okay," I said, standing straighter. "I'll talk to him, and then I'm heading home. See you tomorrow."

He grunted and waved, and I stepped out of the office. Within five minutes, I had the file boxes in my truck. Second Avenue wasn't far away, so it didn't take long to drive. Darius Adams had an office in the basement. I knocked before opening the door.

The interior was musty but neat. Late afternoon sunlight filtered through the windows near the ceiling and cascaded down on the thin gray carpet. It was a simple room with two wooden desks pushed against opposite walls. There were gray metal file cabinets everywhere. A man spun around on a rolling chair as I entered. He had dark skin and black hair, and he wore an olive-green vest, a white shirt, and jeans. He was twenty or twenty-five years older than me, but he was still handsome, even more so when he smiled.

"Can I help you?" he asked.

"Are you Darius Adams?" I asked, pushing my jacket back to expose the badge on my hip. "I'm Detective Joe Court. Harry Grainger sent me."

"Nice to meet you, Detective Court," he said, turning back around to close a document open on his computer.

"How's Harry doing these days? I hear they made him sheriff."

"They did. He's still adjusting to the role."

"I'll bet," he said, removing his gold-rimmed glasses and placing them on the desk. "What can I do for the Sheriff's Department?"

"I need help with a case," I said. I looked to the empty desk opposite Adams's. He nodded, so I pulled out a chair and sat down as I led him through what I had found so far. When I finished speaking, he crossed his arms and leaned back.

"So you've got bodies on the ground, and boxes of receipts and documents in your truck, and you don't know what to do with them," he said. "How would I fit in here?"

"I'm not sure," I said. "My victim, Laura Rojas, was investigating Reid Chemical, but I don't know what she was looking for. She wouldn't have kept all these documents unless she thought she could use them, though. I need someone to look through them and find whatever she found."

Adams considered before nodding. "All right. Let's see what we've got."

Adams helped me carry the boxes to his office, where he looked through what we had.

"Two boxes aren't interesting," he said after a few minutes. "You can leave them here, but I don't think they have anything I can use. The other two, though, might be helpful. It'll take time to look through them, but your lawyer was hunting for something."

"You have any idea what?"

"Not a clue," he said.

"So you think you can help?"

"I'll need two to three days to get oriented," he said. "Do you have a number I can reach you at?"

I fished through my purse until I found my business cards. "This has my office number and email address. If you can't reach me, just leave a message. It also has the station's address. When you're done, send us a bill. Harry's authorized the expense."

"Okay, Detective," he said, slipping my business card into his pocket. "Tell Harry I appreciate the business. I'll get right on this."

"Thanks, Mr. Adams," I said.

"Darius," he said, holding out his hand. "My friends call me Darius."

I shook his hand. He had the calloused skin of a carpenter. Surprising from an accountant.

"Joe," I said. "And it's nice to meet you, Darius."

"A girl named Joe," he said, leaning back in his chair again. "Bet there's a story behind that name."

"There is," I said. "It's not very exciting, though."

"Maybe one day, I'll hear it," he said. "Goodbye, Joe. I'll get started on your case tomorrow morning. My wife made shepherd's pie for dinner, and I've got two teenage boys. If I don't come home right on time, I'll starve."

"Have a nice dinner," I said. "I'll see you later."

He smiled as I walked out of the office. Outside, my feet felt light, and I even smiled hello to a woman pushing a stroller up the sidewalk. Only as I opened my door did I realize that I had enjoyed meeting somebody new. That rarely happened. I spent my entire day talking to people, but it was never fun.

Even with my colleagues, I always had to stay on guard. My department had few choice assignments, so everybody jostled for a position at the department trough. I had friends at work—Trisha, Harry, Sasquatch, and a few others—but I never relaxed around them. It felt nice to let my guard down.

I drove home, but as I pulled into my driveway, the smile left my face. With Roger at the vet's office, I was alone. I stayed in my truck for a few minutes, feeling the solitude creep into my bones. As I opened my truck's door, I took my phone from my purse and called Dr. Johnson. He answered on the third ring.

"Doc," I said. "It's Joe Court. I'm calling about Roger."

"Hi, Joe," he said, his voice a little flat. "Roger's with me right now. If it's okay with you, I'd like to keep him with me for observation for the night."

My throat tightened a little. "Everything okay?"

"How long has it been since he stopped eating?"

"Last night," I said, crossing my yard to the mailbox. I had two catalogs and some generic junk mail. They'd go straight into the recycling bin. "He's been drinking, though."

"Yeah," he said, his voice low. "Roger's not a puppy anymore."

"I know," I said, walking toward the porch. I sat down on the edge so my feet were on the grass. "He's a happy dog, though. He likes it here."

"And I've seen you with him. He loves you," said the vet. He paused. "I'd like you to come by the office tomorrow if possible. Tonight, though, make a list of things Roger likes to do. His five favorite things."

I didn't have to think. I knew what he was getting at and already had the list written by my back door. Roger wasn't the only old dog to enter my life. My dad used to have a golden retriever named Benji. Dad had loved him. They went for walks every day—rain, snow, or shine—and Benji used to sit at Dad's side every time he came home from work. When Benji got old, Dad wrote down Benji's five favorite things to do. When Benji stopped doing those things, Dad knew he had to let him go.

I swallowed hard.

"Roger likes to retrieve his ball, he likes to sit with my neighbor on her front porch, he likes to run with me in the woods, he likes to greet me when I come home, and he likes to chase small animals."

Dr. Johnson paused.

"Does he still do those things?"

For a moment, the lump in my throat prevented me from answering.

"You still there, Joe?"

I nodded and forced myself to suck in a breath.

"He's my friend," I said, rubbing another tear from my eyes.

"I know, but he's in pain. His kidneys are failing, and his arthritis is just getting worse. His health will not improve. We need to consider his quality of life."

I drew in a long breath, forcing myself to calm down.

"Can we talk tomorrow?"

"Sure," he said.

I thanked him and then hung up. Part of me knew I needed to get something to eat, but I couldn't force myself to move. So I stayed there as the sun set and let myself think back to my conversation with Harry. I came to St. Augustine when I finished college because I had needed a job, and the Sheriff's Department had offered me one. The town became my home, though, when I adopted Roger.

He was six when he came to live with me, which meant he had already been middle-aged for a dog his size. When I brought him home, he ran into the doghouse I had built for him in the backyard and refused to come out no matter what I did. I almost asked the shelter to take him back, but my dad persuaded me not to. I think Dad understood that I needed Roger as much as he needed me.

Every day, I brought Roger food and put it a little farther from his house so he'd come out farther each day. It took time, but he accepted me. He didn't trust me, but he didn't run when he saw me, either. I couldn't blame him. Roger's previous owner shot him with a BB gun so often he had pellets lodged all over his body, and he trembled whenever he met someone new for the first time. If someone had done that to me, I'd have trust issues, too.

It wasn't always easy, but I earned my dog's trust and affection. Roger became my best friend. He and I walked all over the county together, we ran through the woods together, and we sat beside each other on the porch to look at the stars. When I got Roger, I had been just as broken as him. I had adopted parents and siblings, but I had never let myself be a part of their family. I had acquaintances but no real friends. I had been alone in the world, and I hadn't even known it.

Bit by bit, I fixed up my crappy old house and turned my day-to-day existence into a life that was worth living. Roger was with me the whole time. Every good memory I had in St. Augustine involved Roger. Now that I was losing him, I wondered whether Harry was right. Maybe I should leave and start over. Without my buddy beside me, this didn't feel like home anymore.

Chapter 30

When I went to bed that night, I slept so fitfully it was almost a relief when my phone rang, waking me up from a nightmare. In my dream, somebody had been chasing me, but his face was blurry. Every time I thought I got away from him, he'd appear in front of me once more. I had been crying in my sleep, but no one heard or cared.

My phone rang again. I blinked my eyes open. It still felt like my nightmare assailant's hands were on my breasts, arms, and back. Sweat soaked my pillowcase and sheets. I swallowed hard and stayed still, forcing my racing heart to slow down and my breath to calm. Then I swung my legs off the bed and reached for my cell phone on the end table.

"Yeah," I said, rubbing sleep out of my eyes.

"Hey, Detective. This is Nicole Bryant. Sorry to wake you up, but we've got an issue."

Nicole was one of the uniformed officers assigned to the night shift. I didn't envy her hours, but the night shift came with a pay raise, and she and her husband were saving up to put their kids through college. Nicole worked hard and did her job well. If she'd had the ambition, she could have made sergeant easily, but she didn't want to become a supervisor. I couldn't blame her.

"That's all right. Tell me what's going on."

"Sasquatch and I have been following the two men you met earlier. They've spent most of the afternoon at a hotel by the interstate, but a few minutes ago they broke into the train yard out on River Road."

I pictured the area in my head.

"What are they doing at the train yard?"

"We don't know. They cut the chain on the gate, and then they drove in. Now they're opening a cargo car. What do you want to do?"

"Watch them for now. If they do anything, use your judgment. Remember these are bad men who will not hesitate to kill you. I'm on my way."

"See you soon."

I hung up and dressed in jeans and a T-shirt and pulled my hair into a ponytail behind my head before heading out. The night air cooled my skin. Stars stretched from one end of the horizon to the other without even a wisp of cloud cover. On most nights, I liked looking at the stars. Tonight, though, I didn't have time for reverie. I made sure my pistol had a full magazine and that my badge hung on my belt, and then I hopped in my truck and drove.

The train yard was about twenty minutes away. The railroad owned more property in St. Augustine County than any other business or person, but it employed so few people it didn't have the political clout commensurate with its investment. I could burn every building it owned to the ground, and the members of the County Council would simply shrug their shoulders. That was how politics worked around here. Cash and campaign contributions were king. Little else mattered.

As I approached the yard, I called Nicole on my cell phone.

"Where are you guys?"

"Base of the billboard on the north edge of the property. It's dark, and our lights are off so the bad guys can't see us."

"I'm on my way."

From a distance, the rail yard looked like a junkyard, but as I got closer, the individual tracks and cars became clear. Nobody worked there at night, so the company hadn't even installed overhead lights. A tall chain-link fence topped with barbed wire surrounded the property. No night watchmen patrolled that rail yard. If somebody wanted to steal a four-hundred-thousand-pound locomotive, they were welcome to try.

As Nicole had said, she and Sasquatch had parked beneath a billboard near the edge of the property. I parked beside them and joined them at the front of Sasquatch's cruiser. The north edge of the property had a slight rise, which gave us a clear view inside the property. There must have been a thousand train cars inside the yard, creating a maze of steel and dirt. A four-door sedan had conspicuously parked on its outskirts.

"That car belong to our bad guys?" I asked.

"Yeah," said Sasquatch. "Sorry to wake you up, Joe."

"Sorry for keeping you up," I said. "You've had a long day."

"I'm pulling a double and covering for Gary Faulk. He's got the flu," said Sasquatch, pointing toward the rail yard. "They're in the red car, and they've got a light."

I focused on the yard until I found a red train car with a faint glimmer of light spilling beneath its closed door.

"How long have they been in there?"

"Almost an hour," said Nicole. "Before that, they were at their hotel. What do you think they're doing?"

"I don't know," I said, shaking my head.

"Want to let them know we're here?" said Sasquatch. "We could knock."

Again, I shook my head. "No. Those train cars are solid steel. If they pull firearms on us, they'll be in a hardened position with cover, and we'll be out in the open. Once they're done inside, they'll come out. We'll wait."

Sasquatch nodded before yawning.

"If you two don't mind, I'll take a nap."

"Go ahead," I said. "If anybody moves, we'll let you know."

He nodded and went to the front seat of his cruiser, while Nicole and I sat on the bumper of hers. We talked for a while. I liked Nicole, but we came from different worlds.

She got married when she was seventeen and had her first kid—a girl—six months later. Now that little girl was getting married to her college boyfriend. Nicole's other kids were in high school. I didn't have kids or a husband or loved ones to talk about, and I didn't want to talk about Roger. So I nodded along, smiled, and asked questions until Nicole ran out of things to say.

A little over an hour after I arrived, two men emerged from the railroad car. They looked around, but they didn't notice us. Nicole crept around Sasquatch's car and woke him up. I joined the two beside the cruiser.

"Should we follow them or check out the car?" asked Nicole. The two men climbed into their sedan. A second later, their taillights lit up, and they drove toward the gate. They kept their headlights off, making them difficult to follow in the starlight.

"They're up to something, so follow them," I said. "I'll check out the train car. If we need to, we'll call in backup. Go now before they're gone. And be careful."

Sasquatch didn't hesitate before turning on his car. I took a step back as Nicole hurried to the passenger side. Once the bad guys reached the highway, they turned on their headlights and sped up. This patch of the highway had a few curves and a few hills, so Sasquatch let them drive over a hill before turning on his own headlights. At night, nobody would see their paint job or the unlit light bar on top of their cruiser. They'd be fine.

I let them both disappear around a bend before making sure Nicole had locked her cruiser. Then I got in my truck and headed toward the rail yard. The bad guys had pulled the front gate shut, but they hadn't locked it. Within moments of pulling into the lot, I opened the rolling door of a freight car and peered inside.

Blue plastic tarps covered the car's walls, ceiling, and floor. Duct tape joined the seams. In the center of the car, they had placed a wooden chair, the kind my teachers had kept behind their desks in elementary school. It was a good place to kill somebody. The train car was remote, but more than that, by the time we realized we had a body, our crime scene would be thousands of miles away.

I ran out of there and ripped my phone from my pocket. Sasquatch's phone rang three times before he answered.

"Where are you?" I asked.

"In a neighborhood off River Road," he said. "What did you find in the car?"

"Tarps. They plan to kill somebody. I'll call the station for backup. Stay on these guys, but don't engage them unless you have to."

Sasquatch hesitated.

"They split up. One guy got out of the car about half a mile away. Nicole followed him into some woods. I'm following the guy who's in the car."

"Leave the guy in the car. Go back and get Nicole. I'll send backup to you as soon as I can."

I hung up on him and threw open my door. It took a moment to find Nicole's number in my address book, but I punched in her entry as my old truck roared to life.

"Come on, Nicole," I said. "Pick up. Pick up. Pick up."

I put the truck in gear and floored the accelerator. Dust flew behind me as the rear tires spun in the loose soil before gaining traction. My truck rocketed forward. Finally, I heard Nicole's soft breath on the phone.

"Joe," she said. "I'm following one of 'em on foot."

"Back off," I said. "They've set up a kill room in the train. You've got backup en route, but you're not safe on your own. Get back to River Road. Sasquatch will pick you up."

For a few seconds, Nicole said nothing. Then her breath caught in her throat, and she jostled the phone.

"Police officer!" she screamed. "Put your hands in the air."

"Fuck," I said. My entire body tingled, and I willed my car to speed up. I hit the asphalt at thirty miles an hour and floored the accelerator. Sasquatch and Nicole couldn't have driven far.

"Hands in the air. Now."

Nicole's voice was strident, almost to the point of breaking. Then somebody fired a gun. It was deeper and louder than Nicole's pistol. I held my breath and waited for return fire.

"Shoot him, Nicole," I whispered.

No shots came, so I ended the call and dialed my station's number with trembling fingers. The moment someone picked up, I shouted orders.

"We've got shots fired. Trace Preston Cain's cruiser and send everybody we've got to that area. We have at least two armed suspects and two officers in the area. I am en route right now in my truck. Repeat, we have shots fired. We need EMS and backup."

Jason Zuckerburg, our night dispatcher, pounded on his keyboard.

"The GPS says Preston is near River Road. Does that sound right?"

"Yeah," I said. "Send everybody on duty. And call the Highway Patrol. We need tactical help and a bird in the air."

He continued to type. "I'm routing eight officers and an ambulance toward that area. The nearest officer is..." He paused. When he spoke again, his voice was crestfallen. "...seven miles away. We're going lights and sirens. We'll get there as soon as we can."

"Understood."

I hung up and tossed my phone onto the seat beside me as cold anger flooded through my system. Even at this time of night, it would take our cruisers at least five minutes to cross seven miles on the county's decrepit, narrow roads. If someone had shot Nicole, she didn't have that kind of time, and Sasquatch was alone against two gunmen who had already taken out one officer.

I had to move.

Chapter 31

I kept the accelerator floored until I located Sasquatch's cruiser on the side of the road. Fields and patches of thick woods surrounded us. There were few homes. Sasquatch had parked in front of a rambling single-story brick home with a big front porch. I screeched to a halt near his cruiser and positioned my truck at an angle so Sasquatch's vehicle gave me cover from the left and my truck's engine block gave me cover from the right. Then I climbed out and pulled my firearm out of its holster.

Sasquatch wasn't here, but the driver's door and trunk of his cruiser were both open. I peered into the trunk. Each of our cruisers had a rack for an M4 carbine on the lid. Sasquatch's was empty.

I didn't care if the bad guys saw me. I needed to keep my officers safe, so I opened the passenger door of Sasquatch's cruiser and leaned inside to turn on the light. Red, blue, and white lights lit the world around me like a fireworks show.

"Preston!" I shouted. Nobody answered, and nobody came out of the houses. "Nicole! Preston!"

I turned, hoping I'd see movement somewhere. Then the distant, staccato report of a rifle echoed against the nearby trees. A shotgun answered with a deep booming blast. Then a pistol fired.

"Shit."

I sprinted toward the noise. My mind screamed at me that this was the stupidest thing I had ever done, but I didn't care. I wouldn't lose somebody else tonight.

I streaked across the lawn and plunged into a deep thicket of woods. Poplar, walnut, cherry, and other trees I didn't recognize surrounded me. Weeds and thorny vines covered the ground, creating a tangled mess of tripping hazards. I couldn't stop moving, though.

I sprinted and paused only long enough to duck behind trees to listen. My department had sent backup almost five minutes ago, but I couldn't hear their sirens yet. I did, though, hear gunfire. It wasn't far now.

I ran another hundred yards and pressed my back against an ancient silver maple tree.

"Preston, where are you?"

A pistol blasted to the west, far closer than I had expected. Bark and wood exploded around me. I yelped and ducked before returning fire in the general direction the shot had come from. Then I sprinted to another big tree to the east of my original location.

Fresh rounds thwacked into the woods around me. Sasquatch returned fire with his carbine from the north.

"Joe!" he shouted. "Stay down."

"Where's Nicole?"

"I don't know," he said. The man with the pistol fired again. It hit my tree at an angle, sending bark flying. Debris raked my face and bit into my skin. I blinked dirt and bark out of my eyes as I knelt down to get my bearings.

As best I could tell, the four of us had positioned ourselves in a box-like shape. Sasquatch hid behind a tree to the north, while the man with the shotgun had ducked into a ravine to the northwest. The man with the pistol hid somewhere to the west. Everyone had cover, which meant we had a stalemate. Sasquatch and I only needed to survive until our backup arrived.

The bad guys shouted to one another in a language I didn't recognize.

"You understand any of that?" I shouted.

"No. You?" asked Sasquatch.

Broadcasting our ignorance at the moment didn't seem to matter.

"No."

As I spoke, the man with the pistol popped off two rounds. They hit my tree. Then he popped off two more. These thwacked into the tree Sasquatch had hidden behind. As the pistol shooter gave him covering fire, the man with the shotgun took off.

So did Sasquatch.

"Preston, get to cover!" I shouted.

Sasquatch didn't acknowledge me. He kept running after the man with the shotgun. I didn't know what he was thinking. He was right in the open. The pistol shooter raised his weapon. I fired at his hands but missed.

The bad guy's pistol barked once and then twice more. The world slowed. With each shot, the orange glow of his muzzle flash lit up the surrounding woods. Preston stumbled and fell as if he had tripped on a tree root.

Raw, hot rage overcame me. I screamed and squeezed the trigger on my firearm as I sprinted forward. I didn't know what I was doing, and I didn't have a plan. If Sasquatch was still alive, he needed help, and he wouldn't get it if people were shooting at us still. With each step I took, I fired again, driving the shooter back. The man with the shotgun kept running. He was getting away, but I couldn't stop him.

The pistol shooter wasn't far—maybe thirty feet from where I started. My pistol had few rounds left, but I only needed one. I stopped squeezing the trigger and darted behind the trunk of a gnarled oak tree. Thanks to all my early morning runs through the woods behind my house, I was in good shape. Already my heart was slowing down.

Nobody fired a gun for a moment. I crept forward, giving myself a better view of my target. The barrel of his firearm extended beyond the tree. His partner had left the woods.

In the distance, I heard the first sirens of my approaching team.

"Toss your weapon down and put your hands in the air!" I shouted. "I have two officers down. You're not walking away from this. If you keep fighting, you will die."

I didn't expect him to give up, but I sure didn't expect him to chuckle, either.

"You're out of rounds, aren't you?" said the shooter. I recognized him by his accent. It was Stephan Kushnir, the younger of the two men I had met at Rise and Grind. "I've been counting."

I hadn't been counting, but by its weight, I knew I had several rounds left in my firearm.

"Throw down your weapon and put your hands in the air," I said. "I'm not playing here."

"You first," said Kushnir. I heard a twig snap and leaves crunch as he exited his position. He was walking toward me with his firearm held at his side. I stepped out from the tree's cover and raised my pistol.

"I've got at least one round in the chamber, buddy," I said. "Drop your weapon and put your hands in the air."

"We've already killed two of your friends tonight," he said, smirking. "You think I get a medal for taking out one more?"

"Are you this stupid?" I asked, raising my eyebrows. "I don't want to shoot you. Lie down. I've got a dozen or more officers inbound right now."

He raised his weapon. It was almost a lazy movement. My finger slipped from the trigger guard to the trigger. Before I squeezed my trigger, three staccato shots rang out behind me. One round struck a tree, but the other two hit Kushnir in the back. He fell forward. I looked behind me to see Sasquatch about forty feet away. He leaned against a tree, but he gave me a thumbs-up before dropping his rifle and collapsing.

I kicked Kushnir's hand to dislodge his firearm. Then I kicked the gun so he couldn't reach it. He was alive, but Sasquatch had shot him in the back twice with an M4 carbine. The muscles of his back wouldn't have even slowed the rounds down before they reached his lungs. He coughed, splattering blood in the night air. He was dead in all but name.

I ran to Sasquatch. He had taken a round to his rib cage. Blood dribbled down his chin. I pressed a hand to his wound to stop the bleeding. His blood trickled through my fingers and down my wrist.

"I saved your life, Joe," he said, almost smiling. "I heard him talking."

"Don't speak," I said, pulling my T-shirt over my head. I pressed the fabric hard against his rib cage, hoping that would help stanch the blood flow. He licked his lips. As I held the shirt, I checked his neck for a pulse. It felt weak and thready. Unless we got him to a doctor, he would die. "You're a hero, Preston. If you make it out of this, I'll tell everybody."

He closed his eyes and swallowed. "And I'll tell everybody you showed me your boobs."

I was wearing a bra, but I didn't want to quibble with him. A moment later, people shouted behind me. Our backup had finally arrived.

"I'm here, and I need help."

Officers Dave Skelton, Bill Wharton, and Louise Ortega sprinted through the woods toward me. Skelton carried a first-aid kit, and he knelt beside Sasquatch. Before becoming a police officer, he had been an Army Ranger and had spent a lot of time overseas. He rarely talked about it, but he had seen people hurt before and had the training to help. I stood and backed off.

"One shooter is dead, but the second shooter escaped," I said. "I can't find Nicole Bryant. She's hurt. I need an air ambulance. Louise, call that in. Bill, work with Dave Skelton and tend to Sasquatch. Any of you guys have a shirt or windbreaker in your car?"

Nobody had extra clothing, so I crossed my arms and watched them get to work. Ortega sprinted toward the road while Skelton and Wharton started emergency medical treatment on Sasquatch. I wasn't any use there, so I started walking in the direction I presumed Nicole Bryant was.

Even I knew it was pointless. The woods were dark, and I was just walking in circles. Every time I stopped, though, my mind flashed to a mental image of Nicole dying on the ground.

As time passed, more officers arrived. Several of them cast long glances at me, but I didn't care. I was wearing a sports bra. People of people went jogging in less.

Eventually, Harry and Trisha found me. She handed me a navy St. Augustine County Sheriff's Department shirt. I thanked her and slipped it over my head.

"Nicole's somewhere around here," I said, my voice coming out quicker than I intended. I wanted to slow down, but, for some reason, I couldn't. "She was following a guy named Kurt Wilkinson. He had a shotgun, but I don't think she knew. I was on the phone with her when the bad guy shot her. She identified herself and ordered him to drop his weapon. He shot her instead. He didn't even warn her. She was just doing her job."

The longer I spoke, the harder it became to form the words. I realized I was crying when I tasted my tears. Trisha put a hand on my shoulder.

"It's okay," she said. "You did everything you could."

"We've got to find her," I said. "She's here somewhere."

"We already have found her," said Harry, his voice soft. "She probably died instantly. Sasquatch is still alive, and that's because of you. A helicopter is taking him to a hospital in St. Louis right now. You saved his life."

My legs felt weak, and my head felt light, but I didn't let myself fall. Every muscle in my body felt tense.

"You need to call the Highway Patrol. We need helicopters, and we need officers to go door to door for Kurt Wilkinson. He's armed and dangerous."

"We're already on it," said Harry. "We need you to calm down and come with us. We think you're in shock, so we're going to—"

"I'm fine," I said, interrupting him. My fingers trembled, so I balled them into fists at my sides. "I was disoriented at first, but I'm better now. Okay?"

"The paramedics need to check you out anyway," said Harry. "I understand that you want to find Wilkinson, but you're no good to anybody if you're hurt."

My breath felt short, and my skin felt warm.

"I'm fine," I said. "I'm just a little hot."

"This isn't a suggestion," said Harry, following along as I plodded through the woods. "Talk to the paramedics. That's an order. If you refuse, I'll put you in handcuffs. Please don't make me do that."

I said nothing, but I kept walking. Then, I ran into a tree. It was like it had just jumped in front of me. I put my forehead against the bark.

My throat felt thick.

"Nicole and I talked before this happened," I said. "She was working the night shift because she needed more money for her kids. I told her that it sucked. That was the last thing I said to her. 'That sucks.' Like she didn't know that. And then she died."

Neither of them said anything, but Trisha put a hand on my upper arm.

"She was just trying to help her family," I said. My eyes were so glassy with held tears that I could barely see.

"You did your best to take care of her," said Trisha, smiling and leading me away. "Let us take care of you now."

"I'm fine," I said, trying to push away from them both. They both held onto me. There were a dozen or more emergency response vehicles with their lights on at the edge of the woods. I hadn't even known they were there.

"You're not fine," said Trisha. "Let us take care of you."

She squeezed my arm hard. I wanted to fight her and thrash my arms. I wanted to scream at her and tell her to leave me alone. She was just trying to help, though. I nodded and let them take me to the edge of the woods.

"You'll be okay," said Harry. "You're in shock, Detective. We've known you a long time. Trust us. We're here to take care of you."

They led me to an ambulance, where a pair of paramedics checked my blood pressure and flashed a light in my eyes. They even gave me a bottle of water. More than anything else, that cold liquid calmed my racing heart. I may have lost it for a little while, but I was okay.

The ambulance's air conditioning cooled me off and allowed my mind to focus. While they tended to someone else, I slipped out and found Harry at the edge of the woods talking to a trooper from the Highway Patrol. Both looked at me as I approached.

"How are you feeling, Joe?" asked Harry.

"Better. Thank you," I said, drawing in a deep breath and trying to sound confident even though my legs felt weak. "Kurt Wilkinson and Stephan Kushnir covered a train car in tarps. They planned to kill somebody."

"Who?" he asked.

"I don't know," I said. "But we need to find out before Wilkinson finishes the job."

Chapter 32

I stayed at the crime scene for another three or four hours and led four different investigators through what had happened. All the while, I couldn't stop thinking about Nicole Bryant's family. Nicole didn't have superpowers, and she couldn't shake off fatal wounds, but she still risked and lost her life to protect other people. She died a hero in every sense of the word. Someone needed to tell them what had happened and why.

After hours of interviews and prodding by the medical staff, I turned my firearm over to a detective with the Highway Patrol and drove home. Harry and a minister from the local Methodist church had already stopped by Nicole's house to inform her family that she had died, so I'd go by in a couple of days when things had settled some.

Tonight was one of those nights that I most needed someone, but nobody came to the porch as my truck pulled into the driveway. Judging by the already brightening skyline, sunrise was about an hour away. I stripped off my clothes, showered with water so hot it turned my skin red and raw, and then slipped into the softest pajamas I owned. As I went to bed afterwards, I hugged my pillow and prayed the nightmares wouldn't be too bad.

With no one to wake me up, I slept until almost eleven the next morning. The sun poured through my windows, striking me in the face. My head hurt, and my body ached. Sleep had been a welcome respite, but the moment I opened my eyes, a weight pressed down on me again. I had been so self-absorbed at the crime scene I hadn't even asked about Sasquatch. I hoped he was alive.

As I swung my legs over the bed, birds sang outside my window. I liked wildlife, but today, I needed silence. I closed my eyes and took two deep breaths before standing and getting dressed. Half an hour after waking up, I left my house and drove downtown.

When I got to the station, I found a Cadillac sedan parked in the loading zone out front. Police officers parked there all the time when they had to run into the station for something quick, but it was rare to see a civilian with gall enough to park in a spot that even law enforcement officers tried to avoid for over five minutes at a time.

Trisha was at the front desk, talking on the phone when I walked inside. She smiled, but she was directing officers toward a car accident out by the interstate, limiting her ability to talk. I mouthed hello to her before taking the steps upstairs to my boss's office. The county had yet to appropriate funding to renovate the entire second floor of our station, so Harry was the only person with an office up there. He liked the solitude and the quiet. Today, voices carried up and down the hallway.

I followed the sound and found Councilman Rogers, Detective Delgado, and Harry outside his office, talking. All three men turned as I walked toward them. Councilman Rogers held out his hand for me to shake.

"Detective Court," he said, smiling as he took my hand and covered it with both of his own. "I hear congratulations are in order."

I glanced at Harry with my eyebrows raised before looking to Rogers.

"What have you heard?"

"That you closed your case," he said. "You got 'em. This Kushnir fellow and his friend Kurt Wilkinson. They killed that naked girl you found out at Ross Kelly Farms. I hope you understand that there are no hard feelings between us. Sometimes I let the emotion of the situation get to me."

I looked to Harry again, my brow furrowed. Then I looked at Rogers again.

"Why do you think Wilkinson and Kushnir killed Laura Rojas?"

Rogers looked to Detective Delgado.

"You think it's a coincidence that these two roll into town right after your victim goes down?" asked Delgado. "I don't. They killed Laura Rojas, and then they killed her boyfriend, Aldon McKenzie. Jennifer McKenzie probably got in the way, so they killed her, too."

"That's a good theory, I guess," I said, nodding, "but what evidence do you have?"

"Evidence is for trials, and there won't be one," said Rogers before Delgado could respond. "Kushnir died last night, and Wilkinson died this morning in a shootout with the State Highway Patrol. We have everything we need to close these cases. You don't need to harass anyone else, Detective."

"I'm not harassing anyone," I said. "I've been working a homicide, and I've been following the evidence. Back me up, Harry."

"Sheriff Grainger won't be with us too much longer. He's retiring with full honors," said Rogers, smiling as he put a hand on Delgado's shoulder. "As soon as we can swear him in, Detective Delgado will be your new boss."

Delgado's smile held more than a hint of malice.

"I hope that's not a problem for you, Detective," he said. "You weren't gunning for the job, were you?"

"No. I'm happy being a detective," I said, glancing from Harry and then to Councilman Rogers. I took a step back to give myself some space. "Let's back up a minute. Can you give me any reason to close my investigation of Laura Rojas? Other than that it upsets your clients."

Rogers's smile turned into a glower before returning to a malevolent grin.

"I'm a county councilman, and I don't have clients. I have constituents."

"No matter what you call them, they still pay your mortgage," I said, looking to Harry. "Step in here, please. You may be retiring, but you're still the sheriff. Act like it."

He looked down and scratched his brow. "At Councilman Rogers's suggestion, I'm using my stored personal leave to take a vacation until my retirement. You should direct your questions to my successor."

"Sheriff Grainger's going on a cruise," said Rogers, smiling and raising his eyebrows. "It was a little gift from St. Augustine County to commemorate his years of honorable service."

"Well, congratulations, Harry," I said. "A retirement and a cruise. You're making off like a bandit."

"I understand that you're upset about Officer Bryant's death, Detective, so I'll cut you some slack," said Rogers. "In the future, though, you would be wise to avoid speaking to your superiors with that insubordinate tone."

"Harry's on leave pending his retirement, so I wasn't talking to my superior in an insubordinate tone," I said. "You're a civilian, so you're not my superior officer, either. Detective Delgado, as superior as he thinks he is, still holds the same rank I do and does not supervise me. By definition, Councilman, I'm not insubordinate, although I appreciate your advice."

He narrowed his gaze. "You are clever, aren't you, young lady? Things are going to change around here. We might not have room for clever young ladies in our department too much longer."

"Fine," I said, raising my eyebrows. "Until you fire me, though, I have work to do."

"The Laura Rojas case," said Delgado, lowering his chin.

"Yes," I said, nodding. "I'm working the Laura Rojas case. Though I appreciate your theory about Kushnir and Wilkinson, I'd like to see evidence before I believe it."

"All right," said Roger. "I'm not an unreasonable man. I think that's a fine idea. Find evidence and close this case to your satisfaction."

"Thank you for your permission to do my job," I said. "I appreciate it."

He smiled that malevolent grin once more and put a hand on Delgado's shoulder again. "Sheriff Delgado and I have projects to discuss. The county cleared funds to renovate this old place, and we're talking about the future. And let me tell you, Detective Court, the future is looking up. St. Augustine's going to become the new Branson. We'll be an Orlando in the Midwest. I can see it now."

"How nice," I said. "I look forward to seeing what your brain trust comes up with for the building."

The smile slipped off his face. "I told you when we met before that you ought to smile more often. Men like women who smile occasionally. Might make for a more pleasant workplace."

"One of my colleagues died last night," I said. "Another is in the hospital. I don't even know whether he's alive. You'll forgive me, but I don't have a lot to smile about at the moment. Our soon-to-be sheriff should take heed and wipe the smirk off his face. He lost a colleague, too."

Delgado's lips tightened to a thin line.

"As you were, Detective," he said. "I'm sure you have better things to do than sit and chat with us."

"Yeah, I do," I said. I turned around and started toward the stairs. A pair of heavy footsteps followed as Delgado and Councilman Rogers continued speaking in hushed tones. As I reached the landing between the first and second floors, I turned and looked at Harry. "Something you want to tell me?"

"Sorry," he said. "Things happened fast last night."

"Seems like it," I said, crossing my arms. "So you're out and Delgado's in. You warned me, so I guess I shouldn't be surprised. Your timing sucks, though."

Harry leaned against the handrail and crossed his arms. "Nicole is dead. Preston is in the hospital. The doctors saved his life, but he lost a lung. He can't work in the field."

The anger I had felt earlier swelled until it made my skin feel hot.

"That doesn't excuse you quitting," I said. "You may not like the job, but you're a decent sheriff. Delgado will be a disaster."

"Councilman Rogers came to my office this morning with a letter signed by every county councilman. If I didn't quit, they planned to call an emergency meeting, where they'd hold a vote of no-confidence in my abilities as sheriff. They were going to fire me for getting Nicole Bryant killed and for allowing Preston to get shot. I'd lose my health insurance, my life insurance, and possibly my pension."

"You had nothing to do with Nicole's death or Sasquatch's injury."

"You think I don't know that?" asked Harry. He sighed disgustedly. "The County Council runs St. Augustine, and they take their marching orders from the people who pay their salaries. That's how it is, that's how it's always been, and that's how it'll be. You'd better get used to it because that's the world you live in."

I looked down. My hot anger had transformed into something cold and sharp.

"Do you even remember when you lost your balls?" I asked. "This is bullshit, and you know it. The guy I used to work with wasn't a coward."

"That's unfair, Joe," he said. "You walk a mile in my shoes, you'll find the world's a much bigger place than you realize."

"I know how much the world sucks, boss," I said. "I just wish you'd try to change it instead of running from it. Enjoy your cruise. You've earned it."

He opened his mouth to say something, but I turned and walked away before he could get a word out. I hurried to the first floor before anyone could stop me and then signed out a marked cruiser. Harry was my friend, and I cared about him, but this wasn't him talking. I'd apologize in time, but I had shit to do. Today was about Laura Rojas, Aldon McKenzie, and Jennifer McKenzie. Today was about the dead. Tomorrow, I'd worry about the future.

Chapter 33

I drove for two or three minutes and parked in front of Rise and Grind. It was late for morning coffee or pastries and too early for those who needed afternoon pick-me-ups, so it was empty. As I walked inside, Sheryl walked around the bar and pulled me into a hug. I rarely let people hug me, but sometimes I needed it. I squeezed her tight.

"A customer told me about Nicky," she said. "I'm so sorry. Are you okay?"

I nodded and took a step back. "Yeah. I'm okay. Thank you for the hug."

She squeezed my arm before walking around the counter to pour me a cup of coffee.

"I never met the other officer who got hurt, but is he okay?"

"He's alive," I said, taking the paper coffee cup from her outstretched hand. I reached for my purse to pay, but she shook her head. I nodded my thanks and took a sip. It was great coffee, but somehow it still tasted like sand in my mouth. "They airlifted him to St. Louis."

"I hope he pulls through."

"Me, too," I said, forcing myself to smile. "Thank you."

She gave me a sympathetic smile. I sat at a table in the front window and pulled out my cell phone. Trisha answered after two rings.

"Hey, it's Joe," I said. "Is Harry around?"

"He's cleaning his office out."

"Can you transfer my call?"

She sighed. "He doesn't want to talk to you. Everybody in the building heard your conversation upstairs."

I grimaced. "I shouldn't have called him a coward. That was wrong."

"You were rude, but you weren't wrong," she said. I looked down at the table and felt my gut twist. "Delgado will ruin this place."

"We'll see," I said. "He deserves a chance."

"You're more generous than I am," she said, drawing in a breath. "You didn't call to gossip, though. What do you need?"

"Information," I said. "Delgado thinks Wilkinson and Kushnir killed Laura Rojas. I'm not ready to jump on that bandwagon, but they came here to kill somebody. We get anywhere on that?"

She typed for a few moments and then hummed. "Best I can tell from their after-action reports, Ortega, Skelton, and Simpson knocked on doors in that area, but they were looking for Kurt Wilkinson. They didn't ask about anything else."

"Okay," I said, nodding. "I've got one more favor to ask you, and it might not be the easiest thing. I need you to find out who owns the houses near the woods where Preston was shot and whether the homeowners work at Reid Chemical."

"Okay," said Trisha, sounding unsure. "Why?"

"Because all of my victims have a connection to Reid Chemical. If a homeowner near the crime scene works for Reid Chemical, he or she might have been Wilkinson and Kushnir's target. You should be able to get the property records from the county assessor's website. Then you can look each person up. Check out LinkedIn, Facebook, and Twitter. If you can't find anything on those sites, search for them on Google. We might get lucky."

"I'll see what I can do," she said. "Are you coming back to the station soon, or do you want me to call you?"

"Call me," I said, picking up my coffee and standing. "After what I said to Harry, it's best if I stay away for a little while."

"All right," she said. "Good luck, Joe."

"You, too," I said, already leaving the shop. Since I was driving a marked police cruiser, people gave me a wide berth on the road. Trisha needed time to work, so I didn't hurry. When I reached the woods in which Nicole had died, twenty minutes had passed. It had been hours, but there were still two marked cruisers from the Highway Patrol, an unmarked black minivan, and two unmarked civilian sedans on the side of the road nearest the woods. I parked near them and flashed my badge to a uniformed trooper as he stepped out of the woods.

"I'm here to talk to the neighbors," I said.

"Good luck," he said.

I nodded my thanks and leaned against my cruiser to make a call. Trisha answered before her phone finished ringing once.

"It's Joe. Harry still locked up in his office?"

"He left," she said. "I looked up the neighbors. As best I can tell, the property on which Nicole was shot is owned by the Gable family. Trent Gable works in IT at Baptist Hospital in St. Louis, and his wife works in marketing at Purina in St. Louis. The residents across the street are teachers. The resident to the west is a minister at a Methodist church in Broward County, and her husband builds custom furniture. The only person with any connection to Reid Chemical lives about a quarter mile to the east. His name is Austin Wright, and he is a chemist."

I let my mind process that before nodding. "Aldon McKenzie was an accountant at Reid Chemical. They must have known each other."

"At least they worked in the same company," said Trisha. She gave me Austin Wright's address and wished me luck. I got back in my cruiser and drove for two or three minutes until I reached a white Garrison Colonial home. It had a red swing in the front yard and nice trees at the corners of the building. I parked in the driveway, walked up the bluestone walkway to the front door, and rang the doorbell. A woman roughly my age answered within a minute. Despite it being the middle of the afternoon, she wore a pink terrycloth bathrobe and no makeup.

"Yes?" she asked, raising her eyebrows. Her voice was sharp and almost angry. A toddler called out for juice somewhere in the house. She softened her voice, turned, and said she'd be there in a minute. I smiled at her once she looked at me again.

"Hi, I'm Detective Joe Court with the St. Augustine County Sheriff's Department. Is this a bad time?"

She closed her eyes and sighed.

"No, but that doesn't matter. What do you want?"

"I need to speak with Austin Wright," I said.

"He's not here."

It was the middle of a workday, so he was probably at the plant.

"Does he still work at Reid Chemical?"

She scoffed and turned her head before shrugging.

"I don't know," she said. "He didn't tell me when he left."

My heart rate kicked up a notch.

"When did your husband leave?"

She raised her eyebrows. "That's none of your business."

"Normally, it wouldn't be. In this case, it is," I said. "When did he leave?"

She rolled her eyes and crossed her arms.

"A few days ago. He wrote me a note while I was at work and the kids were at daycare. He said he was running off with some skank he met on the internet. As an apology, he said he was leaving us a houseboat he had bought in Branson. He suggested we sell it and pay off the house. What kind of a loser buys a houseboat and runs out on his kids and his pregnant wife? I work in a nail salon. Even if I sell his stupid houseboat, how the hell am I going to take care of three kids on my salary?"

I couldn't answer that, so I ignored the question and furrowed my brow.

"Is the name Aldon McKenzie familiar?"

She nodded. "He works with Austin. Don't ask me what they did because I don't know."

"Someone murdered Aldon and his wife," I said. "Have you heard of Laura Rojas?"

This time, she blinked. Her expression softened, and she gave me a thoughtful, lingering look before shaking her head.

"No. I don't know her. Why would someone kill Aldon and Jennifer? And what happened to Daria? She was a sweet little girl."

"Daria's okay," I said. "She's with her grandparents. We're still working on Aldon and Jennifer's murders. So you don't know Laura Rojas?"

"No. Who is she?"

"She's an attorney," I said. "Aldon hired her. She was investigating Reid Chemical, although we're still not sure what was going on there. Have you heard the names Stephan Kushnir or Kurt Wilkinson?"

She shook her head and looked down.

"I don't think so," she said, her voice soft. "What's going on?"

"Kushnir and Wilkinson died in a shootout about a quarter of a mile from here. A couple of people in my department think they killed Laura, Aldon, and Jennifer, although we can't prove that yet."

Her expression shifted from one of confusion to concern as she crossed her arms and took a step back.

"What the hell is going on?"

"Kushnir and Wilkinson worked for a Ukrainian gang in Chicago. They were professional hitters, and they came here to do a job. How much did your husband's houseboat cost?"

She looked taken aback for a second, but then she drew in a breath.

"I don't know. Why?"

"Houseboats aren't cheap. He got the money for it somewhere."

She stood straighter. "What are you accusing us of?"

"I'm not accusing you of anything," I said. "I'm trying to put together pieces. So far, I've got a dead accountant who worked for a pharmaceutical company, a dead attorney who investigated that company, and a presumably expensive houseboat. I've also got two dead Ukrainian gangsters who worked for an organization that bought and sold drugs."

Her face grew pale.

"Are you saying my husband sold drugs?"

"Is that a possibility?"

She reached for the door.

"It's time for you to leave, Detective."

"Those Ukrainians might have been here to kill you," I said. "They died near your house. A police officer died saving your life. A second officer was shot and lost a lung."

She blinked before looking down. "I have to go."

She didn't shut the door, so I kept talking. "Where is your husband?"

"He left me," she said. "That's all I know."

There was more to it than that, so I reached for my purse for a business card. Unfortunately, she shut the door in my face before I could give it to her. I almost knocked again, but that wouldn't get me anywhere. Instead, I put the card into the mailbox beside her door. I doubted she'd call, but it wouldn't hurt to give her the chance.

As I walked back to my car, I called Trisha again.

"Hey, Trisha," I said. "I visited the home of Austin Wright. He's missing."

"You think he's dead?"

"I don't know, but there's something shady going on at Reid Chemical. Dead or alive, Austin Wright's knee deep in shit. Put together an APB on him and send it to the Highway Patrol. We need this guy brought in alive."

"I'll put that together," she said.

"Thank you. If possible, keep this quiet. I don't want Delgado knowing what I'm up to. He and his buddy Councilman Rogers are too likely to stop me."

"What are you doing, Joe?"

I opened my cruiser's door and sat down. "I have no idea, but the more I work, the more I think I'll shut down the largest employer in the county before I'm done."

Chapter 34

I left the Wrights' house and drove back to town. After a few minutes of driving, I pulled off the road in the parking lot of a gas station off Highway 62 and Googled Kevin Rasmussen, Logan Reid's attorney. Once I found his office number, I called and spoke to his receptionist, who patched me through to his cell phone.

"Mr. Rasmussen, this is Detective Joe Court. I was hoping to talk to Logan Reid today."

"Give me a second to check my schedule, Detective," he said. He paused for a moment. When he returned, his voice sounded almost chipper. "I can set up a meeting for the first of next month. How does that sound?"

"That sounds like you're trying to piss me off," I said. "I need to talk to Mr. Reid, and I need to talk to him today."

"Mr. Stewart is a busy man. He's unavailable until the first of next month."

"I don't need to talk to Mr. Stewart. I need to talk to Logan Reid. Can you make that happen? If not, I'll arrest him."

"On what charges?"

"I'll think of something along the way," I said.

"I don't appreciate your attempt at humor."

I nodded and crossed my left hand across my chest. "I'm sorry to hear that. I need to meet with Logan Reid. Can you set that up?"

"Mr. Stewart isn't available until the first of next month."

I gritted my teeth so I wouldn't snap at him.

"As I've told you, I have no interest in talking to Mr. Stewart," I said. "I need to speak to Logan Reid. Is he available today?"

"You won't talk to Mr. Reid without Mr. Stewart present."

I sighed and nodded.

"I get it. Stewart doesn't trust his stepson, so he wants to be in the room when I talk to him."

"I won't dignify that statement with a response."

"Stewart must be sweating," I said. "How many people has he taken out so far, anyway? Three? Four?"

"Goodbye, Detective," said the lawyer. "We won't be cooperating any further."

"You weren't cooperating anyway, so we're cool."

He hung up before I said anything else. I didn't mind. This was a courtesy call. I put my cruiser in gear and drove to Waterford College, where I parked by the school's Public Safety Office. The officer behind the counter raised an eyebrow when I walked in.

"Detective," she said, nodding. "What can I do for you?"

"I need to see Logan Reid," I said.

"Business or personal?" she asked.

"Business," I said. "I need to ask him about his stepfather's company."

She typed at her computer. Then she glanced up at me.

"We've been fielding complaints from alumni and parents for the past two days because of you. The Sigma Iota fraternity has a lot of friends in this area."

I leaned against the counter. "I'm sorry that happened. It wasn't my intent."

She glanced up from the computer. "I'm supposed to call a guy named Kevin Rasmussen if you come by here again. My boss was insistent on that."

"Mr. Rasmussen is an attorney who represents Logan's stepfather."

She nodded before looking at her screen.

"I don't like lawyers," she said. "Logan's in a philosophy class in Rollins Hall. Room 214. I didn't give you that information, though, and if you tell anyone I did, I'll deny it. Please don't pull any fire alarms or ask us to evacuate a building today."

"I'll do my best," I said. "Thank you, Officer."

She looked back to her computer, and I left the small office. I checked out a map of the campus posted outside the Public Safety Office and walked to the classroom building she had mentioned. The interior of Rollins Hall was cold, so goosebumps formed on my arms beneath my shirt. My footsteps carried down the hallways.

Logan's classroom was on the second floor. An older woman stood at a lectern in front of the room, answering questions. I knocked on the door. A dozen pairs of eyes turned to me. Logan drew in a surprised breath.

"Can I help you?" asked the professor.

"Sorry to interrupt, but I need to see Mr. Reid," I said. "He knows what this is about."

The professor looked to her student and raised her eyebrows. "Get a move on, Logan. I'd like to continue my lecture."

Logan stood and hurried out the room. The professor gave me a hard, cold stare before continuing to speak. It didn't make me miss school one bit.

"Am I under arrest?" asked Logan, once he reached the hallway.

"No," I said. "I'm here to talk."

"In that case, I'm going back to class," he said. "My stepfather told me not to talk to you without my lawyer."

"Your stepfather doesn't give a shit about you, and your lawyer's paid to look after your stepfather's interests," I said. "They will douse you in gasoline and light you on fire if it benefits them in the least. You can let them do that, or you and I can talk. Your choice. I don't give a shit at this point. So what's it going to be? Help yourself or help your stepfather?"

"I don't know anything," he said. I nodded and walked.

"Then I won't keep you long," I said. "We'll talk in my car."

He said nothing, but he followed me out of the building and to the parking lot in which I had parked. Once we reached my car, I opened the rear door for him and told him to scoot all the way over so I had somewhere to sit.

"I won't bullshit you," I said upon sitting down. "I'm looking at you for Laura Rojas's murder. Did you kill her?"

He looked down and shook his head. "No."

"Did your stepfather?"

Before answering, he hesitated and shook his head.

"No."

"You sure about that?" I asked. "Because I've found a lot of ties between your stepfather and my victims. Laura was using you. Those nude pictures she texted you weren't her. If you'd slept with her, you'd know that."

"You're lying. She liked me."

"Kid, the girl in your pictures had a tattoo on her rib cage. Laura didn't. She was using you. Did you give her documents?"

"I didn't kill her," he said, his face red as he looked down at his hands.

"Prove it," I said. "She died Saturday night. Where were you?"

"Writing a paper in my room," he said. "Alone."

"Can anyone confirm that?"

"No," he said. "I live on the third floor in a single room. I don't share it with anybody."

"Did anybody see you in your room?"

"No," he said. "I don't make a big deal about it when I go upstairs."

"So your alibi is that you were alone in your room," I said. He nodded. "That's not going to work."

"There are surveillance cameras on every exit," he said. "I went in after dinner at six. Then I stayed in all night. I can't have killed her if I was inside all night."

I couldn't argue with that, so I nodded.

"Where can I see this video?"

"Public Safety Office. They watch everything."

I didn't know whether I believed him, but I nodded again.

"Go back to class," I said. "I'll check out the video."

He left. I wasn't sure what to think. Everywhere I turned with this case, I found smoke and mirrors. This was getting old. I walked to the Office of Public Safety and told the officer at the reception desk what I needed. She called one of the other officers to watch the front desk, and we walked to a small room with four television monitors mounted on the walls. Those cameras allowed them to watch every building on campus. I wondered whether the students knew how well the school spied on them.

I told the officer what I needed, and she spooled up the correct video. The Sigma Iota fraternity had security cameras on each of its four exits. The officer put one camera view on each of the monitors and gave me a paddle that allowed me to speed up, slow down, or stop the video.

It took almost two hours, but I reviewed every frame shot between 6 PM on Saturday and 10 AM on Sunday. As Logan said, he entered the building a little after six and didn't leave until nine the next morning. I pushed back from the table and rubbed my eyes.

Laura had strung Logan along and even sent him nude pictures of another girl to keep him interested in her. She'd manipulated him and used him to get something she wanted. More than anyone I had seen so far, Logan had a reason to want her dead, and he was the only person I had investigated so far who couldn't have done it.

Every lead I found left me banging my head against the wall. I still didn't know what was going on at Reid Chemical, but too many people had gotten hurt because of it. I needed to wrap this up and make some arrests. I just wished I knew how to do that.

Chapter 35

After wasting the afternoon at Waterford College, I needed good news.

I didn't get it.

I drove back to my station and parked in the lot. Almost the moment I opened my door, though, my cell phone buzzed. It was my vet. I closed my eyes as the strength left my arms and legs. He had asked me to stop by and talk about Roger, but I had forgotten. I ran a hand across my brow to wipe away sweat before answering.

"Dr. Johnson, it's Joe Court. Sorry I didn't call earlier. I've been busy at work."

"That's all right," he said, his voice subdued. "Are you free to talk for a minute?"

I swallowed a lump in my throat. "Please tell me Roger didn't die while I was at work."

"He's alive, but he's not drinking or eating. We ran a blood profile and urinalysis on him. Roger has anemia, and his electrolyte levels are abnormal. We ran an ultrasound yesterday to check out his kidneys. They're very small for a dog his size, which—along with his other symptoms—is indicative of chronic renal failure. I'm sorry, but we need to talk about his end of life, and the sooner we talk, the better."

I blinked but said nothing.

"Are you still there, Detective?" he asked after a pause.

"Yeah," I said, my voice a low rasp. It was all I could get out. "I'm here."

"If you'd like to come by, he's awake and alert," said the vet. "This would be a good time to tell him goodbye. He's in a lot of pain. We can talk about the procedure when you get here."

Procedure. It was such a cold, clinical word. It didn't convey what would happen.

"Can I take him home?" I asked. "I can give him a shot or whatever it takes."

The vet hesitated. "It would be kinder if we did it here without moving him."

I closed my eyes and nodded. My throat was tight, and my lip quivered.

"All right," I said. "I'm on my way."

I hung up and drove. When I got to the vet's office, Roger lay on his side on a big pillow. He licked his lips and thumped his tail once when he saw me, but he didn't lift his head. His eyes looked glassy. He didn't seem to know where he was, but he recognized me. For the next hour, I held his head in my lap and told him how much he had brought to my life and how much I loved him.

And then I told him goodbye.

I didn't cry in the office. For the moment, my case didn't matter. I had other things on my mind. After the vet and his assistant wheeled Roger away, I drove home and grabbed a shovel. I dug until my arms and back ached and every muscle of my body screamed at me to stop. Then I kept going until my aches turned to pain and I couldn't move my arms. As the moon rose and the stars appeared, I stopped digging.

The hole was about five feet deep and four feet around. It was big enough for Roger to rest in. I climbed out of it and sat on the edge. The tears came as I looked into the cold, dark earth. I drew from the silence around me and allowed the solitude to creep into my bones.

I didn't like being alone. For years, I had pushed everybody away when they tried to draw close. In my mind, that had made me strong, but it wasn't strength that had persuaded me to keep the world at bay. It was fear. Roger had been hurt, too, but he loved me with reckless abandon even when I didn't love myself. I could never thank him enough for everything he had brought to my life.

A big part of me wanted to drink until I stopped hurting. Booze usually helped me cope. Tonight, I didn't want to run from the pain. I wanted to experience it. I wanted to remember my friend, but I didn't want to be alone.

My hands trembled as I called my mom. She answered on the second ring.

"Hey, Joe," she said, her voice light. "I didn't expect to hear from you. How are you doing?"

"I've had a bad day," I said. "I needed to hear a friendly voice."

"Everything okay?"

I thought about Roger and about my empty house. Part of me wanted to tell her everything was fine and to cut the call short so I could get the vodka from my freezer and drink. I didn't, though. Instead, I did something I hated doing.

"No, it's not okay. Do you havc a minute? I need to talk."

***

It was two in the morning when my phone rang. My eyes refused to focus, and my back and arms still ached from digging Roger's grave. I rolled over and turned on a light on my nightstand before grabbing the phone. According to my caller ID, it was the front desk at my station.

I rubbed my eyes as the phone rang a third time. Then I ran my finger across the screen to answer.

"Yeah?" I said, my voice low.

"Sorry to wake you up, Joe," said Jason Zuckerburg, our night dispatcher. "We've got a shooting at Waterford College. Delgado's in charge, but he asked for you."

"Okay," I said, sighing. Jason wouldn't have called me in the middle of the night for a normal shooting. Something was up. "Was Logan Reid involved?"

"No," he said, his voice low. "This involved a young woman named June Wellman."

My stomach crashed into my feet. I closed my eyes.

"He shot her, didn't he?" I asked, my voice low.

"No, she shot a boy named Chad Hamilton," he said. "You should get over there. She was asking for you."

"Okay," I said. "Tell Delgado I'll be there as soon as I can."

My head sunk into my pillows after I hung up.

"Shit."

I dressed and headed out. The college streets were empty, and I didn't know where I was going until I saw the police cars outside the Sigma Iota fraternity. There were probably a hundred young people in pajamas on the front lawn of the dorm next door. I parked about half a block away and jogged toward the scene.

Bob Reitz and Tracy Carruthers, two of our uniformed officers on the night shift, were stretching crime-scene tape around trees to erect a perimeter. They must have just gotten there. I nodded hello to them both.

"Hey," I said. "Is Delgado around?"

Bob pointed toward the police cruisers.

"Thanks," I said, already turning and hurrying away. As I approached the cruisers, Delgado stepped out of the backseat of one and walked toward me, a scowl on his face.

"Hey," I said. "Dispatch called, so I'm here. What's going on?"

"You tell me," he said, crossing his arms. "Girl only wants to talk to you."

"I know her," I said. "What's the story here?"

Delgado looked toward the fraternity house and pulled a notepad from his pocket. He licked his lips.

"Campus police received reports of shots fired in the Sigma Iota fraternity house at ten after one this morning. They arrived at the house within moments to find dozens of men and women running through the front doors. They corralled the students and called us for assistance.

"Bob Reitz got here at 1:14 AM. Tracy Carruthers got here at 1:16 AM. While campus security dealt with the crowd outside, Bob and Tracy cleared the building's interior. They sent a couple more kids out before coming across the crime scene on the third floor. There, they found a young woman named June Wellman holding a Ruger EC9 pistol. A young man named Chad Hamilton lay on a couch. He had a gunshot wound to the forehead."

A knot grew in my stomach, and I swore under my breath. Delgado cleared his throat.

"You got something to say?" he asked.

"Chad raped her a few days ago," I said. "Let me talk to her. I'll see what's going on."

"You sure you can remain objective?"

I narrowed my gaze at him. "What's that supposed to mean?"

"Someone raped June, and she shot the guy," said Delgado, blinking. "Someone raped you when you were a teenager, and you shot the guy. The parallels are obvious."

I balled my hands into fists in my jean pockets and counted to five in my head before responding.

"I see the parallels, and I understand where you're coming from," I said. "If you want me to talk to her, I will. If you want me to go home, I will. I'll do my job gladly and to the best of my abilities, but you don't get to call me to a crime scene in the middle of the night so you can question my professionalism in front of our colleagues."

Officers Reitz and Carruthers looked away, both trying to seem busy. Delgado's eyes narrowed as I crossed my arms.

"We'll talk about this later," he said. "For now, talk to the shooter. Get me a confession."

"Will do, boss," I said, walking to the cruiser he had just exited. June Wellman sat in the backseat crying. Since I didn't know what had happened, I didn't know how I felt about her at the moment. They had cuffed her hands in front of her. A hair tie held her brunette hair behind her head. She looked tiny in that car. I opened the door and sat beside her. "You okay to talk?"

She nodded, so I shut my door and sighed. I didn't look at her as I ran a hand across my brow.

"So you shot him," I said.

She nodded, and I closed my eyes and swore in my head.

"Okay," I said, reaching into my purse for my phone. I opened a recording app and put my phone on the seat between us. "Before you say anything else, I need you to listen. June Wellman, you are under arrest for the shooting death of Chad Hamilton. You have certain rights. First, you have the right to remain silent. You don't have to talk to anyone. If you choose to talk to me, the prosecutors can use anything you tell me against you in court. You have the right to have an attorney anytime a law enforcement officer interviews you. If you or your family has an attorney, I can call him now and have him come down. If you can't afford an attorney, the court will provide one for you free of charge. Bearing those rights in mind, do you want to talk with me right now?"

I wanted her to say no, but she nodded again.

"I need you to acknowledge your rights aloud," I said.

She nodded once more and cleared her throat.

"Yes," she said. "I want to talk."

I glanced out the window to see George Delgado talking to Bob Reitz on the periphery of the crime scene.

"In your own words, tell me what happened tonight."

"I shot him in the head because he deserved it."

"Okay," I said, trying to think how I should best approach this. "Why did you shoot him?"

Her eyes locked onto mine. They almost pleaded.

"Because of you. I did it because of what you did."

All at once, a heavy weight pressed down on my chest.

"Let's take a step back. Tell it to me from the beginning."

Chapter 36

June's story was simple and tragic. After she and I shared my dinner in front of the Waterford College entrance, she looked me up and read dozens of articles about what had happened to me. She learned that after he got out of prison, Christopher Hughes—my rapist—came to my house. He tried to kill me and might have succeeded had Roger not been there. Instead, I killed him. June thought that made me a hero.

She tried to move on with her life as I had told her, but it was hard to move on when she saw her rapist every day on campus—especially when she saw him with another girl. He had his arm draped across her shoulders, and he smiled at her the same way he had smiled at June.

When she saw that, she said, something within her broke. She said she knew he'd rape her, too. Maybe she was right, but it didn't matter. Since I couldn't put him in prison, she decided she'd take care of the problem.

She went to a sporting goods store in St. Louis and bought a gun. Then, she took it to campus and sneaked into Chad's room at his fraternity. She told him she was sorry and that she wanted to make amends for lying to the police about him.

They watched a movie and had drinks. At eleven, she slipped three Rohypnol pills into his beer. Once he fell asleep, she shot him in the forehead. It was as cold-blooded a murder as I had ever seen. Once she finished speaking, I turned off the recording app on my phone and looked at her.

"I don't know what to say," I said, shaking my head. "You murdered him."

"He would have raped his new girlfriend. I did the right thing."

"No, you didn't," I said. "If his new girlfriend's safety worried you, you should have called me. I would have spoken to her. Your sorority sisters could have spoken to her. You could have warned her about the guy she was dating. You had options. Instead, you shot him. Get a lawyer, June. You need one."

I threw open my door and stepped out. My skin felt both warm and cold. Muscles all over my body had grown tight. I wanted to run and run. Overriding all my anger and my disappointment, though, I felt a profound sense of wrongness.

Delgado came toward me with his eyebrows raised.

"Well?" he asked.

"I got your confession," I said. "She picked up the gun yesterday from a store in St. Louis. Then she sneaked into Chad's fraternity, drugged him, and shot him when he fell asleep."

"Tell me you recorded this confession."

I nodded. "It's on my phone. I'll send you the file. Before letting her talk, I explained her Miranda rights. She acknowledged them and agreed to talk anyway. You should have everything you need to charge her with murder with special circumstances."

Delgado opened his eyes wide.

"You think we should go for the death penalty," he said, lowering his chin and smiling just a little. "This girl must have pissed you off."

"She planned this," I said. "She drugged him and murdered him in his sleep."

Delgado nodded before holding out his hand.

"I owe you an apology," he said. "You did good today."

I shook his hand. "Thank you, but I was just doing my job. I'll go by the Public Safety Office. The fraternity has surveillance cameras on every entrance to the building. We should be able to see her sneaking in."

Delgado whistled and then shook his head before looking to the fraternity.

"This is a bad place to murder your boyfriend," he said.

"He wasn't her boyfriend," I said.

He wished me luck and then walked toward the fraternity. Waterford College owned several thousand acres around St. Augustine County, but its actual campus was small. It only took a few minutes to walk from the fraternity house to the

Public Safety Office. The night air cleared my head, allowing the shock of the shooting to wear off.

I knocked on the door before pulling it open and sticking my head inside. The man behind the counter wore khaki pants and a polo shirt with the college's logo stitched across the breast. He was tall and had a medium build with gray hair swept to the right. Acne scars pockmarked his face, making him look older than he was. He stood up as I walked in.

"I'm Rusty Peterson," he said, shaking my hand. "I'm the director of Public Safety."

"Detective Joe Court. St. Augustine County Sheriff's Department. Are you a sworn officer, Director Peterson, or are you a college administrator?"

"Bit of both," he said. "I spent twenty years with the St. Louis Metropolitan Police. My badge says captain."

"Enjoying your retirement?" I asked.

"Until tonight," he said, drawing in a deep breath. "We haven't had a murder on campus in forty years."

"I need to see the surveillance footage from the Sigma Iota house tonight."

He lowered his chin. "We don't have cameras inside the building, so we didn't capture the murder."

"Not a problem," I said, nodding. "I talked to the shooter, and now I'm trying to verify her story. She said she snuck into the house at eleven. Based on what I've seen of the surveillance cameras around here, it should be on video."

He nodded and motioned for me to follow him around the counter.

“Chad Hamilton was a jerk, but he didn’t deserve to be shot in his sleep.”

“June didn’t deserve to be raped,” I said. “Nobody’s walking away a winner on this one.”

Peterson nodded as we entered the surveillance room. “I left the city so I wouldn’t deal with this kind of shit.”

“You’re preaching to the choir, my friend,” I said, nodding toward the four video monitors on the wall. “If you don’t mind, spool up the video of the Sigma Iota house from nine this evening until now.”

He pulled out a chair from beneath the table near the monitors. I did likewise and sat beside him. We spent an hour watching the film at high speed. From nine to ten, two dozen people entered and left the fraternity. Chad Hamilton came in with a group of men at 9:43 PM. From ten to eleven, the number of people coming in slackened. From eleven to midnight, two young men came in, and both swayed and stumbled as if they were drunk. June didn’t make it onto surveillance once, and Chad didn’t leave.

Peterson looked at me. “You sure your victim came in during this time frame?”

“She said she came in at about eleven,” I said.

“We can rewind,” he said. “She could have gotten the times confused.”

"I think we've looked at enough film," I said. "I'll go talk to her. Thank you, Mr. Peterson."

He nodded, and I left the small office. Back at the Sigma Iota house, the crowds had thinned, as had the police presence. Now, only three police cars and a hearse remained. Sam, Dr. Sheridan's assistant, nodded as I walked to the crime scene.

"Is this your case, Detective?" he asked.

"No, George Delgado's working it," I said. "I'm just assisting. Is Delgado still around?"

"He left about fifteen minutes ago with your suspect."

Delgado was moving things along. Not that I blamed him. June confessed, and we had more than enough corroborating evidence to send her to death row. I thanked Sam and then headed for my truck. It didn't take long to reach the station. Jason gave me a halfhearted smile from the front desk as I walked inside.

"Morning, Joe," he said. "Sorry again for waking you up."

"No problem," I said, hurrying past him toward the bullpen. "Where's Delgado?"

"With Shaun Deveraux in Harry's office."

I nodded and jogged toward the stairwell. The second floor didn't have many working lights, so I had to go along by feel until I saw light spilling out from beneath Harry's door. I knocked before opening the door.

"Detective Delgado, Mr. Deveraux," I said, nodding to both men. Delgado nodded and waved me in.

"We were just talking about what to charge Ms. Wellman with," said Delgado.

"Her rape accusation will make things hard," said Deveraux. "You said you got her confession on tape?"

"Yeah," I said, reaching for my purse. I hesitated before turning on my recording. "There's one problem. She's lying."

Delgado rolled his eyes and sighed. "How did I know this would happen?"

Deveraux held up a hand to keep him from speaking. "What'd she lie about?"

"Getting into the house," I said. "I looked at the security footage. She said she snuck in at about eleven, but she didn't show up on any of the college's surveillance footage."

"Isn't it possible she avoided the cameras?" asked Delgado.

"No," I said, shaking my head. "They're well positioned. Even if she slipped in through an open window, the cameras would have caught her walking toward the building."

"Officers found her with the gun in her hand," said Deveraux. "Could she have come in earlier?"

"Possibly," I said. "I'd like to ask her."

"You think she's lying and covering for somebody else?" asked Deveraux, crossing his arms.

"I doubt it, but who knows?" I said. "Let me talk to her."

Deveraux looked to Delgado. "It's your case. What do you want to do, George?"

He planted his hands on his hips and narrowed his eyes at me.

"You backdoor me, I won't forget."

"I pulled a confession out of a murder suspect who wouldn't even talk to you," I said, speaking slowly so he wouldn't misunderstand me. "I made this case for you. You don't like me—I get it—but that's your problem, not mine. I'm just trying to do my job. Are you going to let me, or are you going to stand in my way because you're threatened by me?"

Delgado sighed and then crossed his arms. "Fine. Talk to her. I'll be watching on video."

"Thank you," I said. I left before either man responded. Our interrogation booths were on the first floor. At one time, they had been storage closets, but we had enlarged and secured them. Now, they had sophisticated surveillance equipment hidden in the walls and locks that could have caged an enraged gorilla. They worked well for our purposes.

When I got downstairs, I found June Wellman sitting on a bench in the bullpen. Someone had cuffed her hands in front of her and shackled her feet to a ring embedded in the floor. I unhooked her and led her to a booth. There, I turned on my cell phone's recording app and sat across from her at a metal table bolted to the floor.

"Thank you for talking earlier. I'm here to follow-up on that conversation. Same rules apply here that did there. You don't have to answer my questions, but if you do, we can use what you say against you in court. You can also have a lawyer here. Do you want one?"

She swallowed and shook her head.

"I fucked up, didn't I?" she asked.

"You sure did," I said. "You can't make that right, but you can help yourself by answering my questions. Given everything that happened to you, the more honest you are, the better. They won't drop the charges against you, but a judge might be more lenient at sentencing. Your lawyer will explain your options, so make sure you get a good one."

She nodded and looked at her hands. "Thanks."

"That's assuming you haven't been lying," I said, raising my eyebrows. "If you've been lying, they'll put a needle in your arm."

Her eyes shot to mine.

"Why would I lie about this? Chad raped me, and then I shot him so he wouldn't hurt anyone else. It was awful."

"When did you sneak into his house?"

"Like I told you," she said, wiping tears from her eyes. "It was a little before eleven. I remember because my roommate wanted our room at eleven so she could hook up with her boyfriend."

"I pulled the surveillance video from the fraternity house from nine to almost two in the morning. You didn't go in at eleven."

She shook her head. "I'm not lying."

"What door did you go through?"

She said nothing for a few seconds, so I repeated the question.

"I didn't use a door," she said. "I went through the tunnel."

"What does that mean?"

"It's a secret entrance. The brothers use it as part of their initiation. Chad told me about it so I could sneak in during special events when girls weren't supposed to be in the house. I didn't think they'd let me through the main door."

I raised my eyebrows and cocked my head to the side. "And where is this secret entrance?"

"The rear parking lot. There's a drainage system that runs beneath the whole campus. The house has a storm drain in the basement big enough for people to climb up. The brothers use it to smuggle in kegs for parties."

This was interesting for more reasons than she realized. I stood up.

"I'll check this tunnel out. Thank you. Remember what I said: get a lawyer," I said, hurrying toward the front desk. June said something as I hurried away, but I couldn't hear her. Jason, the night dispatcher, was typing something as I reached the desk, but he stopped when he saw I needed to talk to him. "Tell Shaun Deveraux and Detective Delgado that I'm going to the college to check something out. Ms. Wellman is in an interrogation booth. They should take her to a cell."

Jason furrowed his brow, but he nodded anyway. "Will do, Detective. Good luck."

I ran to my truck and checked the flashlight I kept in the glove box to make sure its batteries worked. It was time to go exploring.

Chapter 37

The parking lot behind the Sigma Iota house was large enough to hold cars for every resident of both the fraternity and the dorm next door. I parked my old truck near the back and followed the asphalt's slope to a ditch. In one direction, it led to a large basin that was still soggy with rain from the previous week. The other end led to a large, stone culvert that ran beneath the parking lot and straight toward the Sigma Iota fraternity.

I turned on my flashlight. It was six in the morning, and the sun peeked over the horizon. No one watched me, so I crept forward. The culvert was about five feet tall from floor to base, so I didn't need to crouch far. Moss, gravel, and grit covered the floor inside. The air was fetid and thick. I tightened the beam on my light, but even then, I couldn't see the end of the tunnel.

I walked for a hundred yards before finding a small shoot to the right, which ended about twenty feet from the main branch. Those enterprising Sigma Iota brothers had left an aluminum stepladder to allow unseen access to their home. I climbed up and pushed a heavy metal grate out of the way but stayed inside the lip of the pipe so I could flash my light around.

The tunnel ended in an expansive laundry room with concrete walls, exposed pipes near the ceiling, and eight washers and dryers. Heaps of clothes covered every table, chair, and flat surface in the room, while empty laundry detergent containers decorated two of the room's corners. The room smelled like gym socks and mold. I pulled myself up the rest of the way and pushed the grate back over the hole.

Though I hadn't searched this part of the house, I found the stairwell to the first floor quickly. Dr. Sheridan, his assistant Sam, and Officer Tracy Carruthers were in the lobby. Sam saw me first and nodded hello. That caused Tracy and Dr. Sheridan to turn around.

"Detective," said Tracy, stepping forward with her brow furrowed. "I didn't realize you were in the building."

"I wasn't until a moment ago," I said. "There's a tunnel in the basement that leads to the parking lot. I'm guessing none of the brothers mentioned that when you interviewed them."

"Sure didn't," said Tracy.

"I'm tired of people holding back on me," I said. I focused on Tracy. "You guys need anything?"

She shook her head. "We'll be here for a while longer, but we're good."

"Great," I said, already hurrying past them to leave the building. Classes wouldn't start for another couple of hours, but already there were young men and women out and about. I drove back to my station, where the morning exodus had begun as the evening shift left and the day shift arrived. Half a dozen uniformed officers nodded hello before returning to their conversations in the lobby as I stepped inside.

I walked to the front desk. Jason was behind it, but he was yawning as he logged out of the computer.

"Trisha around?"

He glanced up at me. "She's in the locker room. Something I can help you with?"

I considered and shook my head. "It's a woman thing."

He nodded as if he understood. "Whatever it is, good luck."

I nodded and smiled before turning toward the rest of the lobby. Even with Harry on vacation, there'd be a roll call meeting in the bullpen in about ten minutes to go over the day's assignments and to go over the previous night's events. I didn't want to deal with Delgado, so I planned to skip it.

Trisha sauntered up the stairs from the women's locker room in the basement and smiled at me.

"Hey, Joe," she said. "I'm going to get coffee. You want something?"

"No, but I need to talk to you," I said.

"Okay," she said, a concerned look on her face. She looked to Jason, who was still manning the dispatcher's station. "Anything I should know about this morning?"

"Line four was fuzzy last night," he said, slipping around the counter. "If it gets bad, we need to call somebody."

"I'll bear that in mind," she said. "Have a good one, Jason."

"You, too," he said. He left, and I looked to Trisha.

"I need advice about a baby."

She opened her eyes wide and leaned forward on the counter.

"Tell me everything."

"It's for a case," I said. The eager smile on her face slipped away, and she reached for her rolling office chair to sit down.

"Oh," she said. "You're not pregnant. That's okay, too. What's going on?"

"I'm working the Laura Rojas case, but I'm running into walls every where I turn. Laura didn't talk to people. When she died, she was pregnant. So far, I've talked to her mom, her neighbors, her co-worker, and a few friends. Nobody knew she was pregnant."

Trisha looked thoughtful before nodding.

"This was her first pregnancy?"

"I think so," I said. "Her mom claimed she was a virgin and would remain so until her wedding night."

Trisha laughed and smiled as she drew in a breath.

"My mom assumed the same thing when I was young."

"I've never been pregnant, but it's supposed to be exciting. She would have told someone, wouldn't she?"

Trisha curled her lip into a thoughtful frown before shaking her head.

"When I was pregnant with Morgan, I didn't tell my friends until I was twelve weeks along. After the first trimester, the chance of a miscarriage drops. You don't want to tell people you're pregnant and then tell them two weeks later that you're not. A miscarriage is hard enough as is."

"You wouldn't even tell your mom?"

Trisha's lips curled upwards into a faint smile. "My mom and I didn't get along well. If she had found out I was pregnant before Graham and I were married, she would have dragged me to church and waterboarded me in the baptismal font until I repented for my sinful ways. Once I had a ring on my finger, she was fine with it, but before then, she might have cut Graham's penis off."

I sighed. "Sorry. I didn't mean to pry."

"You're not prying. And it's fine. Mom and I made up before she died. She always wanted what was best for me, even if I didn't agree with it."

I rubbed my eyes and nodded before sighing.

"I'm getting frustrated with my case. Laura found something at Reid Chemical, but she didn't tell anybody. She didn't even tell anybody she was pregnant. It's hard to investigate somebody who doesn't talk to anybody."

Trisha smiled and looked down to her computer.

"Does that remind you of anyone?"

I leaned against the counter. "I'm not dead, so it's not a problem."

"Does she have any sisters?"

I nodded. "Yeah, she's got a younger sister named Alma. She's a nurse in St. Louis."

Trisha raised an eyebrow. "Have you talked to her?"

"Not yet," I said. "If she didn't tell her mom she was pregnant, she wouldn't tell her sister."

Trisha laughed and looked at me. "You have a different relationship with your mom than most people. Doesn't your sister talk to you about the men in her life?"

"Well, yeah, but that's Audrey. She thinks I'm celibate and live through her."

"That's not why she tells you those things," said Trisha, shaking her head. "She wants you involved in her life. That's what sisters do. They talk. If Laura needed to talk to someone, she would have gone to her sister."

"Really?"

"Yeah," said Trisha. "Trust me."

I rapped my fingers on the desk before nodding. "Okay. I guess I'm going to St. Louis."

Trisha reached beneath the counter for a clipboard. "You'll want a car."

I thanked her and signed out a marked SUV before heading out. Laura Rojas had a sister, Alma Diaz, and according to the license bureau, she lived in St. Louis's Central West End. It was a vibrant, hip part of town with great bars and restaurants and some very expensive historic homes and condos. If Alma could afford to live there, she did well for herself.

The drive was easy until I reached the city. Once I got off the interstate, I used my GPS to guide me to Alma's house. She lived on an elegant street in a three-story brick home with a portico on the front. Despite the city address, her street was quiet and had little through traffic. I parked out front and walked up a brick path to her front door.

A small Hispanic woman answered my knock. She had a young child with curly black hair on her hip, and she gave me a strained smile.

"Yes?" she asked.

"I'm Detective Joe Court. Are you Alma Diaz?"

She nodded. "Yes."

"Are you Laura Rojas's sister?"

She drew in a deep, slow breath. "I am, but I have nothing to say. I've talked to the police enough."

"Who have you talked to?"

"Ugly man with black hair."

I nodded. "Mathias Blatch. He's from the St. Louis County Police."

"He said my sister was a drug dealer and that she had over a pound of marijuana in her house. If that's what you're here to talk about, then you can contact my attorney. My sister didn't need to sell drugs. She worked for a living."

I scratched the back of my neck. "To be fair, we found drugs in her house, but they weren't hers. Someone set her up."

Alma's expression softened, and she nodded.

"What do you want?"

"Just to talk."

"About?" she asked, raising her eyebrows.

I shifted from one foot to the other and looked down to the brick pavers upon which I stood so I wouldn't have to look her in the face.

"Did you know your sister was pregnant?"

When I looked up, she nodded.

"Do you know who the father is?"

She blinked before nodding again. "A friend from law school. He's an attorney in New York now. He doesn't know."

"So Laura confided in you?" I asked.

"Of course. I'm her sister."

I blinked a few times. Maybe Trisha was right. Maybe most women did talk to their sisters.

"Did she confide anything else to you?"

Alma looked to her daughter and smiled. "Mommy needs to put you down now, okay?"

The little girl nodded, and Alma lowered her to the ground. For a moment, the girl hung onto her mother's pants, then Alma looked down with a gentle smile on her face.

"Go watch *Daniel Tiger*. Mommy and this woman need to talk."

The little girl cast me a wary glance before running into the house. Alma looked at me once more.

"What do you want to know, Detective?"

"Laura was working a case before she died. Do you know anything about it?"

Alma crossed her arms and shook her head. "Work was one thing we couldn't talk about. She took attorney-client privilege seriously."

My heart felt like it had shrunk, and my shoulders slumped.

"Did she ever mention Reid Chemical?" I asked, hoping to mask my disappointment. Alma chuckled a little and furrowed her brow.

"That's where she worked."

Everything ceased moving at once. I raised my eyebrows. "Excuse me?"

"She was the general counsel at Reid Chemical. She even planned to buy a house in St. Augustine."

My entire body tingled, but I tried not to let my surprise show. "Can I come in? We've got a lot to talk about."

Chapter 38

Alma pursed her lips and narrowed her eyes before taking a step back.

"All right," she said. "We can talk inside."

She led me to a kitchen in the back of the home. A pair of French doors opened to the backyard, while an archway led to a family room with a television and couches. Alma's little girl sat on a big red couch and watched *Sesame Street*.

"Can I get you a cup of coffee?" she asked, gesturing toward a small round breakfast table in the kitchen. I sat down.

"I would love a cup if you've got some made," I said. She nodded before pouring two mugs of coffee and sitting down. I took a sip. It tasted sweet and nutty, and I appreciated the caffeine. "Thank you."

She made a noncommittal noise in her throat and watched her daughter for a moment before focusing on me.

"Why are you here?"

I put my mug down and took out a notepad from my jacket.

"You said Laura worked for Reid Chemical."

Alma nodded and then sighed. "You don't seem very well informed about your own case. It doesn't fill me with confidence you'll find her killer."

"We're making steps," I said, nodding. "I thought Laura ran her own private practice."

"She did, but she was closing it down," said Alma. "She liked being her own boss, but after finding out she was pregnant, she wanted something more stable."

"She didn't even tell her assistant."

"She didn't get the chance. That's what happens when you're murdered."

I nodded and gave her a moment before continuing.

"When did she take the job at Reid Chemical?"

Alma crossed her arms. "Four weeks ago."

Aldon hired her six weeks ago. If she got the job at Reid Chemical four weeks ago, we had a problem. Since finding her body in the woods, I had thought of Laura as a victim. I thought she was innocent and that she had died because she was brave enough to fight a major corporation on behalf of her client.

But she wasn't.

She was one of our bad guys. Aldon came to her for help, and she sold him out for a paycheck. Part of me didn't blame her. She was twenty-six and pregnant, and she wrote wills for three hundred bucks a pop out of an office in a strip mall. Even though she owned her own home, she likely had student loans to take care of. A cushy general counsel's job at

Reid Chemical would have seemed like the perfect solution to her problems.

But now Aldon McKenzie and his wife were dead, and so was Laura. So was Austin Wright. So was Nicole Bryant. Sasquatch would never be the same. Everything came back to that company.

"Do you recognize the name Aldon McKenzie?" I asked.

Alma shook her head as I stood.

"No. Why?"

"Just checking," I said. "Thanks for your time."

"What's going on, Detective?" asked Alma.

"I'm working a case," I said, retracing my steps through the kitchen. "I'll see myself out."

"Detective?" she called.

I pretended I hadn't heard her. She didn't deserve my anger, but I couldn't help but feel it. All this time, I had pictured Laura Rojas as a crusader, someone willing to fight for the underdog. All this time, I was wrong. Aldon McKenzie cut her a check and gave her evidence against his employer believing she would protect him. Instead, she took her findings to the company, and they gave her a job—probably to silence her. She sold her client out. And then she died for it.

She didn't deserve to die, but if you sit on the bad guys' bench, you shouldn't be surprised when they call you into the game.

I got in my vehicle and squeezed the steering wheel.

"Shit," I said. I twisted my keys in the ignition and headed out. Other drivers crowded the surface streets, but traffic thinned as I pulled onto the interstate. There, the monotony of the drive calmed me some and allowed me to focus on my case.

I had no physical evidence, I had no murder weapon, and I had no more idea who killed Laura today than I had a week ago. Not only that, my original victim wasn't the innocent victim I had thought she was. She got this whole thing started.

About half an hour into my drive, my cell phone rang. I answered without looking at the screen.

"What?"

The caller hesitated before speaking.

"Detective?"

The voice belonged to Darius Adams, the accountant we had hired to look over Laura's files.

"Yeah, it's Joe Court," I said, softening my voice. "Sorry. I've had a lousy morning. What can I do for you?"

"Sorry to hear about your morning," he said. "I wanted to call you with an update about the files you gave me. I've found something. You okay to talk for a minute?"

"Sure," I said, doubtful that anything he had to tell me would get me anywhere with this case after everything else had failed. "What did you find?"

"Bear in mind, I'm not a chemist. I can answer questions about the numbers, but you need to talk to a chemist about the nuts and bolts of all this."

"Okay," I said, nodding as my curiosity built. "Go on."

"Someone at Reid Chemical has misappropriated almost four hundred thousand dollars' worth of two restricted chemical compounds. One is called 4-anilino-N-phenethylpiperidine, and the other is N-phenethyl-4-piperidone."

I leaned back on the SUV's firm, leather chair. I didn't know what the chemicals were, but I understood cash. If someone stole four hundred grand from me, I'd be pissed. I might even want to kill somebody. This may have been what Aldon found. I blinked and drew in a breath as I tried to fit this new piece into my puzzle.

"I took chemistry in college, but I've never heard of those chemicals."

"They're the chemical precursors for fentanyl," said Adams. "I looked them up. Someone at Reid Chemical is making some very dangerous drugs."

My heart beat a little faster.

"Do we know who stole them?"

"If the invoices are right, we do," said Adams. "The executive vice president of the company. Logan Reid."

I shook my head.

"That can't be right. Logan Reid is twenty-one years old. He's in college. He's not the vice president of the company."

"College student or not, every piece of evidence I've got points to him."

Now I knew why Laura had led Logan on and sent him those dirty pictures. She was setting him up. That bitch.

"Could you talk to my colleagues about this?"

"You'll get a bill for it, but sure."

"I'm on the road now. Let me get back to my station. I'll set up a time there. Thanks for your work on this."

"Anytime," he said. "You drive safe, Detective."

I thanked him and then hung up. The phone call might as well have injected adrenaline into my veins. I almost smiled. The odds in my murder case had always been against me. Without physical evidence to tie a suspect to the crime scene or a murder weapon, my best option to send somebody to prison for Laura Rojas's death was a confession. This was almost as good.

Mason Stewart couldn't run from this. A federal narcotics manufacturing charge would send him to prison for the rest of his life. I had him. More than that, we had official company records—seized from the office of their general counsel, if Alma was right. We had the whole company in a vise. Once we took them down, we could move on to their distribution network. They weren't selling the drugs themselves. They had help. This would be a good day.

My head felt light, and my chest felt loose as I drove back to St. Augustine.

When I got into the office, I called Detective Delgado, Shaun Deveraux, and Darius Adams for a meeting to go over what I'd found. In the meantime, I tried to organize the case in my head. Six weeks ago—or maybe a little earlier—Aldon McKenzie discovered that someone at his workplace was stealing chemicals used to manufacture fentanyl. He then contacted an attorney, Laura Rojas. Laura investigated and confirmed Aldon's findings.

Instead of working with Aldon to protect his interests, she turned on him. She went to Reid Chemical with her findings, and they offered her a job in their general counsel's office—probably on the condition that she destroy her evidence. Newly pregnant and still unsure of her future, she accepted.

I was a little unsure what happened next. Maybe Laura realized she couldn't cover this up. Or maybe Mason Stewart just got paranoid. Either way, the company added Logan Reid to their staff as a vice president. He was just a kid, so he didn't know his asshole from his elbow. Suddenly, though, a beautiful, sophisticated woman was talking to him and sending him naked pictures of herself. All the while, she was setting him up to take a fall so she and her boss wouldn't.

Only, Mason Stewart didn't trust Laura. She had already turned on one client for money. Not only that, she didn't destroy the evidence in her possession. She made herself dangerous. I didn't know who pulled the trigger to kill her, but I would bet Mason Stewart ordered the hit. Then he ordered

Aldon's murder. The other names on Laura's list—Austin Wright, Mike Brees, and Ruby Laskey—must have known more than they should have, so Mason ordered them killed, too.

It was still just the outline of a case, but it would be enough to get the DEA and US Attorney's Office involved. They'd take over and send everybody involved to prison for the rest of their natural lives. They might even solve our murder cases for us. This wasn't how I anticipated things going, but I'd take it.

At eleven, Deveraux, Delgado, and Adams met me in the conference room, where I laid out my case. Delgado might have dismissed me, but it was hard to ignore the evidence Adams presented. By the time he and I finished talking at noon, Deveraux was already on the phone with the US Attorney's Office in St. Louis to schedule a meeting.

I left the room while Delgado and Deveraux dug into the evidence with Mr. Adams. I had important strings to tie up. Downstairs, I smiled hello to Trisha at the front desk before taking out my cell phone. Logan Reid's phone didn't even ring before dropping me to voicemail.

"Mr. Reid, it's Detective Joe Court. It's very important that you call me or come down to my station. There are things we need to talk about. It'd be helpful if you had an attorney. Thanks."

I hung up and waited a moment to see whether he'd call me back. He didn't. With as many dead people as we had so far, I felt nervous, so I walked to my truck and climbed in. Waterford College wasn't far, so I drove over and parked outside the Public Safety Office. Rusty Peterson, the director of public safety, was behind the desk.

"Hey," I said. "Remember me?"

"Hard to forget when you come by every day," he said, smiling. "What can I do for you, Detective?"

I leaned against the counter.

"I need to talk to Logan Reid."

"Is he in trouble?"

"More than he could realize, but not from me," I said.

Rusty hesitated. "Is there a threat to my campus?"

I shook my head. "I wouldn't think so, but if we don't find him soon, there's a reasonable shot somebody will help him disappear for an extended period."

"How extended?" asked Rusty, lowering his chin.

"Eternity."

He grunted and picked up his phone to call his team. I stayed with him for about an hour while five public safety officers scoured the campus, but neither Logan nor his car was on the grounds. As before, his phone dropped me to voicemail the instant I called it. This time, I left him another message requesting a return call, but I didn't expect a response. Hopefully, they hadn't killed him yet.

I left the college at about one and drove back to my station, where I caught up on paperwork until five that evening. As the evening's swing shift trickled in, I stood up and stretched. I had done everything I could. I hadn't found Laura's murderer, but I had taken the case as far as I could. Other people had it now, and they'd do their best.

I nodded greetings to several people on my way out the door and headed to my car with my head held high. On the way home, I stopped by the grocery store and picked up bread, eggs, butter, and a sandwich from the deli for dinner. With the case over, life would settle into a new normal under interim Sheriff George Delgado. I didn't know what the future held, but I still had a job I believed in. That was enough for now.

As I approached my house, I slowed when I saw a white Mercedes in my driveway. An unfamiliar woman sat on the rocking chair on my front porch. She wore a fashionable black dress and impeccable makeup. I parked beside her car and stepped out of my truck with my hand over my firearm. The woman stood.

"Detective Court," she said, walking toward me. I held up a hand flat toward her as if I were directing traffic. She stopped in her tracks. "I'm Debra Reid. I'm Logan Reid's mother."

My muscles relaxed, but I didn't take my hand from my firearm.

"What can I do for you, Mrs. Reid?"

"I need you to help me find my son," she said, taking a step toward me again. "I'm worried that my husband has done something stupid."

My shoulders relaxed, and I nodded.

"Yeah, I am, too," I said. "I stopped by his college—"

A shadow moved in my peripheral vision.

I stopped speaking midsentence and whirled around. Before I could even focus, pain exploded across my head. I gasped and fell to my knees. Then my assailant pressed a cloth to my mouth. It smelled sweet, but it had a chemical undertone. I reached for my gun and drew in a breath to scream without thinking. That sweet, thick, chemical odor flowed into my lungs.

My limbs grew weak, and my vision narrowed. I pulled my firearm from its holster, but I didn't have the strength to lift it. I couldn't think or focus.

My eyelids grew heavier and heavier, and my vision grew darker and darker until the world disappeared.

Chapter 39

My mouth felt dry, and my head throbbed as my eyes fluttered open. I was in a dark, wood-paneled room with floor-to-ceiling windows. Bookshelves lined the walls, while my chair faced a heavy wooden desk. The sun had long since set, so a dim desk lamp served as the room's only light source. I blinked hard, orienting myself to the surroundings. I was sitting on a sturdy wooden chair. A rough rope held my hands behind me, while something similar bound my ankles to the legs of the chair. My head throbbed.

They had taken my weapon, but I still had the holster on my belt. My keys, purse, and cell phone were gone. This was bad. No one would even realize I was missing until tomorrow morning when I didn't show up for work. I wriggled my wrists, trying to free them from the rope, but that only tightened the knots.

"Hey, looks like Sleeping Beauty is awake."

I held my breath. The speaker was behind me, and his voice sounded almost jovial. It was the security consultant from Reid Chemical.

"If you kill me, you might as well kiss your life goodbye because you're dead. You can't get away with killing a police officer."

"Your threat's misdirected, sweetheart. How'd they get you? They stabbed me with a paralytic and threw me in the back of an SUV."

I turned my head, hoping to catch sight of him out of the corner of my eye. Something moved, but it may have been one of my eyelashes. I didn't trust him, but I didn't know why he'd lie given the situation.

"Chloroform or something like it," I said. "They hit me in the head as I came home."

He grunted. "That sucks. Mason Stewart's here, too. I think he's still alive, but he hasn't moved since they brought him in."

I nodded. A ton of questions floated through my mind, but they were for later. I was dead if I stayed here tied to a chair.

"Are you tied up?" I asked.

"I am."

"What's your name again?" I asked. The desk was about ten feet in front of me, and the windows were another ten feet beyond that. The desktop held a coffee cup and a stack of papers, but no letter opener, knives, or scissors. This didn't look good.

"Nick Sumner," he said. "It's nice to be memorable."

I grunted. "How am I bound to this chair?"

"Your hands are both tied with a rope, and that rope is wound around a slat in your chair. They bound your feet to the chair legs. I assume I'm tied up the same way, but I can't see behind me."

This wasn't the time to panic, but already my heart rate ticked up. I twisted my wrists, testing the knots and the rope again. As before, the braided rope bit into my skin but didn't loosen. My abductors knew what they were doing.

"Does anybody know you're here?" I asked.

"Just you," said Sumner. "How about yourself? Did you think to alert your colleagues before being kidnapped?"

"They think I'm at home," I said. My mouth felt dry, and an empty pit grew in my stomach. "They won't check on me until tomorrow morning. You think Stewart's people will look for him?"

"Mason Stewart is an asshole who alienates, overworks, and underpays everyone around him. If his people saw somebody kidnapping him, they'd cheer for the new management."

I grunted, twisted my arms, and tried to kick my legs again. As before, nothing moved. Sumner cleared his throat.

"You're only tightening the knots," he said. "This is a quarter-inch nylon rope. The minimum breaking strength is well over a thousand pounds."

I stopped moving and clenched my jaw. My face and neck felt hot, and my fingers tingled.

"You seem to know a lot about it," I said.

"This isn't my first rodeo," he said. "And they got the rope from my trunk."

I tried looking over my shoulder at him, but I still couldn't see him.

"If you've done this before, how do we escape?" I asked.

"There's a knife in my shoe, but I can't reach it."

I cocked my head to the side and furrowed my brow. "Why do you have a knife in your shoe?"

He paused. "We're tied to chairs in Debra Reid's library, and that's your question?"

I clenched my jaw before drawing in a breath. "Fine. How do you propose I get it?"

"Scoot your hips forward to give yourself room to extend your legs. Then lean the front of the chair back and slip the ropes off the legs. Your arms will be the problem. They won't be easy to free."

I visualized what he expected me to do. It sounded possible—if painful. I took a deep breath and used the muscles in my lower back to push my hips forward. With my hands secured behind me, my shoulders stretched. That gave me room to move my legs.

"Tip back, but take it easy," he said. "If you fall over, you'll break your arms."

I gritted my teeth and pressed up with my legs, lifting the front of the chair. The ropes on my ankles were tight, so it took work to slide them down the chair legs, but I got them off. Unfortunately, that didn't help free my hands.

"What now?" I asked.

"Lean forward so the chair's on your back and come toward me. I'll kick my shoe off. The knife is between the lining and sole over the heel. Get that and cut us out."

I did as he suggested and sat straight before pitching myself forward so that my feet were on the ground and the chair was strapped to my back. It wasn't comfortable, but it let me stand and move. As Sumner had said, someone had tied him to a chair behind me. Mason Stewart lay on a couch beside the fireplace on the far side of the room. His chest rose and fell with his breath, but he didn't otherwise move.

Sumner kicked off his right shoe. Then he used his feet to prop it in the air. I walked toward him and sat down again.

"Your best bet is to sit with your back to me and then knock your chair over," he said. "That'll let you reach my shoe."

"This is delightful," I said, getting into position.

"Beats dying."

I grunted my affirmative and rocked left and right until gravity took over. My chair, arm, and side hit the ground with a thud that reverberated against the walls. Pain lanced up my shoulder, almost knocking the breath out of me.

"You've got to move," he said. "They'll have heard that."

I forced a breath into my lungs and felt along the ground for his shoe.

"To the left."

I scrambled until I touched something leather. Once I had his shoe, I peeled the sole back from the heel. There, my fingers touched a curved, flat knife with a sharp edge. The knife was so short I could hide it in my palm, but I had to bend my wrist at an awkward angle for the blade to touch the rope.

"Cut the rope and scoot away from me. We don't want them to think we're working together."

I nodded and thrashed on the ground to move the chair a few feet from him. Because the blade was so short, it barely kissed the rope. Still, each flick cut a few fibers.

"What do you use a knife this short for?" I asked.

"It's a last-resort knife," he said. "I use it to gut fish. My kids and I go fishing once a month. We're from Miami. It's our thing."

"Are you always this chatty?"

"Only when I think I'll die," he said. "If you make it out of here, tell my wife and kids I love them."

I tilted my head to the side and raised my eyebrows. "If you die here, there's a good chance I'm dead, too."

"Just promise me," he said.

"Okay," I said, shaking my head. "Will do."

"You got a boyfriend or husband you want me to contact?"

I shook my head. "No."

"Girlfriend?"

He almost sounded hopeful. I gritted my teeth before speaking. "No."

"That's sad," he said. "A woman your age should have somebody."

I grunted once more. "You kill people, and you're tied to a chair. You're hardly qualified to give me life advice."

"Touché."

Heavy footsteps pounded down the hallway. I couldn't see the door, but I palmed the knife to hide it anyway. The new arrival sighed as soon as he opened the door.

"Hey, Mom!" shouted Logan. "She's up."

Logan's footsteps came nearer. My heart thudded, and waves of adrenaline pounded through me so hard that my entire body tingled. Cold sweat beaded on my chest and back. The pain in my arm, side, and shoulder diminished as my adrenaline took over.

Logan stood over me and cocked his head to the side.

"Have a little accident?" he asked, his voice strong and confident. He stepped behind me and righted the chair. Then Debra Reid entered the library. She wore a red skirt and a white shirt with a gold necklace. If I'd had any saliva in my mouth, I would have spit at her. She ran a finger across my face, so I pulled away.

"Feisty," she said, glancing at her son and then back. "I'm sorry my husband dragged you into this, Detective. Normally, I like to keep family business within the family."

"I'm sorry, too," I said. "If you let me go, I promise to pretend I didn't see anything."

She laughed.

"I wish it were that easy," she said, turning to walk toward the desk. Logan stepped around me and joined his mother. Since they couldn't see my hands anymore, I began flicking the knife against the rope again. Debra looked at me with a wistful smile on her lips. "I have to hand it to you, Ms. Court. You found us out."

"It was easy," said Sumner before I could respond. "You guys are shitty criminals."

"So says the man who thought my husband ran my company," she said, sliding a drawer open behind the desk. She pulled out a firearm and aimed it at Sumner. "Goodbye, Mr. Sumner."

Every muscle in my body tensed as she pulled the trigger. A spray of blood hit me on the back and side. I sawed furiously on the rope.

Fuck.

Debra swung the barrel toward me. Her hand didn't even shake.

"You didn't have to kill him," I said.

"He was a mercenary," said Debra. "He would have killed you and us without a second thought."

I had almost cut my way through the cord, but I needed another moment.

"Sorry about Laura," I said, looking to Logan. "You loved her, didn't you?"

"Laura was a slut," said Debra.

"Slut or not, it must be hard knowing the woman your son loves is boning some guy behind his back," I said.

Logan vaulted across the room so quickly I didn't have time to brace myself. He slapped my cheek hard enough to knock my chair over. My face burned, my ears rang, and stars flashed before my eyes as pain radiated through my body and shoulder.

"Laura's dead," said Logan, his voice flat. "Tell her hello for me when you get to Hell."

I spit salty blood. One of my front teeth was loose. My hand was wet. At first, the pain in my neck and cheek made it hard to understand what had happened, and then I felt the throbbing from my hand and wrist. I must have cut myself as I fell. Worse, I had dropped the knife.

"Takes a real man to beat up a woman tied to a chair," I said. "Must suck knowing your mom has bigger balls than you."

"Give me the gun, Mom," said Logan. "I'll take care of this one myself."

Debra held the butt end of the weapon toward her son. He took it from her outstretched hand.

I twisted my arms, trying to work them free. My blood was slick and warm, and my hand slipped a fraction of an inch.

"If you kill me, the police will hunt you for the rest of your life," I said. "Is that what you want? You want to spend the rest of your life on the run?"

His lips curled into a smile. "I'm not taking the fall for this. Mr. Sumner and my stepfather are the bad guys here. We'll tell the police Mom and I walked into a massacre."

"I'm pretty sure Mason will dispute those events."

Without taking his eyes from me, Logan swung the pistol toward his stepfather. He fired three times. The rounds hit Stewart in the side and chest.

My ears rang, and I yanked on my restraints. I almost gasped as my right hand popped out. That loosened the ring enough to free my left.

"Just kill her, Logan," said Debra. "We've wasted enough time here."

Logan turned toward his mom. It gave me the opening I needed. My shoulders throbbed, but I had a chair that weighed fifteen or twenty pounds. That meant I had a fifteen- to twenty-pound club.

Now that my hands were free, I whipped the chair around, hoping to bring it crashing down on his back.

"Logan!" Debra screamed.

Logan turned at the last second and pointed his firearm toward me. My chair caught him in the arm and shoulder instead of his back and head. He fired, but the shot went wide and thudded into a bookcase.

I shoved the base of the chair straight at him, catching him in the nose with a rail. Logan staggered back.

That was the only opening I needed.

I kicked him in the balls and thrust the chair at his face again, screaming as I did. The chair slammed into him once more, this time just below the eye and across the bridge of his nose. He groaned and blinked. I threw the chair and lunged for the pistol he was holding.

In my mad scramble, I had lost track of Debra. I put a hand on the base of the gun and another on the barrel and twisted hard. Logan wasn't a big man, but even in his disoriented state, he had forty pounds on me.

He also had his mother.

As I fought for control of the weapon, Debra grabbed the lamp from the desk and swung it at my back. The blow threw off my balance just enough for Logan to toss me to the side. I tripped over the legs of my chair and fell hard onto the ground, knocking the breath out of me.

I sucked in air, but my lungs wouldn't inflate. It didn't matter. I had to move. I had to get to cover. As I pushed up, my hands touched something cold and metallic. It was Sumner's knife. I palmed it, but strong fingers grabbed me by the hair before I could stand. Pain exploded along my scalp line. Logan wrenched me to my knees and shoved a pistol against my forehead.

"You broke my nose."

I tried to pull away from him, but his fingers tightened in my hair, and he slammed the gun hard against my cheek, inches from my eye. Pain coursed through my body. My eyes began to close as my consciousness ebbed away. Then Logan twisted my hair.

"Look at me!" he screamed, his voice a wicked snarl. I looked at his black, hate-filled eyes. Blood ran down his face and to his chin in a steady stream. His nose would never be straight again. He cocked the hammer back on the pistol as if it were an old revolver. My face throbbed. "You have any last words?"

Time seemed to slow down. Logan was just a foot from me. He had one hand in my hair and the other wrapped around a pistol.

His belly was unprotected.

My hand shot out. Sumner's knife dug into his soft flesh with little resistance. Then, its curved tip tore through his bowels as I ripped it to the left. He gasped as his eyes popped open. I swept my arm up and to the right, slashing at his wrists. For a split second, the fingers intertwined in my hair tightened. Then they relaxed as Logan's life slipped away.

I pulled the gun from his hands as he fell to his knees. Debra ran around the desk for her son. Blood covered my face and arms, but I didn't care. I took a step back and raised the weapon as Debra sobbed and wailed. Her mascara ran down her cheeks, and her son's blood stained her white shirt.

I swallowed hard, trying to get my racing heart and breath under control.

"Debra Reid," I said, my voice shaky. "You're under arrest, but tell your son goodbye before he dies."

She sobbed and looked at her son, cupping his face in her hands. She whispered that she loved him and then held him as he died. I checked Sumner's pulse, but he was already dead. So was Mason Stewart.

When I had picked up this case, I suspected that it would be hard. I didn't expect this. I didn't know who had squeezed the trigger to kill Laura Rojas and Aldon McKenzie, but it didn't matter. The dead would take their secrets to the grave.

"Where's my cell phone?"

Debra didn't look up, so I searched the desk. My phone, keys, and badge were in the center drawer. Jason Zuckerburg at my station answered before the phone finished ringing once.

"Hey, Joe," he said, his voice cheerful. "What can I do for you?"

"I'm at the home of Logan and Debra Reid," I said, swallowing. "Send every officer we've got on duty to my location. And tell Detective Delgado that I've closed the Laura Rojas investigation."

"Okay," he said. "Do you need an ambulance?"

"No. Everybody's dead."

Chapter 40

In the days that followed Debra Reid's arrest, dozens of DEA and FBI agents came to St. Augustine to sort through Reid Chemical's finances. They interviewed everyone who worked at the company and subpoenaed every financial record the company held going back at least ten years. If anyone at the company had committed financial impropriety, they'd find it.

Already, the federal government had begun procedures to seize Reid Chemical's assets. There'd be lawsuits, but in the meantime, they'd auction off the company's assets and put hundreds of people in my community out of work. Nobody won.

To avoid the death penalty for killing Nick Sumner, Debra Reid filled in details for us, giving us a pretty clear picture of what happened.

This whole mess started with Mason Stewart. He slept around on his wife and destroyed her business. Reid Chemical, under his stewardship, lost five to ten million dollars a year. Debra could put up with a cheating spouse, but not one who destroyed her family's firm. Mason learned she planned to divorce him and leave him penniless, so he hatched a plan.

To fund his retirement, Mason persuaded chemists at the plant to make and sell fentanyl. He took half the proceeds of the drug sales and gave the other half to the chemists. Together, they made millions at Reid Chemical's expense. The arrangement worked well until Aldon McKenzie found the discrepancies in the accounting books. Aldon told his superiors, but more than that, he hired Laura Rojas to protect his interests.

Having recently learned of her pregnancy, Laura was desperate and broke. She learned everything she could about Reid Chemical and its problems and contacted Mason Stewart. He made her a deal: If she stopped investigating his company, he'd give her a cushy job in the legal department.

Laura agreed, but she didn't trust Mason completely. She kept investigating and even persuaded Aldon to steal additional information from the company mainframe. When the IT department found Aldon's data breach, they came to Debra Reid, which led her to open her own investigation into the company's accounting books.

Her accountants uncovered the problem within hours. Debra might have been able to handle things in-house, but by then, the company's silent partners had learned of Reid Chemical's problems. They brought in Nick Sumner to assess the situation and eliminate any threats. Sumner, not knowing how deep the problems ran, kicked a hornet's nest and opened the case wide.

Everybody lost in the end, St. Augustine included.

Already, organizations and businesses around town felt the pinch. Fewer people came into Rise and Grind for coffee, fewer customers patronized the county's bars and restaurants, and Reid Chemical's former employees began using the area food banks they had once helped fund. Worst of all, the number of domestic violence cases had already started rising. St. Augustine would pull through, but it would take work and time. We'd have to change, but we'd come out stronger in the end. We always did.

Delgado put me on desk duty pending a psychological evaluation. I didn't put a lot of stock into therapy, but I had just disemboweled a man who had held a weapon to my forehead. Therapy seemed like a good idea.

Two days after the incident at Reid Chemical, I called Allison Sumner in Miami with her husband's last message. Before learning of Nick Sumner's death, she hadn't known what her husband truly did for a living. She was glad he had died.

Closer to home, June Wellman's attorneys negotiated a plea with Shaun Deveraux at the county prosecutor's office. June pled guilty to voluntary manslaughter and would spend eight years in prison. In exchange, the county dropped all other charges against her. Deveraux could have pushed for a stiffer sentence, but nobody wanted to take a rape victim to trial.

Chad Hamilton's family had already filed civil wrongful-death proceedings against her, the college, and my department. That case would drag on for years. They'd subpoena me to testify eventually, but I'd worry about that another day.

For the moment, I had time to relax on my front porch. It was six in the evening, and I held a glass of vodka in my hand and an empty salad bowl in my lap. Roger had died a week ago. I missed him, but the sting of his death had passed. I hadn't gotten over losing him, but I would in time. Until I did, he had left me with wonderful memories.

As I sat and watched the sun sink lower in the early evening skyline, a black pickup appeared on the horizon. I thought nothing of it until it slowed and then pulled into my driveway. Trisha and Harry sat in the front seats.

I stood as they opened their doors.

"Hey, guys," I said, smiling. "If you had called ahead, I would have ordered pizza."

"That's all right," said Harry, walking to the porch. He put a hand on my shoulder and squeezed. "How are you holding up?"

"My new boss is an asshole, but I'm good."

"You mean that?" asked Trisha.

I considered her for a moment and then nodded. "Yeah. George Delgado is the biggest asshole I've ever met."

She shook her head and said I was terrible. I laughed. Trisha hadn't visited since I killed Logan Reid, but this was Harry's third trip. His first visit had gone poorly because I had been mad at him for quitting, but his second had been better.

Harry had taught me how to be a detective. He had been my partner, and it had felt like a betrayal when he had quit. That was my problem, though. He had done the right thing for himself and his family. I'd be a terrible friend if I couldn't accept that.

"You mind if we come inside?" he asked.

"Not at all," I said, nodding and holding open the screen door. My house was hot, but it was clean and comfortable. Harry picked up a coffee mug from my coffee table to clear it and then looked at Trisha. That was when I noticed she held a rolled piece of paper under her arm. She put it on the table and unfurled a detailed road map of Missouri and the surrounding states.

"Trisha and I have been working on something," said Harry. "You promise to keep this quiet?"

"Sure," I said, furrowing my brow. "What's going on?"

Trisha pulled a black marker from her purse and then focused on the map before drawing a large dot over St. Augustine.

"You're working a missing-person case still, right?" she asked. I nodded.

"Paige Maxwell and Jude Lewis," I said. "They were teenagers."

"And they disappeared from St. Augustine on March 13, correct?"

She looked up, and I shrugged and then nodded.

"That sounds right," I said.

"We haven't found them yet, but we have found their car. They're presumed dead," said Harry, taking a notepad from his pocket. He flipped through a couple of pages before focusing on me. "Since my retirement, I've had a little more free time than usual. Trisha and I have been researching similar disappearances, and we've found something disturbing.

"On May 13 of last year, Olivia King and John Rodgers were reported missing from Hannibal, Illinois," he said. "Both went to the same high school. They were a couple, so their parents thought they had run away so they could be together. Despite a manhunt, neither was seen again."

I nodded, and Trisha marked the town on the map with a dot.

"On July 15 of last year, Tayla Walker and her boyfriend, Matthew Bridges, disappeared from Kennett, Missouri," said Harry, reading from his notepad. "Both were seventeen, they were dating, and they attended the same high school.

"On September 14, Amy Hoffman and her boyfriend, James Tyler, were reported missing from Decatur, Illinois. Amy was eighteen, and James was seventeen. Both, again, attended the same high school. Again, they were dating.

"On November 15, Jordan Fitzgerald and Simon Fisher were abducted from Mountain Grove, Missouri. As before, both were dating, and they attended the same high school.

"On January 13 of this year, Nicole Moore and her boyfriend, Andrew White, were abducted from Sturgis, Kentucky. Both were seventeen."

As Harry read, Trisha marked off the locations. My stomach churned. When they finished, I slowly looked up at them both.

"These kids are all still missing?" I asked.

"Yeah," said Harry. "Here's what we know: The victims are all roughly the same age; in every case, the missing persons were dating; they disappeared in two-month intervals; and they all disappeared after withdrawing money from the bank to make it look as if they had run away. There's something else, though, too."

Harry looked at Trisha, who hesitated before connecting the dots on her map in a near perfect circle around St. Augustine.

"Whatever's going on, we're right in the middle of this," said Harry. "These kids and these locations weren't chosen at random."

I nodded, although I barely heard him. My heart pounded in my chest as I focused on the picture before me.

"Give me those dates and locations again."

Harry read them out. Hannibal, Illinois, the site of the first disappearance, was to the north of St. Augustine, while

Kennett, Missouri, the site of the second abduction, was to the south. Decatur, Illinois, was to the northeast, and Mountain Grove, Missouri, was to the southwest. Finally, Sturgis, Kentucky, was to the southeast.

I connected the dots in that order and took a step back. None of us said anything, but Harry covered his face.

"Shit," he said, his voice low. "It's not a circle."

"No," I said, shaking my head. "It's a pentagram, and we're right in the middle."

"What does that mean?" asked Trisha.

I shook my head. "I have no idea, but I don't think it's good."

***

I hope you liked the book! Joe's adventures continue in *The Boys in the Church*. It's an intense, thrilling novel, and I hope you love it. You can purchase it at my store [store.chrisculver.com], Barnes & Noble, Amazon, and other major retailers.

Or turn the page to get a FREE Joe Court novella....

Get The Girl Who Came Back...

You know what the best part of being an author is? Goofing off while my spouse is at work and my kids are at school. You know what the second part is? Interacting with my readers.

About once a month, I write a newsletter about my books, writing process, research, and funny events from my life. I also include information about sales and discounts. I try to make it fun.

As if hearing from me on a regular basis wasn't enough, if you join, you get a FREE Joe Court novella. The story is a lot of fun, and it's available exclusively to readers on my mailing list. You won't get it anywhere else.

If you're interested, sign up here:

https://www.chrisculver.com/magnet.html

Stay in touch with Chris

As much as I enjoy writing, I like hearing from readers even more. If you want to keep up with my world, there are a couple of ways you can do that.

First and easiest, I've got a mailing list. If you join, you'll receive an email whenever I have a new novel out or when I run sales. You can join that by going to this address:

http://www.indiecrime.com/mailinglist.html

If my mailing list doesn't appeal to you, you can also connect with me on Facebook here:

http://www.facebook.com/ChrisCulverbooks

And you can always email me at chris@indiecrime.com. I love receiving email!

About Chris Culver

Chris Culver is the *New York Times* bestselling author of the Ash Rashid series and other novels. After graduate school, Chris taught courses in ethics and comparative religion at a small liberal arts university in southern Arkansas. While there and when he really should have been grading exams, he wrote *The Abbey*, which spent sixteen weeks on the *New York Times* bestsellers list and introduced the world to Detective Ash Rashid.

Chris has been a storyteller since he was a kid, but he decided to write crime fiction after picking up a dog-eared, coffee-stained paperback copy of Mickey Spillane's *I, the Jury* in a library book sale. Many years later, his wife, despite considerable effort, still can't stop him from bringing more orphan books home. He lives with his family near St. Louis.